JAGGED EDGES

Raine Stockton Dog Mystery #17

Donna Ball

Blue Merle Publishing

ISBN:979-8-9907305-6-4

Published by Blue Merle Publishing
www.buemerlepublishers.com

CHAPTER ONE

From high above, the Smoky Mountain community of Hanover County, North Carolina, looks just like something out of a picture postcard. The snow-covered fields, the blue shadows of the mountains, the farmhouses glittering with holiday lights, the peaceful pasture fences decorated with red bows could all have been painted by Norman Rockwell. In the little town of Hansonville, a Christmas tree stands in the town square, resplendent in multi-colored light bulbs and oversized ornaments. The shop windows are outlined with twinkling lights and their doors sport holiday wreaths. The lawns of the houses along the side streets are all decked out with snowmen and reindeer, and the people who stroll along the sidewalks wear red plaid coats and knit caps with pom-poms on them. You really couldn't ask for more.

Of course, closer to the ground, you see the reality. The snow that has melted into frozen, muddy slush against the side of the road. The Styrofoam snowmen with drooping hats and ragged red bandannas. The Christmas trees turning brown at the curb and the holiday lights that sag from the eaves like unkept promises. And the weary pedestrians, shoulders slumped beneath the weight of post-holiday blues and post-holiday bills, just want to get out of the cold. For many of them, in fact, it's all they can do to keep from tripping over the jagged pieces of their broken lives. It only goes to show that even the prettiest pictures, when examined up close, are rarely what they seem.

The reason I know what our little corner of the world looks like from on high is because my dearly beloved, Miles, who is currently recovering from a badly broken leg—long story—just sent me what has to be the tenth still shot of the morning from his new favorite toy, a super-duper, state-of-the-art, has-to-be-seen-to-be-believed drone. The drone had been his Christmas present to himself, which isn't as self-centered as it sounds because the man is literally impossible to buy for. Naturally, I'm glad he has something to keep him entertained. Miles with nothing to occupy his time is something I wouldn't wish on my worst enemy. But honestly, this new obsession of his is just about to drive me crazy.

I sent him a smiley face, a Christmas tree, and a heart emoji, and put my phone away. I was having a hard time finding new emojis to use as a reply.

"Are you sure you don't want to stop by the house for a little while after this?" I said to Casey, who was driving. I tried not to sound too desperate. "We have all those leftover Christmas cookies in the freezer, and you could play chess with Miles or something."

Casey gave a snort of dismissal. "No way, kiddo. That guy skunks me every time, and he's not even nice about it. Besides, I've got things to do."

"What kinds of things?" I demanded suspiciously.

He shot me a warning look. "I'll think of something."

Casey is my brother—half-brother, actually—and I hadn't even known he existed a year ago. Another long story. Despite that fact, we were already as comfortable together as if we'd been doing the brother-sister thing all our lives. Of course, I suspect a lot of that is trauma-bonding, because in the short time we've known each other, Casey and I have been through hell and back together. Dare I say it? A really long story.

My name is Raine Stockton, and if you lived around here, you'd probably know who I am. Maybe you'd recognize me as the daughter of Judge Stockton, who had quite a reputation in this part of the state before he died. Maybe you would have seen my picture in the paper, along with my search and rescue dog, Cisco, after finding a lost camper or missing child. Or your pup might be a client of Dog Daze, the canine training, boarding and grooming facility I run. I'd like to think so, anyway. I've trained an awful lot of dogs in and around the tri-county area. But sadly, I think most people recognize my name these days because last year I was arrested for killing the very brother who was driving the pickup truck in which I now rode.

Obviously, I didn't kill Casey, or anyone else for that matter, and those closest to me tell me I'm being ridiculous when I say that's all people remember about me. Maybe I am being ridiculous, to a certain extent. I've got to admit my life around law enforcement has made me cynical about people in general, and if you think it's easy to get over being hauled off in handcuffs and standing in front of a judge with your life on the line, I'm here to tell you, it's not. Nonetheless, I've worked hard to move past that whole horrible time in my life, and I'm making progress. For example, I gave a doggie Christmas party last month at Dog Daze with a raffle to benefit the humane society, and it was more successful than I'd hoped. We raised over $700 for the shelter animals which went a long way, I think, toward re-establishing my position in the community. As an added bonus, the Dog Daze phone had actually started ringing again.

I said, "Right at the light."

Casey was driving, because I needed his pickup truck to return two folding tables and a half-dozen folding chairs Aunt Mart had loaned me for the afore-mentioned party. While we were there, Aunt Mart charged us with delivering three bags of clothes collected from the church drive to the women's shelter thrift store. Sad to say, even a post-card- perfect little town like ours had need of a shelter for battered women, and it was consistently one of the most underfunded charities in the county.

Cisco sat between us on the seat of Casey's pickup, his head on a swivel and his tongue hanging out with happy pants as he took in the Christmas banners, giant candy canes, snowmen and reindeer that still adorned every corner as we passed through town. He is a gorgeous golden retriever with a big, blocky head, a lustrous coat, and rich, pale feathering on his tail and underside. He is also insatiably curious and inexhaustibly energetic, both of which get him into more trouble than not. But he loves to travel, and over the years I've gotten accustomed to never getting into a vehicle without Cisco buckled into one of the seats.

Casey pulled into the parking lot of a low, whitewashed building with a sign over the door that read, Welcoming Arms Thrift Store. There were already several other vehicles there, even though it was only a few minutes after 10:00, the stated opening time. A couple of cars I recognized as belonging to volunteers. The other was an ancient two-tone pickup truck that held a man smoking a cigarette, probably waiting for his wife to come out. This time of year, thrift shops do a booming business around here.

Cisco tried to climb over me the minute I opened the door, but fortunately he was secured by his canine seat belt. "Stay here," I told him firmly. "We'll be right back." While Cisco's manners were usually pretty good, especially when he was on leash, I happened to know there were breakables inside the thrift store. No point in taking unnecessary chances.

Just as I started around the back of the truck to help Casey with the bags, my phone pinged with another text. Exasperated, I looked at the photo displayed, then looked again. It was a picture of Casey's pickup truck in the parking lot of the thrift store, Casey getting out of the truck, me with one foot on the ground and one palm raised toward the inside of the truck as I signaled Cisco to stay.

"Oh, for heaven's sake!" I cast my gaze upward, searching the sky for the perpetrator of the unauthorized selfie, but Miles had said that one of the features of this particular model was that it could film from such a height as to be almost undetectable to the naked eye. "Where *is* the damn thing?"

Cisco, my faithful bird dog, stretched his head toward the open door and barked toward the sky. I was pretty sure he couldn't see the drone, but he could probably hear it, and every time the thing was airborne it was all I could do to keep him from chasing it all over the countryside.

Casey came around the truck to stand beside me, a bag in each hand, and followed my gaze upward. "What?"

"That stupid drone," I replied. "Honestly, Miles is like a twelve- year-old boy with that thing."

As I spoke, my phone pinged with two more photos, one of Cisco barking up at the sky that was actually taken through the car windshield, and another of Casey and me standing in the parking lot looking upward. Casey glanced at the pictures and grinned. "Well, it is pretty cool."

"Spoken like a twelve-year-old boy," I muttered, and started to type out a text to Miles.

That's illegal surveillance, I typed.

He returned, *Not if I don't get caught.*

And just then I caught the glint of light on steel against the clouds as the drone sped away.

I stuffed my phone inside my pocket and went to grab the other bag from the back of the truck.

"So how did he know where we were?" Casey asked.

I shrugged as I returned. "He tracks my phone."

Casey lifted an eyebrow and I didn't blame him. Yeah, I know how stalky that sounds, and I hadn't exactly been wild about the idea at first, either. But my search-and-rescue work takes me into remote areas and can sometimes be dangerous. Having somebody else know where I am at all times has saved my butt more than once.

Casey said, "Come on, Raine, we're standing in front of a battered women's shelter and you're telling me this guy is so controlling he tracks your phone?"

Miles and Casey have a complicated relationship —sometimes friends, sometimes rivals, sometimes outright enemies— and I couldn't tell whether his comment was meant to be protective of me or to cast shade on Miles. But it made me grimace in dry amusement. "Not only that, but he takes pictures of me standing in front of the battered women's shelter. Without my permission. What he *does* have is my permission to track my phone."

"Whatever." Casey did not sound mollified. "It still seems disrespectful to me. But at least he's got a hobby."

A huff of disdain was my only reply. If there was one thing my brilliant, billionaire boyfriend was not lacking, it was hobbies. Even as the thought crossed my mind, it was accompanied by an *Oops* because I had momentarily forgotten, as I did too often, that Miles was not exactly my boyfriend anymore. He was, in fact, my husband, and the only member of my family who knew it was Casey. Fortunately, Casey was good at keeping secrets. He'd had a lifetime of experience doing so.

"Also," I pointed out, "this is not the shelter, just the thrift store that supports it. The location of the actual shelter is kept under wraps, for obvious reasons."

The bell chimed as I opened the door to the thrift shop with my free hand and stood back to let Casey precede me. "Hi, Jessie," I called out to the woman behind the counter. "Aunt Mart sent us over with these clothes from the church."

Jessie Crowley was a fifty-eight-year-old woman with a husband and two teenage children, but the minute she saw my brother her face lit up, and she hurried around the counter toward him. "Oh, how sweet! Here, let me help you." She rushed to take one of the bags—from Casey, of course, not me.

Casey had that effect on women, not only because, with his curly blond ponytail, lanky build and pale blue eyes he was—according to my eleven-year-old step-daughter—"dreamy-looking", but because he had enough charm for three or four grown men and he knew how to use it. He hadn't quite been in town a full year, but he'd already had three girlfriends. He'd broken up with each of them before things could get anywhere near serious, of course, but they all still liked him enough to bring him casseroles and bake him cookies. The only other person I'd ever known who had that much charisma was, believe it or not, my ex-husband.

Jessie took one of the bags and led the way to the back room, where a couple of volunteers were sorting through donations at a big table. They were both well into the gray-haired, afternoon- bridge-club stage, but they, too, looked up in delight when Casey came in. I left him to flirt with them and drifted back out into the main store to check out the shelves. Sometimes you could find really good stuff in thrift stores, and I like to keep a collection of dog-related odds and ends on hand to use as prizes in my obedience classes. Assuming, of course, I ever managed to get enough clients together for a class again.

I found a matching set of silver food and water bowls embossed with bones for $5.00, and a ceramic golden retriever holding a bouquet of daisies in its mouth for a dollar. I scooped up both of them and was browsing the glassware—a set of four paw-print coffee mugs for $2.00—when the door chimed again. I heard Jessie come from the back with a cheery, "Good morning! Let me know if I can help you find anything."

A rough male voice replied, "You can help me find my damn wife, that's what you can do." He raised his voice and shouted, "Tina! Tina, you worthless bitch, get out here!"

I stepped out from between the shelves, alarmed. The man who stood inside the door, glaring at Jessie, was the same one who had been smoking in his truck when we drove up. He was thin and wiry, with a scruffy grey-peppered beard, a ruddy face, and greasy tufts of reddish hair. He wore muddy work boots and jeans that had seen better days. He might have looked familiar to me, but as much as I like to say I know everyone in town, there is a certain element even I like to stay away from. That element includes angry, rheumy-eyed men who walk into a room and fill it with the smell of rum.

Jessie said firmly, "There's no one by that name here. I think you'd better leave."

Jessie is a petite woman, barely coming up to the shoulder of the ruffian she confronted, but I've got to hand it to her—she didn't flinch. I had the feeling she had done this before.

"I'll leave when I get good and damn ready," he growled, and shoved past her. Jessie stumbled a little as he bumped her arm.

"Hey!" I said sharply. I stepped in front of him as he strode down the aisle. "She said Tina isn't here." *And even if she was*, I added silently to myself, *there's no way you're getting anywhere near her.* But for once, I had the good sense not to say out loud what I was thinking.

He ignored me. “Tina! Get out here before I have to drag you out!”

I stepped back quickly to avoid being mowed down, juggling my would-be-purchases as I tugged my phone out of my pocket. Jessie followed him anxiously. “Sir, I told you, there’s no one by that name...”

“Dude.” Casey stepped out from the back room, hands in the pockets of his denim jacket, his expression unperturbed. “What’s all the racket about?”

The intruder stopped short a few feet from Casey, glaring at him. “You keeping her back there?” he demanded belligerently. “Are you the one she keeps running off to? Because if you are, you...”

Casey spoke over him calmly. “Man, I don’t know any Tina and I don’t know what you’re talking about. But I think the lady was pretty clear when she said there was nobody here by that name. So maybe you’d better just move on.”

For a long moment, the two men stared at each other. I had 911 pulled up on my phone but did not punch dial. I saw the other man shift his weight awkwardly, starting to lose some of his bravado. I relaxed a little.

I probably should have mentioned that my brother has done time. Granted, it was mostly as an undercover informant for the FBI—mostly— but my ex, who happens to be in law enforcement, once told me that there’s something about the eyes of someone who’s been in prison that always gives them away. Most of the time, Casey has the sweetest eyes I’ve ever seen, but I have also seen that gaze grow hard and, believe me, when it does, you don't want to mess with him.

I'm guessing enough of that look must have penetrated the intruder's rum-soaked brain to make him think twice about challenging a man half his age, because he changed tactics. "Hell, you can keep her. All I want is my damn car. She took off in the middle of the night with my car – my car that I paid for out of my own pocket–and if that ain't thieving, I don't know what is."

"Man, that's harsh," agreed Casey. "I'd call the cops if I were you."

I could tell this was the last thing the intruder wanted to do. He scowled fiercely. "Yeah, well, just maybe I will. You tell her that. You tell her something else, too. You tell her I'm looking for her and when I catch up with her I'm gonna make her wish she'd never messed with me. You tell her that, you hear?"

Casey did not respond, and the man swung around and marched to the door, pushing through it with a clatter. Casey followed, looking out the window to make sure he was leaving. The rest of us breathed a sigh of relief when we heard the squeal of the pickup's tires leaving the parking lot.

"I guess that's our morning excitement," Jessie said, and the other women chuckled nervously.

"Wow," I said to Jessie. "What was his problem? Don't you want to report it to the police?"

Jessie shook her head. "No point," she said. "They won't do anything unless he damages something."

Casey returned from the window and reported, "Well, he's gone now. Has this kind of thing happened before?"

The other women went back to work at the sorting table, and Jessie replied, "Unfortunately, yes. Sometimes men mistake the store for the shelter and come here looking for the women who left them. Most of them aren't as obvious as that one, though. Are you going to take those, Raine?"

I handed over my purchases and followed her to the register. "Do you know who that guy is? Somebody should warn his wife."

"Afraid not," she said. "He's never been in here before that I recall." She wrapped the ceramic piece in brown paper and put it with the dog bowls in a recycled plastic sack. "That'll be $6.25."

"Do you want us to hang around for a little while," Casey volunteered, "in case he comes back?"

Jessie waved the suggestion away as she passed the sack across the counter to me. "Don't worry about it. They never come back, and besides, this place will be full of people in another half hour. I swear, with prices the way they are these days, this is the busiest January we've ever had."

Sure enough, before she finished speaking, the door chimed again with more customers, and Casey and I felt okay about leaving the women alone.

At the door, I looked back. "I don't suppose there's any way you could get word to the shelter, just in case Tina is there?"

Jessie returned a quiet smile. "Don't worry about

her, honey, she'll be fine. It's the ones who don't leave who are really in danger."

I decided right then and there to stop complaining about Miles and his stupid drone.

CHAPTER TWO

Casey said, "So where's the women's shelter?"

I frowned as I glanced at him. "How should I know?"

"Because you know everything," he replied. "And because you're planning to go there to check on Tina. May as well do it while we're out."

"Because you want to check on her, too," I pointed out.

He shrugged one shoulder in careless agreement as he made the turn onto Main Street. I noticed with relief that two men with ladders were starting to take down the Christmas wreaths on the utility poles. No matter how much you love Christmas, most people will admit that by the second week in January, it's time to move on.

I said, "Anyway, you can't just show up there. You have to call ahead and be approved. Cisco and I did a therapy dog visit last year," I explained. "They did a background check and everything." Then I sighed. "They probably won't let me come back, now that I have a criminal record."

"Jeez, girl, will you let that go? You don't get a criminal record for being falsely arrested. You get an apology from the court. And a nice fat settlement, if you're smart."

I slid him a dry look. "You should know."

"Damn straight." He grinned. "You're talking to one of the leading experts in the field."

I took out my phone and started to scroll for the number of the shelter director. "Anyway, she might not even be there. She could have gone to her mother's, or..."

Suddenly, Casey locked up the brakes and laid on the horn. Tires squealed and the truck lurched sideways with a thump and screech of metal. My phone went flying as I flung out my arm to protect Cisco. My seatbelt locked and threw me back against the seat. All of that happened in a single half-breath, and when my vision cleared our truck had come to a stop sideways in the intersection with a big black pickup nosing its front bumper.

"Son of a bitch!" Casey exclaimed. He looked at me, shaken. "You guys okay?"

I nodded, gulping for air, and ran my hands quickly over Cisco. Without his seat belt, he would have gone straight through the windshield. "We're good."

Cisco barked his agreement and shifted nervously on the seat, trying to regain his balance.

"That guy blew right through the stop sign," Casey said, unfastening his seat belt. "Damn it!"

I hadn't seen the accident, but it was pretty clear what had happened from the position of the vehicles. We had the right of way; the stop sign was behind the black truck. Casey got out and slammed the door. I fumbled on the floor for my phone, and when I found it I unfastened Cisco and we followed Casey. It would have been cruel to leave him alone in the truck after such a trauma.

Traffic was starting to back up behind us—if you could call two cars traffic—and I paused to wave them around before joining Casey at the front of the truck. Cisco, who did not appear in the least traumatized, looked around happily as he trotted by my side, always up for another adventure.

The impact had knocked Casey's truck a few inches away from the bumper of the other vehicle, so it was easy to see that the damage was minimal. His fancy chrome bumper was dented, but only a couple of inches, and black paint smeared the shiny silver finish of the front fender. The other guy had absolutely no damage that I could see. That's what you get when you buy premium.

His was a fancy custom job that boasted silver wings painted on the side panels and, just in case there was any doubt about how much he'd spent on the vehicle, a bold "King Ranch Edition" emblem on the tailgate. The man who got out of the hundred-grand pickup was probably in his late fifties, big-shouldered and thick-necked, one of those ex-quarterback types whose enjoyment of life's pleasures had led to a soft jawline and a mild paunch. His thick brown hair was salon-perfect, and he wore a tan cashmere jacket over wool slacks with shiny oxblood ankle boots. Next to him Casey and I, in our sweatshirts and faded jeans, looked like exactly what we were: a couple of hillbilly locals who couldn't even afford to lease a truck like his for the day. I was really, really glad the accident had not been Casey's fault.

The driver took a moment to assess the damage, then straightened up and said, "Lance Booker." He extended his hand to Casey. "You folks okay?"

"Fine." Casey shook his hand. "You?"

I saw the flash of a gaudy watch on the other man's wrist when he shook Casey's hand, coupled with some kind of gold link bracelet. Clearly, he wasn't from around here. Cisco and I walked casually around to the back of the truck to get a look at the license plate.

"Doesn't look too bad," Booker was saying. "Good thing neither one of us was going fast."

"Well," Casey pointed out mildly, "you were haulin' when you went through that stop sign. Lucky I saw you in time to swerve."

The other man chuckled. "Yeah, I guess I was a little distracted."

At that moment, the passenger door opened and I saw what he had been distracted by. The woman who slid out of the passenger seat was straight out of an ad for an Aspen weekend, with skinny jeans, cowboy boots, and rich blonde hair that cascaded over the fur collar of her white suede coat. She wore a single gold filigree earring in her left ear that looked like a butterfly wing, with sparkling rhinestones for the body. Personally, I'm not a fan of the single-earring look; it always makes me want to search the ground for its lost mate. But on this girl, it looked perfectly appropriate. She couldn't have been more than twenty-five, and she was gorgeous.

"Oh, what a pretty dog!" she exclaimed. "Can I pet him?"

Dogs are the great social equalizers, and even though I felt like a street beggar next to the girl's flashy beauty and expensive clothes, Cisco had no such inhibitions. He wagged his way over to her with a big welcoming grin on his face, and I had no choice but to follow. The girl dropped to her knees to pet him. "Oh, what a sweet doggie! What a good, good boy!"

"His name is Cisco," I told her.

"Hi, Cisco," she said, ruffling his ears with both hands. She smiled up at me. "I think he likes me."

It would have been impolite to tell her that Cisco liked everybody, so I just smiled back. "He's a golden retriever," I supplied.

I heard Casey say, "Are y'all just passing through?"

But instead of answering, Booker said sharply, "Amber! I told you to wait in the truck!"

The delighted expression that had come over the girl's face as she petted Cisco vanished abruptly and she stood, smoothing her hands over her jeans. "Sorry," she mumbled. "I'd better..."

"Is that your dad?" I asked, for no particular

reason except that it didn't take a genius to see the power dynamic between the two of them was not weighted in the girl's favor.

"Um, he's not..." She closed her hand into a fist and stretched out her fingers nervously. "I mean, no. I..."

"Amber!"

She turned and hurried back into the vehicle, still opening and closing her fist as though she wanted to hit something. Him, probably.

The passenger door slammed, and Cisco and I went back to Casey.

"Look," Booker was saying as I approached, "Let's not waste any more time on a fender bender. What do you say we just settle this and get on with our day?" He took a money clip from his jacket pocket that was thick with bills. When I got close, I could see that they were all hundreds. He started peeling them off one by one. "Five hundred ought to take care of your damage, don't you think?"

Casey looked reluctant. "Man, I don't know. It's a new truck."

The other man thumbed back two more bills, holding Casey's gaze. "No cops, no insurance, no hassle," he said.

Casey maintained his poker face. "Gosh, I'd hate to get in trouble with the law. You're supposed to report accidents, you know."

"Maybe just this once," said the other man, "you could let it slide."

Two more bills joined the pile. I tried my best

to remain expressionless, but I'm sure my eyes widened.

Casey remained silent until another bill joined stack, and then he smiled. "Well," he agreed, "maybe just this once." He opened his hand, and Booker placed the money in it.

Booker nodded to me as he turned to get back into his truck. "Y'all have a good day."

"You, too," Casey replied pleasantly.

I didn't say anything at all until Booker had backed up his truck, swerved around Casey's vehicle, and continued through the intersection. "Holy Cow," I said, watching him go. "There must have been five thousand dollars in that money clip. Who carries around that kind of cash?"

Casey shrugged. "Drug dealers, gamblers, mob bosses..." He grinned and folded the cash into his jeans pocket. "And now, me. Did you get the license plate?"

Even though we hadn't known each other that long, Casey and I already made a pretty good team. "Arkansas," I replied. "I took some pictures for insurance, including the tag number, but I guess you don't need it now."

"Hell, I'll have that little ding buffed out before supper," he replied. "But I am kind of curious who that guy was. Maybe I'll come down with whiplash later."

I rolled my eyes and went around to the passenger side. Casey waved an apology to another motorist who inched around our vehicle, and climbed behind the wheel. We made our way back home, speculating half-seriously about what the story behind Mr. Big Spender from Arkansas might be, and I'm ashamed to admit I forgot all about Tina and the women's shelter.

Maybe if I hadn't, things would have gone differently for her.

CHAPTER THREE

I live in the same nineteenth century farmhouse my ancestors built; the house where my parents were married, where I was raised, where my mother entertained the state supreme court, where both my parents died. My business is there, all my memories are there, my life is there. I won't be leaving any time soon.

Miles built a gorgeous contemporary mansion on the mountain overlooking my house and we share, not only a driveway, but our time between the two places. Or at least we did, until Miles's injury. Now I spend most of my time at his place, despite the fact that he has a nurse practitioner, a physical therapist and his own mother also taking care of him. Two months post-op, all that attention was a little redundant, and he had reduced the nurse to once a week and the physical therapist to three times a week. His mother, Rita, had her own place less than half a mile away, and had gradually—and with noticeable relief —begun to move her things back home. In the way of all mothers, however, she still quietly manages to be with Miles whenever she is needed.

Today, for example, I felt okay about running errands and spending some time working on the books at Dog Daze because I knew Rita would be with Miles, working on her needlepoint while he played with his drone until the physical therapist came at noon. Rita, I should mention, is one of the reasons Miles and I have kept our marriage a secret and are going through with a semi-elaborate wedding party in April. The other two reasons are his daughter Melanie and my own Aunt Mart. The three of them are wedding-obsessed, and have formed a consortium that could have orchestrated the invasion of Normandy if given a chance. The wedding book alone, stuffed with fabric scraps, pages torn from magazines, stationery samples, and menus is over 200 pages. Although neither Miles nor I has much interest in that kind of thing, it would be cruel to deny them all the fun they're having. So we're having a big wedding in April and not saying a word about the fact that we will have been married for almost six months by then. After all, a party is a party.

January is the dead season for most businesses in small towns like mine, particularly when you run a business that barely keeps its head above water in the good times. Everyone is broke after Christmas, with no money to travel and no reason to board their dogs. The unpredictable weather keeps my out-of-town clients who come for agility or tracking lessons off the roads, and those adorable puppies everyone got for Christmas won't be old enough for puppy class until spring. Corny, my head groomer and general manager, still has his regular clients, of course, which is a good thing since I'd had to cut his salary to almost nothing when I closed the kennel last spring. He has a small apartment in the back of the kennel where he lives rent-free and I'm sure that helps, but, still, I'd expected him to quit at any moment all year long. I wouldn't have blamed him, but I would have hated it. I'd come to depend on him more than I ever intended to.

Dog Daze is located behind a cute picket fence with pawprints painted on the path about a hundred feet from my back door. It's a former horse stable now painted bright yellow with colorful, playful pups stenciled on the front. I have ten roomy indoor/outdoor kennels, an outdoor play yard that doubles as an agility training arena, an indoor play room, two training rooms, and a grooming room. It's all fully air-conditioned with under-floor heating, and the floors are carpeted in bright yellow, red and green puzzle matting. I worked hard to make it a place where dogs love to come and I love to work and, yes, I'm proud of it. I'm also ashamed that I neglected it for so long.

Corny had Georgia Edge's miniature poodle on the table when I came in, and a fluffy golden mix in a drying cage. My two Australian Shepherds, Mischief and Magic, came bouncing and wagging their tailless butts to greet me, and I dropped to my knees to pet them. Cisco bounded ahead toward the gate that separated the lobby from the grooming room to check out the poodle. The whole place was warm and steamy with the smell of exotic shampoos and just the faintest undertone of wet dog.

The Aussie girls covered my face with sloppy grins and doggie kisses, then raced off to tackle Cisco. Cisco had his paws on the gate, his tail wagging in mad hope that someone would open it so that he could greet the poodle. When the girls body-slammed him, the three of them went over in a playful tangle of barks and fur that was destined to end in a canine attempt to turn my workspace into a racetrack. Before I could draw a breath to head it off, Corny said sternly, "Ladies! Gentleman! Indoor manners, please!"

Instantly, my three dogs separated themselves and went to sit in front of the gate, all three of them grinning happily in the direction from which the voice had come. I have no idea how Corny does this. I have been a dog trainer all my life and, while I certainly could have distracted these three from the riot they were intent on creating, I could never have done it with the efficiency and, frankly, the level of delighted cooperation that Corny had managed.

He's something of a curiosity around here, with his bright red Ronald McDonald mop of curls and his tendency to dress in primary colors—not to mention his over-the-top enthusiasm for just about any challenge put in front of him—but five minutes in his presence and you can't help but love him. And anybody who can demand the kind of devotion from a dog that Corny does should be President, as far as I'm concerned.

I took three treats from the canister on the check-in counter and tossed them one by one to my dogs, because you can never over-reward for good behavior, and said to Corny, "You know you could make a fortune on the show circuit with the way you handle dogs."

Corny's grandfather had been a legend in the dog world as both a handler and a judge, and no doubt that was where Corny had inherited his talent. But he just gave a dismissive wave with the scissors, stepped back to critically examine the shape of the poodle's beard, and replied, "Oh, my word, Miss Stockton, if you knew the stories I've heard. Not for me, I can tell you that much." He moved in to make a minuscule adjustment to one of the poodle's curls with the trimming scissors. "Besides, I couldn't leave Mr. Cisco and the Princesses Mischief and Magic, now could I? Not to mention Miss Holly Bell here." He picked up the poodle and kissed her on the nose, then returned her gently to the table.

I grinned and scooped up the mail from the counter. "I'll be in the office for a few hours," I told Corny, "working on my taxes." I called to the dogs, who were sniffing the floor for dropped treat crumbs. "Come on, guys, let's go."

"Yes, ma'am." He held up two bottles of canine nail polish for Holly Bell's inspection. "What do you think, Miss Holly Bell? Precious Peach or Salsa Flame? What are you feeling today?"

I grinned to myself as I went into my office, the dogs following close behind.

Mischief and Magic know how to entertain themselves and immediately picked up a tug toy from the basket in the corner and began a spirited game of tug. Cisco, who had never won in the two-against-one tug contest, nonetheless gamely grabbed the center of the toy and gave it his best shot. Fortunately, I'm accustomed to working in chaos and barely noticed the playful barks, growls and scuffling as I sat down to sort the mail.

It was mostly bills, a few dog supply catalogues that I put aside to peruse later, and the usual amount of junk mail. There was also a window envelope addressed to Corny, which I glanced at and started to put aside, then I looked again. The return address was from Miles's accounting firm. Puzzled, I took the envelope back into the grooming room.

"Corny," I said, holding it out, "this is addressed to you."

He glanced up from putting the last stroke of Precious Peach polish on Miss Holly Bell's nails. He was very fast; when painting a dog's nails, you have to be.

"Oh, yes, ma'am," he said, "I saw it. It's just my W-2 from Mr. Young. I meant to put it away."

He took the envelope and tucked it into his shirt pocket beneath the yellow-and-red pawprint apron. I stared at him.

"Why is Miles sending you a W-2?"

He picked up Holly Bell and transferred her to one of the small-dog crates in the bank against the wall. "I suppose because my paycheck has been coming from him? That's what you agreed to, isn't it? That the grooming fees would be come through Dog Daze and my salary would be issued by Mr. Young's accountants?"

It took me a moment to get that stupid look of incomprehension off my face. As I saw the puzzlement grow on Corny's, I gave him a quick, stiff smile and said, "Right. Sorry. I just forgot who was doing what."

"Maybe you should have Mr. Young's accountants do your taxes," Corny suggested helpfully as I turned to go. "They're really very efficient."

"Maybe I will," I replied, and kept the smile frozen on my face until I closed the door of my office behind me.

Miles and I have one simple rule: he doesn't interfere in my business or my finances, and I don't interfere in his. Not that I would know how to interfere in his business if I wanted to, but you know what I mean. He had gone behind my back and started paying *my* employee's salary because he knew I couldn't afford to and he had deliberately kept it from me and that was definitely not okay. I jerked out my phone and texted him angrily: *We need to talk*.

In former times, I would have stormed up the hill and confronted him in person, but since Miles worked from home now—not to mention his multiple appointments with medical professionals—this approach had left me cooling my heels, and my temper, outside his closed door once too often. I now knew enough to make an appointment if I wanted to fight with him.

You sound mad, he replied.

I am.

Damn. I'm in a Zoom with Zurich and I don't want to miss the fight. Hold on to that feeling.

Don't worry.

Free at 3:00. Looking forward to getting pummeled by you.

I slammed the phone down on my desk as though doing so would let Miles know just how annoyed I was. All it did was crack a corner of my brand-new golden retriever phone case. I spent a moment glaring at the damage, then looked at Cisco, who had given up his quest for the tug toy and was regarding me with that absolutely adorable, half-quizzical head tilt that some dogs—Cisco among them—have mastered. Evolution being what it is, I'm pretty sure that as soon as every dog in the world learns how to call up that expression at will, there will be peace on earth.

I smiled, ruefully at first, then with more warmth. "Come on, Cisco," I said, pushing up from my desk. "Let's go play."

CHAPTER FOUR

What Cisco calls play, I call training, and when done right, there shouldn't be much difference between the two. Apparently, I wasn't doing it right, because I was disappointed in my training session with Cisco. We worked on seek-and-find, which is part of his tracking regimen, and he missed two of the three objects of his search. That's definitely not good for a dog who's been tracking as long as he has, but he just wasn't interested. I'd worked with him only sporadically these last few months, and now I was paying for it.

For a change of pace, we worked on curtsy, which is a more complex version of the bow, with the two front paws crossed. Cisco is a certified therapy dog and often entertains at schools and nursing homes with his repertoire of tricks. Usually, he loves learning new things, but today he refused to catch on. Every dog has an off-day, I guess, and it's important not to get frustrated. To cheer myself up, I brought the girls in after lunch and did some agility runs, and they didn't let me down. By the time we finished, I was having a very hard time being mad about anything.

I kept Miles waiting until 4:00, then loaded the crew into my SUV and drove the short distance to his house. Generally, I would have walked, but living in the shadow of the mountain as we do, it starts to get dark around 4:30 this time of year, and the wind was already bitterly cold. I saw Rita's car parked in the circular driveway as I pulled around into the garage. An RFID sticker on my sun visor opened the garage doors automatically and closed them behind me, and when I opened the car door, the dogs tumbled out, their nails clicking eagerly on the shiny white epoxy floor as they raced toward the stairs. There is an elevator, of course, which had come in handy since Miles's injury, but I had never been able to persuade the dogs to get in it. I can't say I blame them. I don't entirely trust it, either.

I pressed my finger to the digital scanner, and the stairway door clicked open. I jumped at the sound of a warm female AI voice coming from the speaker. "Hello, Raine. Everyone is in the kitchen. I'll tell them you're here." I know to expect it, but the damn thing gets me every time.

Frowning a little in embarrassment, I muttered, "Don't bother." and opened the door to let the dogs precede me up the stairs. The AI speaker didn't respond. It has a somewhat limited repertoire.

I'll admit, I'm a little intimidated by Miles's

house, with its high-tech opulence and designer finishes, but the dogs love it here. For one thing, their best canine friend, a golden retriever named Pepper, lives there. For another, Miles has built them a state-of-the-art playroom complete with a selection of toys that puts the Dog Daze playroom to shame. There's a slide that spills into a wading pool filled with foam balls. There's a series of twisting tunnels, a giant herding ball, and a flirt pole. There's a collection of bones, puzzle toys and stuffies that, frankly, make me wish I were a dog. They even have their own TV, tuned twenty-four-seven to The Dog Channel. Swear to God.

Rita doesn't like dogs in the kitchen, which is probably a good thing, since the only meals I've ever had that were free of dog hair were in Miles's house. I therefore hung my outdoor gear in the closet at the top of the stairs and shooed my crew toward the playroom. Pepper met us halfway there, which delayed our progress a good bit. Just as I'd gotten the happy dog greeting mélange untangled, Melanie came around the corner with a cheerful, "Hey, Raine. Dad says you're mad at him again."

"He's right."

My dogs rushed to greet her and she held up an authoritative hand to stop them from bowling her over. They skidded to a sit— even Pepper, who hadn't been part of the onslaught—and waited while she doled out treats. I couldn't help being proud of that—not so much of my dogs, who knew better than to jump on people, but of Melanie, who had been a lot harder to train. She is a cute eleven-year-old with curly dark hair and big glasses who, since her mother was supermodel material, will probably grow up to be beautiful. Heaven help us all when that happens, because she already has her father's Mensa-level IQ and off-the-scale confidence.

"Let me know when you're finished fighting," she said. "I'll take the dogs to the playroom. Pepper and Cisco need to practice their promenade for the wedding."

Melanie was, as mentioned, the main reason we had kept our secret marriage secret. I doubt very much she will invest this much time and energy in her own wedding when the time comes. Her latest project was to teach Cisco and Pepper—ring bearer and flower girl, respectively— to march down the aisle in unison to Pachabel's *Canon in D.* Good thing she was starting four months early.

"Good luck with that," I told her. "Cisco is in a mood. You need to let them play for ten or fifteen minutes, or neither one of them will be able to focus."

She gave me an airy, dismissing wave over her shoulder as she started toward the playroom, a tangle of dogs scampering at her feet. "I've got this, Raine."

I returned an eye shrug she couldn't see and made my way to the kitchen.

Miles has one of those kitchens you only see in magazines: acres of granite, sparkling stainless, light fixtures imported from Belgium, and every appliance and gadget known to man. Some might say this is all wasted on a bachelor, which Miles was when he built it, but it happens that he is a gourmet cook. His mother isn't bad, either.

To that point, the aromas that wafted over me as I entered the kitchen almost made me forget what I had come for.

Miles chopped tomatoes and okra from his wheelchair at the prep island. Onions, celery and green pepper were sautéing with andouille sausage in an iron Dutch oven. Rita, with her pretty platinum hair pulled up in a messy bun and flour on her cheeks, was up to her elbows in bread dough as she kneaded her famous farm-style cheese bread. "Hi, sweetheart," she greeted me, and turned her cheek for a kiss. I obliged, and wiped away a smudge of flour from her face as I did.

"What smells so good?"

"Creole gumbo," Miles replied. "And mom's rosemary-cheese bread. Are you still mad?"

Miles had graduated to crutches a few weeks ago, but he still used the wheelchair in the kitchen for convenience. Even in a wheelchair, with his leg entombed in a black brace and supported by the footrest, Miles is the sexiest man I've ever known. He's good-looking, sure, with spikey salt and pepper hair and dreamy gray eyes. Lately, he's been sporting a scruff of beard that I'm not crazy about, but the deeply sculpted pecs and biceps that are the result of the extra time he's been spending in his home gym since the accident almost make up for it. But that's not what attracts me to him. It's the way he is with his daughter, the way he can solve any problem, the way he always knows what to say, the way he makes me laugh. The way he adores me. Sexy.

Nonetheless, I scowled at him and replied, "Yes, I'm still mad." Even though I was finding it harder and harder to hold on to that feeling.

"Oh-oh," said Rita. "What has he done now?"

"He broke our rule." I turned to Miles, building up steam now, and repeated, "You broke our rule. You've been secretly paying Corny's salary for over a year without telling me! You *know* how I feel about things like that! We keep our finances separate. You don't interfere. And you *certainly* don't do it without even asking me!"

Miles scraped the chopped vegetables into the pot, unimpressed. " 'Thank you, Miles, for saving my business,'" he said, " 'and for not letting my only employee starve to death because he's too humble to complain and too loyal to leave. I don't know what I would have done without you.' 'Why, you're welcome, sweetheart. It's what people who love each other do.'"

My scowl deepened. I hate it when he does that. And by 'that' I mean when he finds a way to be right even when he's absolutely wrong.

"You should have asked me," I told him.

"You would have said no. Hand me that onion, will you, hon? I think this needs another one."

I found the onion he gestured to and refrained from throwing it at him. I plopped the onion down on the cutting board in front of him. “I have a right to say no. It’s my business!”

“Which would be a former business by now if you’d lost Corny so, once again, you’re welcome.”

I drew in a sharp breath for a reply but released it in frustrated silence. The onion disappeared into small, evenly-sized squares beneath the quick tap-tap-tap of his knife. I turned to Rita, but she had already popped in her earbuds and was completely oblivious to our conversation—something she frequently did when Miles and I went at it to avoid taking sides. I knew in this case she would be completely on my side, but, still, I was a little embarrassed to put her in an awkward position.

I turned back to Miles. “Are we going to be arguing about money for the rest of our lives?”

“Only if you continue to be unreasonable.”

Rita covered the ball of dough with a towel and placed it in what I had recently learned was called the proofing drawer. I have no idea what a proofing drawer is, but according to Rita, it makes excellent bread. Evidence suggests she is right.

I lowered my voice to a conversational level just in case her earbuds weren’t completely blocking outside noise. “You know what it is, don’t you?” I said. “A power inequity. You have power and I don’t.”

“That’s not fair.” But I could tell by the faint scowl that crossed his brow that I had hit a nerve. “Or true.”

“Well, that’s how it looks,” I returned irritably, “to me and to anyone else who’s paying attention. It’s like you don't trust me to take care of myself. Just like that tracking app on your phone. It's good for emergencies, sure, but it's also a little like stalking."

"Is that right?"

I was growing tired of the argument and probably should have quit while I was ahead, but I had to score one last point, even if it was a point I didn't particularly care about one way or another. "Yes."

He appeared to think about that for a minute. "Fair enough," he concluded. "Do you want me to turn the app off?"

"Yes," I said, although I wasn't entirely sure why. The app had never really bothered me until Casey remarked on it this morning.

He took out his phone, tapped an icon, and said, "Done."

"Good."

He returned the phone to his pocket. "I love you."

"I love you, too," I said, and came over to kiss him.

Rita, noticing the fight was over, removed her earbuds and began to clean the counter. I picked up a piece of celery and sat at one of the stools. "How did physical therapy go?"

"Great. X-Rays next week and then I transfer to a walking boot."

"That's fabulous," I congratulated him, beaming. "I'll be glad to see the last of that wheelchair."

"I'll be skiing by March," he assured me. "Of course," he admitted, "all the snow will be gone by then."

"Poor baby," said Rita. "I'm so sorry you're missing the chance to break your leg again. Raine, did you get my e-mail about the tasting menu?"

Miles and I shared a secret grin for no particular reason, and I crunched down on the celery stick. I replied, "I'm sorry, I haven't had a chance to look at it. "

She opened the refrigerator and took out a bottle of wine. "No rush. Just let me know if those dates are okay."

Melanie sailed into the room, declaring, "Maybe I'll make an apple tarte tatin for dessert."

"Maybe you'll do your homework first," countered Miles.

"How'd the training go?" I said.

She frowned. "All they wanted to do was play."

I decided to be the bigger person by not saying "I told you so".

"Well, it's going to be adorable when you teach them to do it," Rita assured her. She poured a glass of wine and added, "Can I get anyone anything?"

We all demurred and she said, "Miles, tell that fancy robot of yours to set a timer for one hour on the bread. I'm going to enjoy my wine by the fire."

"We'll join you in a minute," he said, and added to the robot, "Set a reminder on the bread for one hour."

"Can I help with dinner?" Melanie offered, causing both Miles and me to lift an eyebrow. Melanie loved to cook, but volunteering for anything was a sure-fire indicator that she was trying to get out of something else.

"You can," Miles agreed, "by doing your homework."

Melanie wrinkled her nose. "I have to write a stupid essay about a stupid poem," she said. "I don't do poems. I'm a STEM girl."

Miles said, "You know what else you don't do? Fail to turn in an assignment. Get busy."

"Maybe I'll have Chat GPT do it," she said.

"Maybe you'll spend the weekend in your room writing essays for me instead of going to your friend Simone's party."

Melanie scowled and slouched over to the built-in desk where her book bag and laptop were.

I finished off the celery stick. "What's the poem?" I asked.

"Something about a frosty evening and a horse," she replied unhappily. "And woods that are dark and deep."

"And miles to go before I sleep," Miles supplied for her. His electric wheelchair whirred as he moved to the refrigerator, and then to the pantry. "Which is exactly what you have, so get cracking."

"Oh, yeah, I know that one," I said. "Promises to keep, right?"

"Here it is." Melanie read from her laptop. " 'My little horse must think it's queer, stopping when there's no one near.'" She looked over her shoulder at us. "Is that a misappropriation of the word 'queer'?"

"No," we said together, and she shrugged, turning back to her reading.

Miles placed the ingredients he had gathered on the countertop and adjusted the wheelchair lift to counter height. He had one of those cool electronic chairs that did everything but give the weather forecast, and any offer I made to help would have been insulting. Also, the only thing I knew how to do in the kitchen was get in the way.

I said, "Casey and I were in a fender-bender this afternoon. Some rich guy named Lance Booker from Arkansas. Do you know him?"

"I'll have to look him up in my rich-guy directory," Miles responded. "Any damage?"

"Almost none. But he gave Casey a thousand dollars cash not to call the cops."

Miles's eyebrows went up. "Okay. That's not suspicious at all."

"He was probably carrying drugs or guns," Melanie volunteered from her corner. "Didn't want any K-9s sniffing around."

"Homework," Miles said.

"Maybe I'll write it from the horse's point of view," Melanie replied.

I thought that was brilliant, and told her so. I turned back to Miles. "So how was your day? After you finished stalking us, of course."

"Not as interesting as yours." He added broth to the pot, and it bubbled up a delicious-smelling cloud of steam. "Jim Coker is hunting turkeys out of season. Mrs. Henderson over on Persimmon Street has her grandchildren visiting. One of them threw a ball through the neighbor's car window. And somebody's cutting timber illegally on National Forest land, over by Rattlesnake Creek."

I made a disapproving face. "So you spent the day spying on your neighbors? Good heavens, Miles, you're as bad as that guy in that old movie you made me watch."

"Jimmy Stewart in *Rear Window*," Melanie volunteered. "It's a classic."

"Right," I agreed dryly. "And you remember how that turned out? Not so great for the guy in the window."

"Maybe," replied Miles, "but he did learn some interesting things. So did I."

"Oh, yeah? Like what? Aside from the turkeys and the baseball, of course."

"Like the fact that we have a new neighbor."

I reached for another celery stick. "Really? Where?"

"Buck's old house. Some woman, appears to be by herself."

I stopped with the celery stick halfway to my mouth. Buck was my ex-husband and the former sheriff of Hanover County. His house was down the valley from mine, and I could see it from my kitchen window. The house had been empty for over a year now, since he had remarried and moved to South Georgia. It was strange—more than strange—to think of someone else living there now.

I put the cracker down and took out my phone. I texted Buck: *Did you sell your house?*

In a moment he replied, *Rented. Dakota Bradshaw. LE.*

LE stood for law enforcement, and I could see by

the three little dots that he was explaining further. But the text, when it came, said only, *No kids, no dogs. Don't be a pest.*

I scowled my annoyance at him and put my phone away. I was not a pest.

"Buck said he rented his house to a Dakota Bradshaw," I told Miles. "Apparently, she's law enforcement."

"Good deal. It'll be nice to have a cop in the neighborhood."

"Until she catches you spying on her with that drone. Maybe I'll take her some pie." I turned to Melanie. "Is an apple tart the same as a pie?"

"Tarte Tatin," corrected Melanie impatiently. "And it's not the same at all. For one thing..."

"Last warning," said Miles without looking up from the chicken he was deftly deboning.

Melanie turned immediately back to her homework.

"The woman with him looked like a country music star," I said. "She was more of a girl, really. Maybe twenty? And he had to be close to sixty."

"The guy who hit you?"

"Yeah. He was driving a Ford King Ranch, all tricked out with wings painted on the side panels. You just don't see something like that around here every day."

Miles looked up from his work, a small frown between his brows. "Wings?"

"That's right. Why?"

The frown deepened briefly, and then he shook

his head and turned back to the chicken. "Nothing, probably. Do you see that bowl of salt over there by the oven? Can you bring it to me, please?"

I said, "Who keeps their salt in a bowl?" But I went to find it, and between Melanie's homework, Rita's tasting menu, and the amazing dinner we all shared, I forgot all about the guy from Arkansas.

Until Miles brought him up again, that is.

CHAPTER FIVE

Hanover County was a "semi-dry" county, which meant that you were welcome to pick up a bottle of wine or a six-pack of beer at the local grocery, but if you wanted to sit down at a restaurant that served mixed drinks or purchase a bottle of tequila for margaritas, you were out of luck. Most people didn't mind driving a few miles to the next county for a night out, and places like the Borderline Bar—which, as its name implied, sat mere feet across the border from Hanover County—did a booming business with residents of its neighbor.

The Borderline also made a pretty good hamburger, but that was not why Casey went there. There was a waitress named Izzy he'd been trying to score with for over a month. She enjoyed playing hard-to-get and he enjoyed the chase. He was therefore disappointed when he took a seat at the bar, ordered a beer, and looked around. There were only a dozen or so people there on a weeknight: a couple of guys drinking at the bar and a woman eating alone, a table of four finishing up a pitcher of margaritas and a plate of nachos, a man and a woman being served hamburgers and beers. The waitress serving them was plump, fiftyish, red-haired and overly made-up. He didn't see Izzy anywhere.

"Izzy's not working tonight?" he asked the bartender when he delivered his beer.

The bartender shrugged. "As far as I know, she's not working anytime, at least not here. She hasn't shown up for the last three shifts. No call, no nothing. The boss is pretty pissed."

Casey was surprised. When they talked, she said she liked her job and the tips were good. She needed the money after Christmas and was thinking about taking extra shifts. She didn't seem like the kind of girl who would just not show. "She's worked here a while, though, huh?"

"Almost a year. I gotta tell you, it was rough Saturday night with only one waitress. I never thought she'd do us like that."

Casey said, "Did anybody check on her? Maybe she's sick or wrecked her car or something."

"I heard somebody say she's not answering her phone, but not my problem." He nodded toward Casey's beer. "Get you anything else?"

"Nah, I'm good."

The bartender moved away and Casey sipped his beer, letting his gaze wander aimlessly until they settled on the woman eating a hamburger two seats down from him. She was probably in her thirties, with thick, honey colored hair pulled back in a ponytail. She was not a petite woman by any means, but she was fit-looking in skinny jeans and a big sweater. He studied her until she sensed his gaze and turned to look at him. She had a square face with a hard jawline and steady dark eyes. He smiled. She did not.

"Hi," he said. "I'm Casey."

"I'm eating," she said, and turned back to her burger.

He tried again. "I haven't seen you in here before."

She swirled a french fry in a puddle of ketchup and took a bite without looking at him.

The door opened behind them with a blast of cold air but Casey didn't bother to turn to see who'd entered. The newcomer thumped up to the bar in heavy work boots and banged his fist on the surface. Casey didn't look at him as the bartender came over to attend him, but the woman did.

Casey sipped his beer. "So what are you?" he said. "FBI or local?"

She stopped in the process of taking a bite of the hamburger, shifting her gaze toward him.

"It's in the eyes," Casey explained. "I've been around enough cops to recognize it."

She might have actually answered him then, but the bartender stopped in front of Casey and said, "Hey, buddy." He nodded back over his shoulder to the man who had just come in and was sitting at the other end of the bar. "If you're really trying to find Izzy, you should ask him. She left with him after her last shift. But watch yourself. He's kind of a troublemaker."

Casey turned on his stool to look at the man at the end of the bar. "Well, damn," he muttered. It was that guy from the thrift store this morning. He appeared to have sobered up slightly since then, but from the way he tossed back the Jack Daniels in front of him, that wouldn't last long.

Casey turned back to the woman. "It was nice talking to you," he said.

He got up and took his beer to the other end of the bar, leaning against it next to the newcomer. "Did you find your car?" he asked pleasantly.

The man looked up at him with an angry, red-eyed gaze. "Who the hell are you?"

"We met earlier," Casey reminded him, "at the thrift store in town. You were looking for your car. And your wife."

The man shouted, "Hey!" And lifted his glass to the bartender.

When the bartender came to pour another, Casey said, "On me."

The stranger glared at him. "What do you want?"

Casey said, "You know that waitress that used to work here, Izzy? Curly blonde hair, pink on the ends, likes to wear low-cut sweaters and cowboy boots with tassels on them? Real friendly, always smiling."

The man turned back to his drink.

"I just wondered whatever happened to her. Somebody said you might know."

He did not look at Casey. "Why the hell would anybody say that?"

Casey sipped his beer. "Maybe because you were

seen leaving with her after her shift last week?"

The man kept his eyes on the drink in front of him and said nothing for the longest time. Then, "You got a real problem minding your own business, don't you, boy?"

Casey replied easily, "Yeah, I might have been told that a time or two." He took another sip of his beer. "Look, friend, I'm not asking for trouble. I just want to make sure she's okay, that's all."

The man slammed back the rest of his drink and stood, demanding, "Why wouldn't she be?"

Casey held up a hand in self-defense and took a step backward, watching his opponent carefully. "No reason. No reason at all."

The man fumbled some bills out of his pocket and slapped them on the table, but as he did a small paper fluttered to the floor. Casey bent to pick it up, not to be polite, but because he was curious, now, about who this guy was. He reached for the business card on the floor and the man kicked his hand away. Casey shouted, "Hey!" and stumbled back, spilling the beer down the front of his shirt. "What's your problem, dude?"

His adversary, red faced, shoved Casey hard in the shoulder. Casey, regaining his balance, said, very lowly, "I really wish you hadn't done that."

"Oh yeah?" The man took a menacing step closer. "How about you get the hell out of my way, you punk asshole?"

Out of the corner of his eye, Casey saw the woman he'd been talking to at the bar get up, watching them, and reach for something at her waistband. A gun? A badge? *I knew you were a cop,* he thought smugly, just before a fist slammed into his face.

CHAPTER SIX

I flopped onto the bed in my pajamas and let my phone drop face-down beside me. "Tell me again why we're doing this," I demanded.

Cisco, who was curled up in his high-end Orvis dog bed that was custom upholstered to match the décor of the room, looked up at me with pricked ears, just in case I expected him to answer the question. Mischief and Magic, who were far too restless at night to share a room with sleeping humans, were already tucked away in their luxury crates in the playroom.

"What's that, hon?" Miles, who was sitting up in bed beside me, did not glance up from his own phone, and his tone was absent. He was wearing navy sweats that were as soft as cashmere—and probably were, for all I knew—with his injured leg propped up on two pillows. But he wasn't ready for bed. Even before his injury, Miles only slept a few hours a night, and a regular bed was far too uncomfortable for him with the heavy brace. He had an adjustable bed in the guest room next door where he would spend the night, but we liked to end our days together like this, talking or reading or watching TV in bed, and he would stay here until I fell asleep.

I picked up my phone again and read from his mother's e-mail. "'Wedding dinner menu, choose two from each category: cocktails, appetizers, main course starter, main course protein, main course sides, main course desserts, after dinner drinks... there are, like, seven things in each column! And that's before we even get to the wedding dinner. Listen," I said earnestly. I put the phone down and turned on my side to face him, propping up on one elbow. "I've got an idea. We take off this weekend and drive to South Carolina. They only have a twenty-four-hour waiting period for marriages. Then we come back and tell everyone we changed our minds about the wedding and decided to elope instead. That way it doesn't look like we've been lying this whole time, but we don't have to go through with this—this ridiculous royal wedding they're cooking up."

"That would probably work," he agreed, typing something on his phone, "for Mom and your aunt, anyway. But it would break Melanie's heart. After all the work she's put into training those dogs? And I happen to know she has at least three costume changes planned. She'd never forgive us."

My spirits fell and I turned to stare at the ceiling, propping a pillow under my head. "I suppose so," I mumbled.

"Besides, you know what they say. Weddings and funerals are not for the victims. They're for the family."

I raised an eyebrow at him. "Victims?"

He looked up from his phone long enough to grin at me. "What I meant to say was, the wedding is not about us. The marriage is for us." He looped his fingers through three of mine and gave them a squeeze. "The wedding is for everyone else. Let them have their fun. You've got to admit, it's going to be one hell of a party."

I sighed and picked up my phone again, gazing at it glumly. "I still have to pick two from each category."

He held out his hand and I placed my phone in it. In less than fifteen seconds and a dozen clicks, he returned it to me. "Done," he said. "You worry too much about the small stuff. And you know perfectly well that whatever you choose will be changed half a dozen times before the big day, right?"

I cheered a little. "Yeah, that's right." I looked over his selections. "What's an Aperol spritzer, anyway?"

"Beats me. I don't drink, you know." He put his phone aside and looked at me with unexpected thoughtfulness. "Are you sorry yet?"

"For what?"

He gestured to the broken leg. "The whole 'in sickness and in health' thing. I've been laid up since we got married, and you've done nothing but take care of me. This is probably not the way you expected to spend your honeymoon. I'd have a few regrets if I were you."

"Well," I admitted, "You have been a perfect beast the whole time. But it's not like I didn't know what I was getting into."

"Fortunately," he agreed, and then he frowned. "It's just that I hate feeling so damn useless. I don't know how to sit around and do nothing."

"Which is why you decided to take over my business," I said.

"No. That's why I got the drone." He slanted a look at me. "I took over your business because somebody had to. What do you want to do about Corny? Keep him on my payroll, or not?"

I shifted uncomfortably. "I don't know." I was determined to prove to him I could be reasonable. "Maybe… just leave things the way they are for now." I added reluctantly, "I'm sorry I yelled at you before. I know you were trying to help, but when you do things like that it's like you don't think I can run my own business. And I guess I can't blame you. I haven't done a very good job with that this past year. I just don't like having it thrown in my face."

He looked at me seriously. "The opposite is true. I never had any doubt you could run your business. I just wanted to make sure there was something left to run when you got ready to get back to work."

I snuggled up against his cashmere-soft shoulder. "Well, thanks. But could you maybe just ask next time?"

He kissed my hair. "You know," he pointed out, "the best partnerships are structured so that each partner does what he or she is best at. I'm the best at finance and business. You're the best at everything else. I say we each play to our strengths."

I wasn't entirely ready to concede victory to him. "Maybe. Let me think about it. Meantime..." I glanced up at him. "Will you ask your accountants to do my taxes?"

He winked at me. "E-mail me your records."

His phone chimed with a message and he turned to read it while I sat up and resumed looking over the menu. Half the dishes I couldn't pronounce, and the other half I was pretty sure I wouldn't like. But I guess the bride never has time to eat at her own wedding, anyway.

I said, "You know what we should do? Have the whole thing catered by that barbecue place we like. You know the one just over the state line?"

I glanced at him but it was clear he hadn't heard me. He was frowning at the message on his phone.

I scooted closer to him, trying to read from the phone. "What?"

He modulated the scowl lines on his forehead as he looked at me, although they did not entirely disappear. "You know that guy Booker who ran into you this afternoon? Turns out he's the front man for an outfit called Blackwing Acquisition and Development. They're basically land raiders. They buy up under-utilized or abandoned properties and turn them into commercial real estate. He's been here six months and this is the first I'm hearing about it. I can't figure out what he's doing here."

"Because," I countered dryly, "you're the only land raider around here."

He shot me a look that wasn't entirely indulgent. "Right." He looked back at the phone for a minute and then added, "He bought a big house out on the lake. Paid one-point-four million for it."

"Wow." Now I was interested. "I didn't know there were any houses like that on the lake. It's mostly summer cabins, and those are, like, seventy-five years old."

"Right," Miles murmured. "I looked into buying some of them, but the return on investment wasn't high enough for residential real estate." He thumbed a couple of pages thoughtfully. "Looks like the purchase price of his house included six acres, and he's bought five more lots since then."

Now I frowned and sat up straighter. "What for? You said he does commercial real estate. You can't develop anything commercially out on the lake."

"Don't know," Miles said. "He hasn't filed for any permits that I can find. I'll have to do some more research."

I started to say something, but just then my phone rang. I glanced at the caller ID and answered it impatiently.

"Hey, Sis," Casey said before I could ask what he thought he was doing calling at this hour. "I know it's late but I need a favor. Can you come pick me up and drive me back to my truck?"

Immediately, I thought the worst. "What happened? Are you okay? Where are you?"

He answered, “Hanover County jail.”

CHAPTER SEVEN

It should come as a surprise to no one that the Hanover County jail holds no good memories for me. My stomach was in knots from the minute I pulled into the parking lot, just at the sight of the place. Miles had, of course, wanted to come with me, but travel was a nightmare for him unless he was in his physical therapist's specially equipped van. Casey hadn't said anything about bail, but Miles sent me with his credit card anyway. Yes, bail for minor offenses can be paid with a card these days, and I couldn't think of any crime Casey could have committed that Miles's AmEx Black couldn't fix. Or maybe I should say I didn't want to think of one.

Cisco shifted restlessly in the back seat of the SUV as I parked, sensing my distress. Or maybe he had bad memories of the place, too, having visited me there once. I unfastened my seatbelt and took a breath. "It's going to be fine, boy," I told him. "I'll be right back."

The jail was a low tan brick building in the Public Safety complex adjacent to the sheriff's office, which was another place I didn't frequent very much anymore. I had been a regular there most of my adult life, what with my uncle being sheriff and my husband being a deputy. I had been friends with just about everybody on the force. These days, I do my best to avoid the place.

I crossed the brightly lit parking lot with my hands in the pockets of my coat and my shoulders hunched against the cold. I pushed through the glass door into the small reception area, which was empty this time of night, and went up to the window. "I'm here for Casey Macintosh," I told her. "Raine Stockton."

She indicated an opening in the bottom of the window. "Purse, cell phone, weapons," she said.

I pushed my purse and cell phone through the window. "No weapons."

She nodded toward a metal detector in front of another door, and I walked through. As soon as I did, the door buzzed open.

I found myself in another brightly lit room with doors on either side of a short hallway. Casey was leaning against the booking desk, chatting up the duty officer. I had expected him to be in a cell, or at the very most, waiting in an interview room for the bondsman.

"What the hell, Casey?" I demanded as I approached.

"Oh, hey, Raine." He looked around at the sound of my voice. "Thanks for coming." He turned back to the booking officer and said, "My ride's here. Talk to you later."

The deputy, who looked as though he might have been out of high school a good six months, demonstrated why he was sitting behind a desk on the night shift by waving casually at the consummate con artist who was my brother and replying, "See you around, Case."

That's when I noticed the cut on the side of Casey's mouth that spread to an angry red swelling on his lower jaw, and I walked faster. "Are you okay? What happened?"

He started to grin, and then winced and touched the cut on his lip. "You know me, kid. Making friends wherever I go."

"Damn it, Casey," I returned, anxiety turning into impatience. "I was in my pajamas! What's going on?"

He touched my shoulder and indicated the exit door. "So, you know that drunk that was in the thrift store this morning bellowing for his wife? He was also in the Borderline bar tonight. I had a few questions for him about this waitress I know who hadn't been into work for a few days, and I guess he didn't like my tone. Fortunately…"

"Macintosh, hold on."

We both turned at the sharp female voice behind us. A woman in jeans and a chunky sweater came out of one of the rooms with a clipboard in her hand, moving toward us with authority. Her honey blonde hair was tied back at the nape, and she wore a badge around her neck. Casey greeted her with a sweeping bow and declared, "There she is now, my hero. Deputy...?" He paused, obviously waiting for her to supply her name.

The woman ignored him and addressed me instead. "Dakota Bradshaw," she said. "Are you his ride home?"

I eyed her warily. "Raine Stockton," I said. "What's this about? Are there charges? Is he free to go?"

"Right after he signs this." She turned to Casey with the clipboard. "It's a waiver of medical treatment for your injury. If," she muttered almost under her breath, "it can even be called that."

I liked her already.

Casey smiled as he scrawled his name on the form. "Dakota," he repeated. "Cool name. Do they call you Kody?"

She did not smile. "They call me Deputy Bradshaw."

And that's when it struck me. "Wait," I said. "You're my new neighbor. You rented my ex-husband's house. Buck Lawson," I clarified. "I'm in the white house up the hill from you. You can't see it from where you are, but I can see you. Your house, that is. I have the boarding kennel. But the dogs are very quiet, you shouldn't hear them at all. We're very careful about that." I realized I was babbling and stopped abruptly. I was usually much more composed than that with strangers. This place was really unnerving me.

She looked at me for a moment without speaking. Then she said slowly, "Right. Chief Lawson told me about you."

Casey dropped a hand on my shoulder and said cheerfully, "Don't believe a word of it."

I jammed my hands into my coat pockets and tried to regain my equilibrium. "Can you tell me what happened? Is Casey in trouble?"

She looked from me to Casey in a deliberative fashion and replied, "Not at the moment, no. There was a physical altercation at the Borderline Bar between Mr. Macintosh and one..." She flipped over a page on her clipboard and consulted it, "Thomas Lionel Hoggins, also known as Rooster, of Lookout Lane in Hanover County, a driver with Big Mountain Grading and Hauling. No real damage to either of the combatants..."

Here Casey interjected, "The good deputy here intervened before I could get off more than one or two punches."

"And a good thing she did," I told him sharply. "You can go to jail for assault, you know."

He shrugged this away and I turned back to the deputy. "The Borderline Bar is in Wilkes County," I pointed out. "Why weren't they taken there?"

A corner of her lips turned down, indicating that would have been her preference. "It turns out Mr. Hoggins had several outstanding warrants in Hanover County—DUI, domestic abuse, failure to appear—so it was deemed best to straighten it all out here. He's in custody now, and no charges were filed against Mr. Macintosh."

"Because I didn't do anything," Casey asserted. And when the deputy turned her cool gaze on him, he added, "Much."

I said to the deputy, "This man, Rooster, he was drunk at the Welcoming Arms Thrift store this morning, looking for his wife, Tina. We think she might be at the women's shelter. Is there any way you can, I don't know, warn her that he was looking for her?"

She said, "Yes, Mr. Macintosh mentioned that. I'll look into it, but her husband will be in jail for at least a few days, so there shouldn't be anything to worry about. But if she's worried, she can always get a protective order."

She glanced back at Casey. "You can go online in the morning to request a copy of the police report. And now..." She dropped the clipboard to her side and started to turn. "Since my first shift doesn't officially start for another twenty-four hours, I'll say goodnight."

"I was going to bring you a pie," I blurted.

She looked back at me querulously, waiting for me to continue or clarify. But my mind was blank, and when I said nothing, she offered uncertainly, "Thanks?"

I felt my cheeks go hot. "I mean, welcome to the neighborhood. It was nice to meet you."

I thrust out my hand, and she shook it briefly without returning the sentiment.

Casey winked at her. "Thanks for your help, Dakota. I appreciate it."

She didn't answer him, either.

Casey watched her walk away until I elbowed him sharply in the ribs. "Let's go."

I couldn't get out of there fast enough.

We were well away from the bright lights of the county jail when I said, "You scared me to death. What's the matter with you, getting into a bar fight over a girl? You don't have immunity anymore, you know. Nobody's coming to rescue you if you get yourself thrown in jail."

Cisco was straining against his harness to get Casey's attention, and Casey reached over the back of the seat to scratch Cisco's chin, shooting me a grin. "You did."

I glared at him briefly before turning my attention back to the road. "What's so great about this woman, anyway? How long have you been seeing her?"

"I haven't," he admitted. "I don't really even know her that well. We talk at the bar sometimes. I drove her home one night when her car wouldn't start, but she didn't ask me in. I just can't figure out why a girl like her would hook up with a scumbag like Scoggins—and a married one at that. She was young, cute, sassy. She could've done a lot better."

"Case in point," I said, nodding my head toward him.

"Case in point," he agreed with another grin.

"So what makes you think they hooked up? You just said you don't even know her. He could be her uncle or father or, I don't know, a neighbor. Maybe she had car trouble again and he was just trying to help her out, like you did."

"Yeah, I guess." Casey did not sound in the least convinced. "But she missed three shifts and no one can reach her and this guy was really pissed when I asked about her." He touched his jaw gingerly.

I had to admit, none of that sounded good. "Did you tell that to the deputy?"

"I did. She didn't seem very interested."

"Well," I pointed out, "she did say she was off duty."

I thought I caught a twinkle in his eyes in the flash of headlights as I made the turn into the Borderline parking lot. "She was hot, wasn't she?"

I rolled my eyes in muted exasperation. "Oh, for God's sake, Casey, focus, will you?"

I pulled up behind Casey's truck. It was close to midnight, but there were still plenty of cars in the gravel parking lot, and the neon lights were inviting. "Goodnight, Casey," I said firmly. "Go straight home."

He unfastened his seatbelt and got out. "You bet."

But of course, he did not.

CHAPTER EIGHT

In the city, the working class lived in cheap apartments on the bus route. In Hanover County, they lived in single-wide mobile homes. Some of these mobile homes were located in trailer parks or in neighborhoods roughly carved out from the side of a mountain via a network of unpaved roads. The trailer in which Izzy Stedman lived was on a private lot at the end of a short dirt road with only two other residences near it. Both looked unoccupied.

Casey used his bright headlights to navigate the road, and when he pulled into the short dirt clearing that served as a driveway, the lights reflected on the dark windows and illuminated nothing. Izzy's car was in the driveway, a ten-year-old Ford with a dull paint job and a dented fender. Casey closed his door and stepped out into the dark.

The night was cold and unnervingly quiet. His footsteps crunched on the frozen ground as he crossed to the small stoop and knocked on the door.

He gave it a minute, then knocked again and called, "Izzy! It's Casey from the bar. Don't shoot me, okay? Just making sure you're all right."

He counted to sixty and knocked again, loudly. "Izzy?"

Nothing.

He walked to the nearest window and turned on the flashlight app on his phone to look inside. He'd found the kitchen, and it was empty. He moved in the opposite direction toward the next window, and his flashlight beam picked up an unmade bed, a few clothes strewn around, and a dresser scattered with makeup bottles and tubes. He went back to the door and banged on it with his closed fist. "Izzy!"

By this point, he didn't expect an answer, and he got none.

He walked around to the back of the trailer, using his flashlight to navigate the uneven ground. He skirted a couple of trash cans and some rusted-out gardening tools, and climbed a single step to a set of sliding glass doors. They were the cheap, single-pane kind with nothing but a thumb lock. He knocked once again, just to be safe, and then deftly lifted and jiggled the sliding pane until he heard the lock disengage.

"Come on, girl, you have *got* to get a better lock," he muttered. He settled the pane back into its track and slid the door open.

"Izzy!" he called again. "Are you here?"

He stepped inside and was immediately greeted with a foul odor, like an overflowing sewer. He grimaced and shielded his mouth and nose with one hand, fumbling for a light switch with the other. The room sprang to light and he saw he was in the small dining room/kitchen area. He turned off his phone flashlight and put it away, moving around the kitchen. The cereal bowl in the sink was crusted with the dried remains of oatmeal. The coffee pot held maybe half a cup of cold coffee. The odor, whatever it was, was not coming from the kitchen. He felt his gut tighten with dread as he moved carefully toward the back of the house. The putrid odor grew stronger.

"Izzy?" he called again.

He stopped cold as he thought he heard something. It was faint and high, like a muffled cry or squeak. He turned his head and listened hard, but now there was nothing. Maybe a mouse, or the furnace kicking on. He took a few more steps down the hall and he heard it again. Definitely a hoarse, muffled whimper of distress, and it was coming from a small room to his right.

His heart started pounding as his defensive reflexes slammed into gear. He edged along the wall as quickly as he could, cursing himself for leaving his gun locked in the glovebox of his car. He pictured Izzy bound and gagged, possibly alone, possibly being held at gunpoint by her assailant. He had no plan. But he had often found that plans just got in the way.

He reached the open door of what he assumed was a bathroom or a closet. He reached his arm around, searching on the inside wall for the light switch. The minute he found it, he flung himself around the corner, simultaneously flipping on the light. He didn't even get a foot across the threshold.

From out of nowhere, a small dark figure launched itself toward him and slammed into his chest.

CHAPTER NINE

I had barely closed my eyes—or so it seemed—when my phone buzzed again. I groaned out loud when, blurry-eyed, I saw the time was 12:37. And then Casey's face appeared on my screen.

"What?" I demanded gruffly.

Cisco, always ready for an adventure, sprang from his dog bed, shook out his fur with a rattle of his tags, and trotted over to me. He put his chin on the bed and I flopped back against the pillows, closing my eyes and resting my hand on his head.

Casey said, "I found a dog and it's in pretty bad shape. I'm at Dog Daze. Can you come?"

I was awake, sitting up and flinging back the covers. "On my way."

I pulled on sweats, socks and boots over my pajamas, stopped by Miles's room to tell him where I was going, and dashed out into the cold. Cisco and I pulled into the parking lot of Dog Daze next to Casey's truck five minutes later. I unbuckled Cisco from his seat belt and ran around the car to join

Casey just as he was lifting a jacket- wrapped bundle from the back seat of his extended-cab truck.

"Oh, Casey!" I exclaimed in dismay. "What happened? Did you hit a dog?"

He gave me an indignant look. "Of course not. I found it inside Izzy's house. Water bowl was empty, toilet too. I don't think it's had anything to eat or drink since last week."

I got close enough to see the curly black head of a shivering poodle peeking out from beneath the folds of Casey's jacket. I said, "Okay, let's get her inside. It's freezing out here."

"There's something wrong with it, too, " Casey went on as we hurried toward the door, Cisco at our heels. "It looked like it was trying to bark but couldn't make anything but a squeaking sound. I don't know about the vets around here so I thought you'd be the best choice."

The noise we were making must have awakened Corny, because just as we reached the front door the lights went on. A puzzled Corny looked at us from behind the glass entry door. He was wearing fire truck pajamas and cocker spaniel slippers, his hair sticking out in a tangle of orange corkscrews around his head. When he saw the bundle Casey was carrying, his expression quickly turned to alarm, and he unlocked the door for us.

"Oh, Miss Stockton, what in the world?" he exclaimed as we pushed through the door, Cisco leading the way. "Is that a poodle?"

"Put her on the grooming table," I instructed

Casey, "straight ahead through the swinging gate." To Corny, I said, "Abandoned dog. She's starving and probably dehydrated. Shivering, too."

Corny didn't hesitate. "I've got some bone broth in back," he said, rushing off. "And I'll warm some towels in the dryer."

Casey put the dog on the grooming table and carefully unwrapped his jacket. Cisco put his paws on the table, sniffing the newcomer curiously. It was a female, as I had guessed from the pink collar, with a neatly kept curly black coat. She seemed a little small for a standard poodle, maybe 45 pounds, and was obviously emaciated. I could see every one of her ribs. She wore three tags on her collar—a rabies tag, a microchip identifier, and a name tag with her owner's phone number. "Gigi," I read. I smiled and stroked her head. Dogs respond not only to your actions, but to your facial expressions, and I wanted her to know she was safe. "You're a pretty girl, aren't you? Everything's going to be okay now." And to Cisco I added—mildly, so as not to distress the poodle—, "Hey. Paws off."

Reluctantly, Cisco dropped to the floor but remained close by, watching our every move.

The poodle made no attempt to stand, but wagged her short tail feebly when I said her name. Her eyes looked clear, but her gums were dry, and when I gently pinched a small section of skin on the back of her neck it rebounded far too slowly. I found a coffee cup on the shelf with the shampoo and quickly filled it with water.

"Is she going to be okay?" Casey said worriedly. "She looks bad."

I offered the dog the water and she lapped at it eagerly. I took the cup away after a few laps. "Yeah," I said, relieved. "I think so." I offered the cup to her again for a few more laps, and this time she rose up on her elbows to drink.

"Here you go," said Corny. He had a dog bowl in one hand and a container of bone broth in the other. "I crumbled up some saltines with the broth to help her rehydrate."

"Good thinking." I took the water away and Corny replaced it with the dog bowl. The poodle turned to it eagerly. "Not too fast, now," he urged the dog, leaning close to encircle her with his arm. "There's plenty more where that came from."

Casey and I stepped away from the table. "She's eating and drinking," I said. "That's a good sign. But we should get her to the vet in the morning."

"She'd peed and pooped all over the house," Casey said. "Who knows how long she'd been locked in."

Cisco, smelling the broth, eased his way back toward the table to see if he could mooch a bite. I snapped my fingers at him and his ears went down guiltily. He came over to me with a lowly wagging tail.

Corny straightened up and put the bowl away, looking worried. "Who would abandon a sweet dog like this? She's still shivering. If you'll keep an eye on her, Miss Stockton, I'll go check on the towels."

I took Corney's place at the table with my arm

lightly around the dog in case she suddenly decided to stand up and fell off the table. Cisco couldn't resist following me, and this time I let him put his paws on the table to say hello. His tail waved madly as he sniffed the newcomer, and she stretched out her neck to greet him, as well.

I watched the dogs carefully for signs of ill temper and said to Casey, "So what were you doing in this woman Izzy's house?"

"I went to check on her. I told you I was worried."

"Well, she clearly didn't let you in."

"She wasn't there. The door was unlocked."

I stared at him until he admitted, "Maybe I helped it get that way. But come on, Raine, her car was still there, and I'm telling you she never would have left her dog locked up with no food or water. Something has happened to her."

I had to agree with him there. There were plenty of people in this county who would just move away and leave their dogs behind like worn-out furniture, but those people did not go to the trouble of microchipping their dogs and making sure they had regular veterinary care. And no one outside of a sociopath would intentionally lock a dog up for days without food or water. The poor thing had probably lost her voice barking for help.

I said, "You should file a police report. But," I warned him, "if they find her, they're going to charge her with animal cruelty."

"Yeah," he said thoughtfully. "Might be worth it, though, if they take me seriously. But first, I think

I'll have another look around, maybe talk to some people."

"Or," I suggested, "you could leave it to the police."

He looked mildly skeptical. "Would you?"

Before I could answer—not that I was inclined to—Corny returned with an armful of warm towels. "Here we go, princess," he crooned to Gigi. "This will make you feel better." He draped the warm towels over her and then refilled the dog bowl with bone broth. She lapped it up like the princess she was.

"Put a warming pad in one of the medium kennels tonight," I suggested. "She's probably just too malnourished to regulate her body temperature. I'll call the vet first thing in the morning but I think she's going to be all right."

"Oh, I couldn't possibly leave her all alone in a kennel tonight," Corny crooned, stroking her ears as she licked up the broth. "Not after what she's been through. I'll bring a crate into my room. That way I can make sure she gets something to drink every hour or so, and take her out when she needs to go."

I drew a breath to protest, because Corny's room was barely big enough for his own bed and we had an entire boarding kennel standing empty. But it knew any objection would be futile. This was what Corny did. This was why I was so lucky to have him.

He looked at me, his eyes dark with concern. "How do you suppose she managed to get locked in a house all by herself?"

"I don't think it was on purpose," I said. "Her

owner must have run into some kind of …" I searched for the right word. "Difficulty."

He turned back to the poodle as she finished the last of the broth, and he kissed her head. "But we'll keep her until the owner comes for her, right?"

I replied, "Yes, of course we will."

But I didn't think that would be anytime soon. And I could tell by looking at Casey that he didn't think so, either.

CHAPTER TEN

Corny reported that Gigi the poodle had done well overnight, had eaten a hearty breakfast, and had spent the subsequent hour sniffing every blade of grass in the play yard, peeing and pooping and doing the things dogs do. She even took a run at the big herding ball and seemed blissfully grateful to be outside again. I took all of this as a good sign, but made an appointment with the vet anyway for later that morning.

"I'll stop by and take her through her paces after school," Melanie volunteered as she gathered her belongings for the day. The shuttle that took her to her private school was due to appear on the security monitor at any moment. "You know, sit, stay, come —just the basics. It's important to keep her mentally stimulated."

I repressed a smile and poured myself a cup of coffee. Melanie, whose stated life goal was to either train police dogs for the FBI or be a paleontologist, had missed her daily visits to Dog Daze over the past year much more than I had. "I'm sure she'd appreciate that," I said. "But we might locate her owner before then."

Melanie looked horrified. "You would *never* turn a dog back over to an owner who abused her!"

Before I could respond, Miles said, "A little less judgment, please. We don't know what happened. Get your coat on. The shuttle's turning into the driveway." He looked from the monitor on the wall back to the pancakes on the griddle. "Raine, how many of these do you want?"

"Two." I held out my plate for him.

"Well, anyway." Melanie shrugged into her coat, unmollified. "*I* wouldn't release that dog to anybody without a full investigation." She added cheerfully, "Bye, Dad. Bye, Raine."

She gave me a quick hug and kissed her dad, and we both wished her a good day as she raced to the door. Miles transferred two pancakes to my plate and another two to his own, watching the monitor until Melanie was safely aboard the shuttle. This kind of vigilance—also known as paranoia in some circles—was still a little strange to me, although I understood why Miles thought it was necessary. Melanie had been taken once, even though it was only for a few hours and even though she had been returned unharmed. People like Miles lived with the kind of constant threats to their security that I couldn't even imagine. Still, it was hard to get used to.

Miles handed me his plate and Cisco watched me hopefully as I took them both to the breakfast table.

Miles turned off the burners and followed in his wheelchair.

"You know," I said thoughtfully, "it's really hard to just disappear these days." My eyes were on the security monitor, which now showed a six-sectioned, black-and-white view of the peaceful exterior of Miles's house and all entry points. Except for Pepper, Mischief and Magic chasing each other in the fenced section of the back yard, nothing moved. "There are cameras everywhere, even in a rural area like this."

"Well, maybe not everywhere," Miles said. He adjusted his wheelchair to table height and added, "A person can still fade into the woodwork if they want to badly enough. Are you thinking this woman wanted to disappear?"

I poured maple syrup over my pancakes and passed the bottle to Miles. Cisco, accepting his defeat, settled under the table with a disappointed huff. "No. One of the things dog owners have in common is that they're generally responsible people. I'm just thinking that it's odd that she hasn't *reappeared* by now. I mean, that someone hasn't spotted her if she was hurt or needed help."

"It sounds to me like no one has been looking for her. That may change once the police get involved."

"Maybe," I admitted, hoping Casey had not gotten so caught up in his own troubles that he'd forgotten to file the missing person's report as he'd promised. I took a bite of the pancakes. "Say," I added, "did I tell you I met our new neighbor at the jail last night?"

"Great first impression," Miles observed.

I sighed. "Yeah. I really do need to bring her that pie."

"What's she like?"

"She seemed nice. Casey thinks she's hot."

Miles chuckled. "Why am I not surprised?"

I ate my pancakes in silence for a time, thinking about Gigi the poodle and the woman who had abandoned her. It had been dark when Casey was at her house last night. I wondered what he had missed.

When we finished eating, I took our plates to the dishwasher and asked Miles if he wanted more coffee. Cisco followed me, licking his chops forlornly as he watched the syrup-covered plates disappear into the dishwasher.

"No, better not," Miles replied. "I've got people driving up from Atlanta this morning, and I need to get ready for the meeting."

I poured myself half a cup and leaned against the counter, sipping it thoughtfully. I could have started cleaning the kitchen, but Miles's housekeeper was due in a few minutes and she did *not* like the way I did things. I was fine with that.

I said, "Do you remember that woman a couple of years ago who fell down a hill in her own backyard and was missing for four days? She got lost in the woods trying to find a place to climb back up. When Cisco and I found her, two miles away from her house, she was suffering from exposure and dehydration and had a twisted ankle, but otherwise she was just fine."

Miles nodded, turning his chair toward the door.

"So what time do you think you'll be back?"

"From the vet?"

"From searching the woods around the missing woman's house."

I smiled, a little embarrassed that I was so predictable. "It can't hurt, right?"

Miles paused as he passed us and reached a hand up toward me. I leaned down and he encircled my neck, pulled my face toward his, and kissed me. "You're a good woman, Raine Stockton."

I shrugged in pretend modesty. "Sometimes," I admitted. I kissed him back and put my coffee cup in the sink. "See you this afternoon. Come on, Cisco. We've got work to do."

It was good to be able to say that again.

Doc Witherspoon pronounced Gigi the poodle to be malnourished and still a little dehydrated, and he agreed with me that her lost voice was probably a combination of over-stressed vocal cords and dehydration. Otherwise, she appeared to be in good shape, all things considered, and predicted her voice would return after a few days of rest. He scanned her microchip and found it matched the name and address on her ID tag, and her rabies tag traced back to a vet in Wilkes County. He prescribed electrolytes for a couple of days and a high-calorie diet. We both agreed she was one lucky dog.

I dropped Gigi off at Dog Daze and stayed long enough to make sure she was playing well with

Pepper and the Aussies, who were staying with Corny while Miles had his meeting. Corny, of course, couldn't be dragged away from the playroom as long as Gigi was there, so I felt comfortable leaving them all to their fun.

When Cisco saw me get out his tracking harness and line he was so excited he stood on his hind legs, tail wagging madly, while I fastened him into it. I couldn't help feeling guilty about that. We'd practiced scent work and made a few half-hearted forays into the woods over the summer, but Cisco knew the difference between working and play. He did both with enthusiasm, but he was a working dog. He missed his job.

The address on Gigi's tag was 175 Wandering Way, Hansonville, and I plugged it into my GPS. I wasn't surprised that someone who worked in Wilkes County, just over the line, lived in Hanover County; a lot of people did for affordability reasons. I also wasn't surprised, when I made my way down the bumpy road to the driveway on the edge of the woods, to find Casey's truck already there.

The mobile home was a fairly typical rental for this part of the country. It sat on cinder blocks in a narrow dirt clearing surrounded on three sides by winter-bare woodlands and scraggly bushes. It had white aluminum siding, now dull and mud-spattered from recent rains, narrow windows, and a storm door that didn't quite close. The drive and parking area had once been paved with gravel, but were now mostly mud and ruts. I had noticed a few other residences as I drove in: one falling-down shack that was definitely unoccupied, and two other mobile homes that looked empty, as well. All of them were too far away for their residents to have heard poor Gigi barking herself into laryngitis.

Casey came around the corner of the building as I was unbuckling Cisco's seat belt. Cisco rocketed to him as though it had been weeks, instead of hours, since they'd seen each other. Then again, Cisco greeted most people like that. Casey dropped to one knee to give Cisco a full-body rub, and Cisco made a fool of himself wiggling with delight.

I snapped on Cisco's tracking lead and said, "Find anything?"

Casey tried to look innocent for about half a second, then decided it wasn't worth the effort. He gave Cisco a final pat and stood. "Not really. No phone, no purse. There was an extra set of keys by the door, and I used one of them to try to start her car. Dead battery. What are you doing here?"

I looked around, examining the terrain. "I wondered if she might have had some kind of accident nearby, and thought it might not hurt to let Cisco sniff around."

Casey nodded, his expression grim. "I checked with the manager at the bar, and she's been missing at least four days. I'd hate to think of anybody out in the weather that long."

"People have survived worse." I tried to sound reassuring, but I think we both knew better.

He said, "It looks to me like she got a ride to work

with somebody when her car wouldn't start, and then let that scumbag Hoggins drive her home—or wherever he drove her."

"Did you file the missing persons report?" I asked. "And tell them about her leaving with Hoggins?"

A corner of his mouth turned down bitterly. "For all the good it will do."

"I'm sure they'll at least question him. He's sitting right there in their jail."

Casey's shrug was less a demonstration of uncertainty than hopelessness. "How's the pup?"

"Doc said she'll be good as new in a few days. I left her running around the playroom with the other three, acting like nothing had ever happened. Dogs are pretty amazing."

"Well, that's something anyhow." He shoved his hands in the pockets of his jacket, glancing up and down the road. "I stopped by those trailers you see on the way down the road. Nobody answered my knock. Looks like Izzy was the only person living out here."

I said, "How about going back inside and bringing me something of hers—a sock from the laundry hamper, maybe—that Cisco can use as a scent object."

"I just locked the door," he objected.

"Well, unlock it."

"That's breaking and entering."

I gave him an exasperated look. "You think?"

"There's a pair of gloves in the car," he offered.

"Let's have them," I replied impatiently.

I knew it wouldn't take long to determine whether Izzy had left the property on foot or had ventured into the woods, accidentally or on purpose. After Cisco got her scent from the gloves, he eagerly tracked her up and down the front stairs, to her empty car, around the yard, and to the mailbox at the end of the short driveway and back. All he found was a single gold filigree earring, half buried in the mud beside the steps. I picked it up and stuffed it in my pocket, keeping my eyes on Cisco. He made the circuit several times, never once venturing toward the woods, until I could sense his growing frustration and called him back. I've got to say, I was disappointed. Cisco used to be better than this. I didn't blame him. I blamed myself.

"Okay, finish!" I told him, and tossed his rope toy into the air. He caught it expertly, gave it a happy shake, ran around in circles with it for a few minutes, and then brought it back to me for a game of tug. Any search effort, even if it is unsuccessful, is always rewarded. I want my dog to constantly be looking forward to the next search. And I intended to do a *lot* more practice searches with him. He was a talented dog. I couldn't let him lose his touch.

"So I guess my theory was bogus," I told Casey, winding up the tug game with Cisco. "She didn't get lost in the woods, at least not around here."

"We had rain over the weekend," he pointed out. "Maybe..."

I shrugged, appreciating his effort to excuse our mediocre performance, and returned the tug toy to my backpack. "Well, it was a lot to hope for."

"It was worth a try," he said. "Thanks, anyway. You didn't have to."

"It's what we do," I told him, and the truth was, it did feel good to have tried.

We both turned at the sound of an approaching car, and when a Sheriff's Office cruiser turned into the driveway, Casey muttered, "Terrific."

"Hey, at least they're taking you seriously," I said. But the truth is, I was no more happy to be caught trespassing than he was.

I quickly exchanged Cisco's tracking line for a short leash while the two deputies got out of their vehicle. We waited by Casey's truck while they did the usual cop-sweep of their surroundings with their eyes and approached us at their own pace. There had been a lot of turnover in the sheriff's office since Buck left and Marshall took over as sheriff, and I no longer knew everyone who worked there. But as it happened, I did know one of the deputies, a slightly rotund, easygoing fellow by the name of Jimbo Darrow. He had been a couple of years ahead of me in high school and had joined the sheriff's office while my uncle was still in charge. I greeted him as he reached us.

"Hey, Raine," he said, and reached down to scratch Cisco's chin. Cisco's tail went wild. "What're you doing out here?"

I explained about the abandoned dog, and Casey being my brother, and my theory that the missing woman might have somehow been lost or injured in the woods around her house. He gave a considering nod and said, “Not a bad theory. You didn’t find anything?”

I admitted we had not.

Jimbo jerked a thumb in the direction of his colleague, another twenty-year-old who was trying hard to look tougher than his baby face would allow. I guessed law enforcement was taking what they could get these days. “You know Deputy Thomas, here?”

I gave the kid a brief, vague smile, but Casey spoke up. “I do. He’s the one that took my missing person report.”

“And I told you we’d follow up,” said Thomas. “You shouldn’t be here, Mr. Macintosh.”

“Yeah, I thought I’d leave a note on the door,” Casey lied effortlessly, “in case she comes back. She doesn’t even know anybody’s looking for her.”

Jimbo nodded. “Good idea. We’ll do it, though. Have her call the sheriff’s office.”

“Did you ask Rooster Hoggins about her?” Casey said.

Thomas answered that one. “He made bond early this morning. We’ll track him down.”

I stared at him. “How does a man like Hoggins make bond that quick on outstanding warrants?”

Thomas shrugged. “People do.”

I said, “Why are y’all running this down? Don’t you have a criminal investigator who does this kind of thing?”

I happened to know that the last sheriff’s office

investigator had resigned in disgrace when a supposed murder victim had walked into the courtroom in the middle of his own murder trial. I would be the accused, of course, and Casey the murder victim. Coincidentally, the prosecutor who pressured law enforcement into bringing the case had also left the county—and possibly the state—shortly after the case was resolved. I won't deny a little bit of smug satisfaction at both outcomes. And I'll tell you something else. As much as I've complained about Miles interfering in my affairs, I'm not in the least bit embarrassed to admit that he probably had a hand in the fate of both men. After all, I'm the one who talked Miles out of filing an 80 million dollar lawsuit against the county on my behalf; I figured what he did beyond that was one of my business.

Jimbo answered my question. "Yeah, we're getting one, but she doesn't officially start for a week or two. You know the sheriff likes to rotate all rookies through a week of nights and a week of days, no matter how high their rank is."

"She?" I latched on to that quickly. "Do you mean the new deputy, Dakota Bradshaw? The one who moved into Buck's old house?"

"Hey, that's right, she's a neighbor of yours," agreed Jimbo easily. "I hear she's really sharp. The sheriff stole her away from the Raleigh-Durham PD and he was real excited to get her, too. Meantime, though, we're all kind of taking turns working investigations."

Casey looked like he wanted to say something

pithy about that, so I spoke up quickly, “Well, we’d better let you get to it. You’ll let us know if you find anything?”

“Sure thing, Raine,” replied Jimbo.

Thomas said nothing at all, just walked up the front steps and rattled the doorknob importantly. “Locked,” he reported to his colleague.

Casey and I exchanged a look. Clearly, the new investigator couldn’t take over soon enough.

Casey and I walked back toward our vehicles. “Do you want to stop by Miss Meg’s for lunch?” I asked.

“You buying?”

I made a face. “You’re the one who just came into a thousand-dollar windfall. You’re buying.”

“What about the big guy?” He nodded toward Cisco.

“Meg will let him sit in the back room if it’s not too busy and we go in the side door.”

“Yeah, okay,” he agreed with a shrug. “I’ll meet you there.”

I was parked behind Casey, so I hurried to my vehicle, stuffing my cold hands into my jacket pockets as I did. Cisco bounced along beside me, pleased with his morning’s adventure and looking forward to whatever was to come. As I pulled my hand out of my pocket to unlock the car, something pricked my finger. I took out the earring Cisco had found, wiped off the mud, and looked at it closely for the first time. It was a single lacey gold butterfly wing with three glittery stones representing the body.

And I knew exactly where I had seen its mate

before.

CHAPTER ELEVEN

Miss Meg's is a home-style cafe located in the center of Main Street. She offers daily specials like pork chops and gravy or fried catfish, always with your choice of three sides, and she makes the best French fries in town. Also, the banana pudding is to die for. She does a brisk business all year long, but on a weekday in the middle of January there just weren't that many people in town. Casey, Cisco, and I had the back room all to ourselves.

I'm not the kind of person who likes to impose her dog on other people, even though Cisco was a certified therapy dog and even though his manners were, shall we say, improving. But he had been to Miss Meg's enough times that I could trust him to behave himself in a room devoid of other diners, despite the tantalizing aromas that wafted from the kitchen. I called out to Meg that we were there and got Cisco settled under the table. "Under" is one of the first commands he learned as a puppy, and it really is the key to being able to take him places he normally wouldn't be allowed.

No sooner had we removed our coats and settled at a table by the window than Meg appeared, pad and pencil in hand. "Hello, handsome," she greeted Casey. "What brings you out this way?"

Meg was sixtyish, tall and thin with the lined, leather face of a lifelong smoker and avid gardener. She flirted with all her customers, but it was no surprise that she seemed to have a particular fondness for Casey.

Casey grinned at her. "Couldn't stay away from you a minute longer," he replied.

She pursed her lips and informed him archly, "I was talking to the dog."

We all laughed and Cisco pricked up his ears and panted happily, seeming to sense the joke was about him. A slight tug on his leash discouraged him from wriggling out from under the table and showing Meg just how cute he could be.

She said, "Y'all know what you want, or do you need a minute? Special today is country-fried steak with mashed potatoes and green beans, apple cobbler for dessert."

Casey said, "Sounds good to me."

I ordered a hamburger and fries, and a turkey club to go for Corny.

She jotted all that down and nodded toward Cisco. "How about a nice big steak for my favorite fella, there?"

Cisco swished his tail back and forth enthusiastically, but I said, "In his dreams. A bowl of water wouldn't hurt, though, if you get a chance."

When she was gone, I said to Casey, "You remember that girl that was with Lance Booker yesterday?"

He replied, "I saw her, sure. Great hair, cute butt. His daughter, right?"

"She said no." I lifted a cautionary hand as much to keep myself from leaping to conclusions as for him. "Which is not to say she isn't his niece or a family friend or whatever, but it didn't seem like that, if you know what I mean."

He grunted. "Good for him, I guess. Only goes to prove money *can* buy you love."

"Or a reasonable facsimile." I dug the earring out of my pocket, polished most of the mud off with a tissue and placed it on the table. "Anyway, she was wearing an earring just like this. Only one. I thought it was a fashion statement at the time, but now I think she might have lost the other one. Cisco found this…" I tapped the earring with my index finger, "in the mud by Izzy's front steps."

Casey's interest seemed to quicken and he reached across the table to pick up the earring. He examined it curiously. "What's it supposed to be?"

"One half of a butterfly, I think. The other earring was the other wing."

"It could be Izzy's," he offered, pushing the earring back across the table to me.

"Sure," I agreed. "I mean, two women could definitely have the same pair of earrings. Maybe bought them online or at the drugstore."

Meg returned to set a glass of sweet tea in front of each of us, eyeing the earring with interest. "Honey, if you're talking about that piece, it didn't come from no drugstore."

I looked up at her. "Yeah? How can you tell?"

She gave a small chuckle. "Babydoll, you don't get to be this age without being able to tell a diamond from a rhinestone. Those are diamonds, quarter karat each if I'm any judge. Back in a minute with water for the pup."

She sashayed off, and I picked up the earring again, eyeing it with new respect. "Makes sense, I guess," I said. "The way Booker was throwing money around, why wouldn't he throw a little at his girlfriend?"

"Well, I can tell you right now Izzy didn't have the money for diamonds. So…" he frowned thoughtfully and took a sip of his tea. "Either somebody gave her a pair of earrings just like the ones that other girl was wearing, or…"

"The girl dropped the earring at Izzy's house," I supplied. "Which means they knew each other."

"Not out of the question," Casey agreed. "Everybody goes to The Borderline, and Izzy was a real friendly girl."

"Miles said Booker works for this real estate company called Blackwing Investments. He bought a big house out on the lake, and a bunch of lots there, too."

Casey picked up the earring and turned it over in

his hand thoughtfully. "Okay, that's interesting. Last night, when Rooster Hoggins went to pay for his drink he dropped a business card. I didn't get a real good look at it, but it had the same kind of wing logo on it that Booker had on his truck."

"Maybe Hoggins was working for him. Didn't I hear he was a driver for a grading and hauling company? And if Booker is getting ready to clear some of those lots, that might be just the kind of man he's looking for."

"Yeah," agreed Casey. "Something else to ask ol' Rooster about when I see him."

"You need to stay away from Hoggins," I warned him. I retrieved the earring and placed it carefully in the zipper compartment of my purse.

"Like you're going to stay away from Booker?"

I shrugged. "If I get a chance, I might try to return the earring. Diamonds, after all. But you've got no business fooling around with a man who punched you in the face the last time you tried to ask him a question. Besides, you don't even know where he lives."

Casey smiled benignly. "Sure I do. Police report. And how do you think you're going to find Booker's girlfriend?"

I returned his innocent smile. "Miles isn't the only one who knows how to look up public property tax records."

Casey held up his hand for a high-five and, with a rueful smile, I slapped his palm.

This is exactly what Miles means when he says

Casey and I are a bad influence on each other.

CHAPTER TWELVE

You would think lake property in the mountains would be enthusiastically sought after and highly valuable. In some places, I suppose it is. But the small chain of lakes in our particular county is the natural consequence of tens of thousands of years of shifting tectonic plates, volcanic eruptions, floods and slow erosion. They are difficult to access and even more difficult to build upon. The surrounding shoreline is steep and craggy, and the water depth is unpredictable, which makes recreational use uncertain at best. Sure, if you're determined enough to brave the poison ivy and the copperheads, you can drag a john boat or canoe through the woods to a launch spot and enjoy some of the best fishing in the country, but few people are that dedicated. There are no utilities or paved roads around the lake, and the few summer cabins that are scattered around it operate on well water and generators. Frankly, I couldn't understand why anybody would want to live out here.

I followed the GPS around the lake on a mostly unpaved, mostly one-way road until it led me to another unpaved road which, after about a mile, led to an unmarked gravel drive. It occurred to me that whoever had decided to build a house out here did not want to be found. That speculation was borne out when, after another five hundred feet, I came to a tall iron gate.

I lowered my window on a blast of cold air and stretched to push the button on the monitor. In a moment a voice said, "Yes?"

I leaned toward the speaker. "My name is Raine Stockton," I said, loudly and clearly. "I have something that belongs to Amber. May I come up and give it to her?"

A long period passed in which I imagined I was being examined by the camera, and my name was being searched in some kind of list or database. These kinds of monitored gates used to bother me until Miles installed one on his property and I got used to it. Of course, I had my own RFID entry to Miles's gate, and when there was an event, the gate was monitored by guards. Honestly, I preferred dealing with guards to waiting for the nameless, faceless voice on the other end of the monitor to decide whether or not to admit me.

Finally, the voice came again. "What do you have?"

I dug in my purse until I found the earring, then held it up to the camera.

Another thirty or forty seconds passed, then the voice said, "Leave it in the package receptacle just to your right."

I scowled. Of course I'd always known there was a possibility I wouldn't be admitted, or that Amber wouldn't be home, but after driving all this way on bad roads, I was annoyed. "No," I said. "It's too valuable." I put the earring back in my purse. "Tell her I'm the woman she met the other day after the accident. The one with the dog," I added, remembering how enchanted she had been by Cisco.

Cisco, on cue, shifted his position in the back seat and stretched his grinning, happily panting face toward the camera. For a time it seemed as though Cisco's efforts were in vain, but then, without another word from the disembodied voice, the gate slowly rolled open. I drove through.

The house was a two-story, timber-framed lodge-like structure, with rustic wooden siding and laurel railings along the balconies and the wide front porch. It was situated on a knoll overlooking the lake, with a paved parking lot and custom garage on a terrace below. I had to climb two sets of steps before I reached the winter-brown square of lawn upon which the house sat, and as I did, I saw a woman looking down from an upper window. It had to be Amber—same blonde hair and lithe figure—and I raised my hand in greeting. She stepped quickly away from the window without returning my wave.

One more set of steps took me to the porch and the oversized front door which was, interestingly enough, inset with a stained glass panel depicting a set of gold wings against a sunset sky. I rang the doorbell, and it was answered in a minute by a bald, burly-looking man in a suit who was not Mr. Booker. Security?

I opened my mouth to introduce myself again, but the man opened the door wider and gestured for me to go inside. I'd barely had a moment to appreciate the black marble foyer—yes, black marble from floor to ceiling—with its laurelwood chandelier and beautifully carved deadwood table when Mr. Booker strode in, his hand extended in greeting.

"Miss Stockton," he welcomed me. His tone was pleasant, as was his demeanor, but there still was something a little smarmy about him. He wore a cashmere sweater that was not at all suited to his overfed form, and a thick gold chain around his neck. Did *anyone* wear gold chains anymore? Certainly not around here.

"Good of you to come all the way out here to return Amber's little trinket." He smiled as he shook my hand. It was one of those smiles that crinkled the edges of his eyes but didn't quite reach them. "How did you know where to find us?"

"It's a small town," I replied, giving him a false smile of my own. "It wasn't that hard." I looked around appreciatively. "This place is really something. Not many like it this far from town."

"Yes," he agreed. "I was lucky to find it." His manner remained relaxed and agreeable, but that phony smile was becoming strained with impatience. He added, "Amber isn't here just now, but I'll be sure she gets the earring." He held out his hand for it.

"Oh, but..." I stopped before pointing out I'd just seen her at the window for two reasons. First, I couldn't be entirely sure it *was* Amber, could I? After all, I'd only met the woman once. Secondly, a certain hardness had come over the man's eyes that I didn't like at all. And it was awfully isolated out here.

I unzipped the compartment of my purse and brought out the earring. I handed it to him with a brief, weak smile. "They're lovely earrings," I offered. "I'm sure she missed this."

He took the earring without comment.

"Actually," I pushed on, "it's a funny thing where I found it. You probably think it was at the scene of yesterday's accident, but it wasn't. It was at this girl's house, Izzy Stedman? She's a waitress at the Borderline bar. Do you know her?"

He replied coolly, "I'm afraid not."

"Well, I guess Amber does." I worked hard at keeping the smile on my face. "I was wondering if..."

He spoke over me. "Wilkins will see you out. Thank you again for your trouble."

Out of nowhere, the bald man in the suit appeared, and I had no choice but to follow him the few feet to the door. As soon as I was on the other side, he closed it firmly behind me, but I could feel someone watching me all the way back to my car. As soon as I reached it, I couldn't help glancing back at the house. I was just in time to see the flutter of a curtain as someone stepped away, once again, from that upstairs window where I thought I had seen Amber before.

I didn't realize it then, but that was the second time in twenty-four hours I had turned my back on a woman who needed me.

CHAPTER THIRTEEN

The shabby frame farmhouse in which Rooster Coggins lived looked desolate beneath the lead colored sky. It was reached via a rutted dirt road and sat on a rocky plot of cleared land that was dotted with winter-brown weeds and frozen mudholes. A dump truck and an excavator stood idle in the front yard, and a long commercial-grade chicken house with a caved-in roof sat less than a hundred yards from the main house. Closer to the house was a shed-type carport with a two-toned beige and brown pickup inside. There was a metal barn at the back edge of the property that looked fairly new, and Casey wondered, as he got out of his truck, why the man didn't keep his commercial vehicles there, instead of sitting out in the weather as they now did.

Woodsmoke was coming from a bare metal

chimney, indicating someone was probably at home. Casey climbed the three shallow steps and knocked on the door. No answer. He knocked harder. After a moment, he saw a brief flicker of a shadow cross in front of a window, but no one came to the door. He knocked again and called out, "Mr. Hoggins! I have something of yours!"

In his life, Casey had occasionally been called upon to play a role that wasn't strictly legitimate. This simple claim had often served to get him into places that he would not have been able to enter if he'd told the truth. He knocked again. "Mr. Hoggins!"

He saw another shadow move behind the window, and in a moment the door opened a crack. A thin woman with a narrow face and a dishwater blond, badly cut bob looked out at him. She had pulled her hair forward to partially disguise a fading bruise on her cheek, but she couldn't disguise the purple circles under her eyes. Those eyes were filled with fear as she looked at him. Instantly, Casey knew this was Rooster Hoggins' wife. Tina.

She said, "He ain't here."

She had mostly blocked his view of the interior of the house with her body, so that might or might not be true. He suspected, however, that if Hoggins was here he would have already stormed the door and demanded to know what Casey was doing here.

Casey gave her his most charming smile and said, "I'm sorry to bother you, ma'am. My name is Casey Macintosh. Mr. Lance Booker said I ought to see your husband about some grading I need done. Mr. Hoggins does work for Booker, right? I have the right place?"

Her eyes flitted back and forth nervously, as though she was worried about something behind her. Was she being watched? Was she being held against her will?

She said, "I, um, I guess so. I don't know. Like I said, he's not here."

He nodded, trying to look behind her into the house. All he could see was a slice of the kitchen —dirty dishes in the sink, empty dog bowls on the floor, a half-eaten meal on the aluminum-legged dinette table. No sign that anyone else was at home. No sign that anyone else was not.

He said, still smiling, "You're Tina, right? I think you might know a friend of mine. Izzy Stedman? She works over at the Borderline bar."

She gave a quick, short shake of her head and started to close the door. "No. I don't know her."

As she lifted her hand to close the door, Casey saw an unmistakable smear of blood on the side of her hand, and another dried smear on her sweatshirt. He quickly stepped forward, slipping his boot over the threshold to prevent the door from closing. His smile vanished.

"Ma'am," he said quietly, "are you all right? Do you need help?"

She looked alarmed, although whether it was because of his question or his foot in the door Casey couldn't be sure. "No! No, I'm fine. I just... I need you to leave. I don't know you and I need you to get off my porch before I call the police!"

Casey raised his hands in a placating gesture and stepped back. He didn't suppose she could be any clearer than that. "Okay," he said. "It's just..." He glanced toward the car shed. "Isn't that your husband's truck?"

She slammed the door in his face.

He muttered, "Damn it." Then he called, "Tell him I stopped by when he gets back!"

Casey didn't expect a reply, and he didn't get one. He waited a few more minutes, but no further sounds or movements came from inside the house. "Damn it," he said again, and went back down the steps to his truck. There was nothing else he could do.

CHAPTER FOURTEEN

You know what they say: it never rains, but it pours. This time yesterday, I had a completely empty kennel and no prospects of that changing any time soon. But on the way home, Corny texted to say that the Werners had had an out-of-town emergency and had brought their two border collies to board for an undetermined amount of time. Then one of his grooming clients, who had been planning to take their Shih Tzu with them to visit relatives in Florida, had discovered the relative was allergic to dogs. Corny had naturally suggested they leave little Popcorn with us, and they had naturally been delighted and relieved to do so. All his clients loved Corny.

I was congratulating myself on having four out of my ten kennels occupied—three of them by actual paying clients—when my phone rang. I was startled to hear the caller identify herself as Millie Caldron, from the Welcoming Arms Women's Shelter. She was the person I'd been planning to call when Lance Booker ran into Casey's truck yesterday. Sometimes things happen like that.

"Raine, I'm sorry to bother you, but I'm afraid we have another situation here," she said. "A sweet little bird dog. I don't have anyone who can bring him out to you right now. I don't suppose you could...?"

She didn't have to finish that sentence. "I'm headed to town right now," I told her. "I could be there in maybe ten minutes."

"Oh, Raine, bless you. I'll have him waiting at the front desk for you."

Like I said, when it rains, it pours.

Several years back, I'd organized a fundraiser to help Welcoming Arms provide refuge for women seeking shelter with their dogs. You'd be surprised how many abused women will delay leaving a dangerous situation because they're afraid to leave their pets behind. I can certainly relate, and it just kills me to think anyone would have to make that decision. Working with a corporate sponsor, we were able to dedicate four of the ground-floor bedrooms in the big old house that is Welcoming Arms as pet-friendly accommodations. We added waterproof flooring, crates, bedding, dog bowls and other necessities. We fenced in the backyard, and keep the pantry stocked with dog food donated by pet food companies and local grocery stores. Sadly, four rooms are often not enough, and when that happens, I volunteer to keep the overflow for free. This is not ideal, of course, because in such a stressful time the traumatized woman often needs her dog as much as the dog needs to be with its family. But still, knowing that their dog is in good hands can often make the difference between staying and leaving.

The shelter is located in a fourteen-room house on High Street that was built by a timber baron sometime around 1920. It has variously served as a hotel, a law office, a medical clinic, and a bank over the decades. When the charity bought it ten years ago, it was in fairly rundown condition and required a lot of renovation to make it habitable, but the location was perfect: directly across the street from the county impound lot, which also happened to be where the sheriff's office kept its vehicle inventory. Such an impressive display of police cruisers, SUVs and vans did a lot to discourage loitering by persons of ill intent and, as an added bonus, the sheriff's office allowed women who were staying at the shelter to park their cars there. You'd be surprised how many men try to control the women in their lives by disabling or confiscating their vehicles. Or maybe you wouldn't.

The big brick mansion was not visible from the street, but accessed via a narrow, shrub-lined lane between two brick posts. I pushed an intercom button by the front door, identified myself, and waited until Millie opened the door for me.

"Come on in out of the cold, Raine." She waved me inside. "Thanks for doing this. I hate to ask, but we really have our hands full this week and we're just not equipped to..." She gestured helplessly toward a corner of the room, where a boy and a girl sat on the rug petting a nervous-looking pointer-mix.

I smiled at the kids, but it was the dog I was really trying to make comfortable. "No problem," I said. "Glad to help. Is that the family?"

She shook her head. "No, they just came in with their mom last night from over in Hollifield County. We're the closest shelter to them and we're glad to help out whenever we can. You know, Raine, this program to allow pets doesn't just help the family that brings them. It helps everyone." She smiled at the children and added, "He's really a very sweet dog. Of course, they were only here a few nights, but not a sound out of him."

I was confused. "Wait. I thought they were just arriving, and you didn't have room."

She frowned a little and glanced at the children, lowering her voice. "This has really only happened one time before, when the client knew she couldn't take her dog to her new housing and asked us to find a good home for him. You remember, Raine, it was that cute little spaniel mix a couple of years ago."

I nodded my agreement. It *had* been a cute dog, and we had found a home for it within a matter of weeks.

"So," I said, "this woman couldn't take her dog with her when she left the shelter?"

Millie gave a helpless shake of her head. "I don't know. She must have left before I got in this morning. She left a note on the desk saying, 'Please take care of my dog', but that was it. I tried calling her, but no answer. Under the circumstances, well, I didn't know what to do except call you."

I went over to the dog and squatted down a few feet away so as not to startle him. "Hey," I said to the kids. "Nice dog."

"His name is Riley," said the little boy solemnly. He was probably around eight. "It says so on his collar."

"Hi, Riley," I said. I took a liver treat from my pocket and placed it on the floor a few inches in front of the dog's nose. He sniffed it suspiciously and, after a moment, lapped it up. I smiled and offered him another treat, this time from my palm. He took it tentatively. "Would you like to come home with me for a little while?"

"He likes it here," the little girl protested.

"I know he does," I said. "But I have a little girl at home too for him to play with, and lots of other dogs with a big playground and treats every day."

"What if his mom comes back?" insisted the boy.

"Then she'll know where to find him," I assured him. "She'll just come to my house and pick him up."

I took the leash that I had draped around my neck and snapped it onto Riley's collar. I lured him to his feet with another treat.

"Don't go, Riley!" cried the little girl.

"Now, sweetheart," said Millie, "you know Riley can't stay here forever."

The little girl started to cry. I felt like the Grinch

who stole Christmas. And New Year's. And Valentine's Day and the birthday of every kid in the country who was under twelve.

"I'll tell you what," I said quickly. "I have somebody in the car who's just been dying to show off his tricks to some smart kids like you. Just let me get Riley fastened into his car seat and I'll be right back, okay?"

I glanced a question at Millie, and she smiled her consent. The little girl sniffled hopefully.

Riley followed me willingly to the door, or I should say he followed the liver treat in my hand. As I passed Millie, I said, "I'll need the name and address of Riley's owner so I'll know who to release him to if she comes for him."

Millie frowned a little in dismay. "Oh, dear. Legally, I can't give you that information without permission. But hold on." She went to her desk, looked up something on the computer, and then fumbled around for something to write on. She finally came up with one of the shelter's brochures and copied something from the computer onto the back of it.

"This is her birth date," Millie told me, handing over the brochure. "I put her phone number on there, too, but the birth date should be enough, right? You ask for her birthdate, and if it matches, you know it's the right person. I know it might seem silly, but this is a small community, and we have to be very careful about our clients' privacy—and safety."

I glanced at the numbers and thought that was

actually a pretty clever way of identifying someone who didn't want her name used. "Sure," I said. "No problem. I'll be right back with Cisco." I stuffed the brochure in my pocket and didn't look at it again for days.

Strike Three for me.

CHAPTER FIFTEEN

I always keep an extra crate, leashes, blankets and collapsible dog bowls in my car along with other emergency supplies. It was clear Riley wasn't accustomed to riding in a crate and I took a few minutes to make sure he was comfortable with blankets and a chew toy before I left him. It was starting to sprinkle snow by the time I left him, but I knew I wouldn't be gone long.

The truth is, I'm not that wild about kids and don't think I'm very good with them. But Cisco is both of those things, which is why we end up doing so many programs for schools and libraries. Those few minutes we spent entertaining the two kids at the shelter reminded me how important it was for Cisco to do things like this and how much he enjoyed them. As a matter of fact, I was feeling pretty good about myself, too, when we left.

Melanie came bounding out of Dog Daze to greet me as I pulled up in front of the building, her unzipped coat flapping around her. "Hey, Raine!" she called. "Tonight's homemade pizza night. Can we invite Uncle Casey? He loves my pizza!"

I got out of the car and unfastened Cisco's seatbelt. "It's okay with me. What does your dad say?"

She wrinkled up her nose. "He's busy playing with his drone and talking on the phone."

"He's never too busy to listen to you," I replied, which was true. "Text him."

She thought about that for a minute, then pulled out her phone. "You're right. The best time to ask him anything is when he's not paying attention."

That made me chuckle. Miles was *always* paying attention.

Cisco wiggled and wagged his way around the car to get his usual pets from Melanie, and she obliged him while she waited for a reply from her father. "I took Gigi through her paces while you were gone," she informed me. "She's a smart dog, but she doesn't know much. Is she going to stay long? I'll bet she can really jump. Say, Raine, when are we..."

She broke off with an exclamation of delight as I led the pointer out of his crate and around the car. "Don't rush him," I warned her. "He's shy and a little confused."

"Where'd you get him?" Melanie inquired, approaching the dog with her hand extended, palm down, as I had taught her. "Is he a German shorthair? Are you going to train him? What's his name?"

"He's mostly pointer, as far as I can tell," I replied. "His owner was staying in the women's shelter, but she couldn't take him with her when she left. His name is Riley."

"Oh, Riley," Melanie cooed. "Poor thing." She knelt down to let him sniff her hand, and Cisco nudged his way under her arm, no doubt to show the newcomer that he, and only he, had first dibs on any affection that was being doled out.

"Why would she move somewhere she couldn't take her dog?" Melanie demanded, standing up. "That's just mean. I would never leave Pepper behind."

"I know you wouldn't," I told her, "but not everyone has that choice. Besides, his owner might come back for Riley. We don't really know what happened yet."

"Huh," said Melanie. Her phone chimed and she glanced at it. "Dad says okay, but Uncle Casey better have snow tires on his truck. 4 inches of snow tonight."

Snow was beginning to accumulate in Melanie's hair and creep down the back of my neck beneath the collar of my coat. "Come on, let's go inside," I said. "I'll text Casey about dinner."

Melanie opened the gate and raced Cisco to the door. I took my time with the pointer, allowing him to sniff and pee and proceed at his own delicate pace. Someone had once told me that family trauma usually affects the youngest member of the household the most. Usually, this means the youngest child, but I think it can also be the family dog. Clearly, it would take some time for Riley to learn to trust anything again—his environment, humans, even himself.

I sent Casey a quick text about dinner, and he responded with, *Sounds good. Need to talk to you anyway.*

I took that to mean his attempt to talk to Hoggins had gone no better than mine with Amber.

Corny was waiting for us at the door, drying the snow off Cisco's coat with a chamois, while Melanie told him all about Riley. Corny's face was immediately filled with compassion, and it occurred to me that maybe Riley's luck was changing, now that he had both Corny and Melanie on his side.

"Well now, young fellow," Corny said, kneeling to stroke Riley's ears, "don't you worry about a thing. Everything is going to be just fine now."

The dog leaned into Corny's touch, almost seeming to believe him.

"All Riley has is a rabies tag," I told Corny. "It's current, probably from the county free rabies clinic."

"They always include DA2P and parvo," Corny pointed out. "He should be okay."

"No Bordetella, though," I pointed out. "I'm just not crazy about taking in dogs with no shot records, especially when we've got boarders."

Melanie said, "It's funny you ended up with two dogs from two women, and nobody knows where they are. The women, I mean."

As a matter of fact, that *was* a little strange, and a part of me filed away her comment for further inspection. I replied, “A lot of women depend on their dogs for security and companionship. That’s why I thought it was so important that the women’s shelter be able to accommodate pets. Oh, that reminds me.”

I pulled the brochure out of my pocket and handed it to Corny, pointing out the birthdate written on the back. “This is the ID number for the woman who owns Riley, in case she comes for him. Just ask her what her birthday is.”

“Yes, ma’am.” He stood and took both the brochure and Riley’s leash from me. “I’ll put it on the desk where we can find it. Meanwhile…” He inclined his head toward Riley. “Let’s get you settled into your new accommodations, young sir. I’ve been holding our finest room for you.”

He led the pointer away, and Melanie watched them go thoughtfully. “Do you think she’ll come back for him?”

“I would, if it were my dog.” That was the best I could do, given the fact that I knew once a dog was surrendered, its owner hardly ever came back.

“The problem,” Melanie decided, “is that the shelter is only temporary. If they have to leave their dogs behind when they move into a new house, what good is it?”

Again, there were some things better left unsaid, especially to an eleven-year-old who still had hope for the world. The truth was that most women who left the shelter did not go on to a better life, but returned to their husbands and the nightmare they had left behind. Besides, she had a point, and I started to wonder uneasily how many women went back to the place they'd run away from because, all things considered, it was just easier.

I said, "You know something? That sounds like something we could ask your dad about. I thought he had meetings all day. What's he doing playing with that drone, anyway?"

She shrugged. "He thinks he can take pictures of snowflakes with it or something."

I gave a brief sniff of laughter. "Knowing him, he probably can."

"If he gets the perfect video, we're going to use it to illustrate the Koch snowflake for an extra-credit paper I'm writing. It's a famous fractal," she explained importantly.

"Oh," I said, having no idea what a Koch was and little to no idea about a fractal. "How's that poem essay coming along?"

She scowled, annoyed. "I got a B-minus. The teacher said I didn't follow instructions."

I lifted an eyebrow. I would have killed for a B-minus at her age. "That's pretty good for someone who didn't follow instructions."

She gave me a disdainful look. "I," she informed me archly, "am not a B-minus student."

I murmured, "I stand corrected." Then, "Is a not-B-minus student too good to take the dogs out to run in the snow?"

Her expression cleared. “I think I can manage that.”

And for the rest of the afternoon, that’s what we did.

CHAPTER SIXTEEN

I have a confession to make. I am not, and never will be, a fan of drones. Miles says I'm jealous, which is ridiculous, but ever since the sheriff's department bought two of them to use in search missions, I can't help looking at them as competition. I mean, it's one thing to use them to track down contraband or fleeing criminals, but more and more they're being used for legitimate rescue missions. The claim is that they are faster and more efficient than human or human/canine search teams, and they have the added advantage of being able to spot thermal signatures from the air. Okay, I admit, that's a pretty big advantage. But they have a limited range and tend to crash for lack of battery power if their human operator isn't paying attention. They can't see details in the dark and they can't fly in bad weather. Their view is limited to what they can see from the sky, which means if there is a thick tree canopy or heavy underbrush they are virtually useless. A good tracking dog has none of these limitations. I have explained all this to the sheriff but so far this past season, given the fact that Cisco and I were out of commission, the score is drone:12, tracking dog:0. So maybe I am a little resentful. Not jealous, just annoyed.

I was particularly annoyed when, as I was driving Melanie and the dogs back up the drive to Miles's house, the stupid drone buzzed me and almost caused the front tires to veer off the pavement. I was even more irritated when I stormed into the sunroom and found that it was not Miles at the controls of the drone but Casey.

"Seriously?" I demanded. "You could've made me wreck the car!"

Casey shot me a sideways grin, his eyes still on the control monitor. "Sorry. Still getting the hang of it."

With a wry lift of his brow, Miles held out his hand for the controls and Casey passed them over as Melanie and the dogs ran in, a virtual stampede of excited greetings. "Hi, Uncle Casey!" Melanie cried. "Did you hear about all the new dogs?"

While Casey balanced hugs, swishing dog tails and Melanie's report on all the events of the day, Miles carefully and expertly brought the drone into the garage he had had built for it on the patio outside the sunroom, safe from the snow. "Like having one adolescent with a dangerous toy in the house isn't enough," I grumbled, and gave Miles a quick, one-armed hug. "How was your day?"

"Boring," he replied. "How was yours?"

"Interesting."

Before he could ask for details, Melanie abandoned Casey to announce, "Raine and I had a great idea while we were driving over here, Dad. It involves you."

"Then I guess you'd better tell me about it." He put the drone controls away in a cabinet and turned his wheelchair to face her, his hands planted on his knees in a listening posture. "I'm ready."

Melanie, who was accustomed to giving presentations to her class, squared her shoulders and folded her hands. "We think you should build a bunch of little houses..."

"Tiny houses," I corrected. "Each with an attached fenced area for dogs."

Melanie slanted me an annoyed look. "*Tiny* houses," she went on, "for the women's shelter. People could live there with their dogs, instead of in the big house with everybody else. And when they got jobs, they could stay there and start paying rent instead of having to move to an apartment that doesn't allow dogs."

"You could get ten tiny houses on a flat acre of land," I pointed out helpfully. "And they go up really fast. At least, that's what I hear on TV."

"*And*," Melanie put in loudly, giving me another quelling look, "we think Uncle Casey should build them."

"I thought I was going to build them," objected Miles.

"You'd still be in charge," Melanie explained. "But Uncle Casey would do the work."

"In other words," said Miles, "I supply the money, and Casey has all the fun."

Casey sat on the floor with one arm around Mischief and the other around Magic while Cisco and Pepper pawed at his legs for attention. He grinned and stretched out one hand to scratch Cisco's ear. "I can get behind that."

Before Casey came here and started living off a government settlement, he had worked as a carpenter, builder, and all-around handyman. His adoptive father had owned a successful construction business until his death, and had expected Casey to take it over. But life intervened. I thought it was about time Casey got a real job, and, apparently, he didn't mind the idea.

"It could be a real community for these women who are trying to get a fresh start," I said. "They'd all have each other for support, and it would show them it's possible to have a future without, you know, going back to the life they had before."

"We could call it Hope Acres," Melanie added with a flourish, because the name had been her idea and we'd agreed she should be the one to announce it.

Miles nodded appreciatively. "And you two thought all this up on your way over from the kennel?"

"It still needs some refining," I admitted.

"Some," repeated Miles with an amused quirk of his lips.

"I like it," decided Casey. "We could put in a playground for the kids, and maybe even a dog park."

"Yeah!" agreed Melanie enthusiastically.

Miles said, "What is this 'we' business?"

"All we need is the right piece of property," Casey said.

"You've been looking for a project," I pointed out. "And something like this would make you a real hero around here."

"I'm already a hero around here," Miles objected, and then he smiled at Melanie. "But it's not a half-bad idea. Let me look into it."

Melanie squealed and threw her arms around Miles's neck. "I knew you'd say yes!"

The dogs wiggled out of Casey's grasp and rushed to join the excitement. I hurried to pull them away and Miles gave me a look over Melanie's shoulder that said, *What have you gotten me into?*

I smiled back innocently. "I'm sure it will be a *lot* more fun than taking pictures of snowflakes with your drone," I said.

Casey and Melanie kept a lively conversation going through the pizza-making process, designing ever more elaborate versions of Hope Acres. Occasionally, Miles would interject a voice of reason, but I could tell he didn't want to dampen Melanie's enthusiasm any more than Casey did. Melanie could be obnoxious sometimes, and she definitely had a mouth on her that could use some taming. But when she developed a passion, whether it be for dogs or dinosaurs or cooking or the women's shelter, she did so with one hundred percent of everything she had in her. That was something I hoped never changed, and I knew Miles felt the same.

After dinner, which included a gooey fudge brownie dessert topped with marshmallows, Melanie went upstairs to finish her homework while the rest of us lingered around the table over coffee and the pan of brownies. Pepper, Mischief and Magic raced up the stairs with Melanie, no doubt remembering the tasty bones they had left in the playroom. Cisco, ever hopeful, remained glued to my feet beneath the table just in case someone dropped a crumb.

I said, softening the observation with a rueful smile, "Hope Acres isn't going to happen, is it?"

Miles answered, "Oh, we can build it. It'll take a while to get the permits and work out the financing, but it can be done." He dipped his fork into the pan of brownies and cut off another slice, transferring it to his plate. "It's just not going to solve the problem."

"Security," agreed Casey. He broke off a corner of a brownie and ate it from the pan. "There's no way to make it safe."

"The men always find them," Miles said. "The violence always follows. And, more often than not, the women just give up and go back home." He closed his eyes briefly and shook his head. "I hate that I'm raising a daughter in a world where she has to be afraid of half the population."

And that was about as depressing a thought as I'd heard all day. Glumly, I stabbed another corner of the brownie and moved it to my plate.

Casey said, "Speaking of which, I went by the Hoggins place this afternoon."

"One beating wasn't enough?" inquired Miles.

Casey scoffed. "I could flatten him with one punch if I had to. Would've done it the first time if it hadn't been for the lady cop. I didn't want to make a bad impression, you know."

He started to slice off another corner with his fork and I reprimanded him with a tap of my fork on his. "Don't eat all the corners," I said. "There's a serving knife, you know."

Casey cut a healthy serving—with corners, naturally—and transferred it to his plate. "Anyway," he said, "he wasn't there. At least, that's what his wife said."

I paused in the process of cutting my own, slightly smaller second or third brownie. "His wife? Tina?"

Casey nodded. "It was a little weird. No, a lot weird. Like I said, she claimed he wasn't there, but his truck was in the carport. She would only open the door a crack, and she looked scared to death—like maybe he was standing behind her, waiting for her to say something wrong. I felt like shit, leaving her there, but what else could I do? She said she was fine. She told me to get off her porch."

"Damn," I said. Then, "Well, you told the police about her situation. We both did. Surely they'll check on her?"

Casey took a bite of his brownie, shaking his head. "They think she's safe and sound in the shelter."

"And I thought her husband was locked up," Miles put in.

"He made bail," I explained. "I guess Tina didn't know that. She must've heard he was in jail and thought it was safe to go home."

"It looked like she had a cut on her hand," Casey added. "Some blood on her shirt. So I'm guessing it wasn't that safe after all." He took another bite of brownie. "Something else strange. I saw dog bowls in the kitchen, but no dog."

I put down my fork. "Riley," I said. "The pointer I picked up from Welcoming Arms this afternoon. He has to be hers. There weren't any other dogs in the women's shelter." I crumpled my napkin in my lap and started to rise. "Millie gave me his owner's phone number. I should try to call her."

Miles put a hand on my knee. "And say what? If the pointer is this woman's dog, she left him behind because she didn't think it was safe to take him with her. According to Casey, it's still not safe. Leave it alone." He helped himself to another brownie. "And maybe ask the sheriff's office to do a welfare check in the morning."

"So bottom line," Casey said, "I didn't find out anything—not about Izzy, not about what Hoggins was doing with Booker's business card in his pocket."

"I can answer that," replied Miles, finishing off his brownie. "You said Hoggins works for Mountain Hauling and Excavation, right? They're the ones who put in Booker's driveway last year."

"How do you know that?" I asked.

"Research." He frowned a little as he picked up his coffee cup. "There's something that doesn't quite add up about that guy. For one thing, the owner of the company he works for, Blackwing, has been called before a grand jury twice, once for racketeering and once for financial fraud. Failed to indict both times, which never happens unless somebody is being paid off behind the scenes somewhere. Aside from that, I talked to one of the bankers in town and it seems Booker has been making inquiries about development permits—but not for the lake property. He was talking about a commercial development closer to town on property that he doesn't even own, and then he never followed through. I just can't figure out what he's up to."

Reluctantly, I told Miles about my encounter with Booker when I returned the earring. "I'm pretty sure he was lying about Amber not being there," I said. "I just don't know why."

"Just like Tina was lying about her husband not being there," pointed out Casey.

"Yeah, well," said Miles, "any way you look at it, you're talking about two bad hombres and it would make me very happy if you stayed away from both of them."

"Always striving to make you happy, dear," I replied demurely over the rim of my coffee cup, and Miles kicked my ankle under the table.

Casey grinned at that, then looked over his shoulder at the snow-spotted night through the window. He drained his coffee cup. "I'd better get going while I still can," he said, pushing up from the table. "Thanks for dinner. Tell the munchkin goodnight for me. Do you need help with the dishes?"

I waved him off and told him to be careful on the roads. The snow wasn't that difficult to navigate under the right conditions, but some of the steeper roads could get slippery.

Casey replied, "Are you kidding? A snow like this doesn't even make the weather report in Colorado."

"Yeah, well, they have snow plows in Colorado, too," I told him, "and *our* weather report is telling people to stay off the roads."

He shrugged it off as he started toward the door to get his jacket. There he was met by Melanie and the three dogs who thundered down the stairs after her. The dogs, of course, greeted Casey as though it had been months since they'd seen him, bouncing and wiggling and yipping for attention while he laughed and petted them and tried not to trip over the melee.

"Finished my homework," Melanie announced happily. "And guess what? Snow day tomorrow! I just got the e-mail."

"Remote learning," her father corrected. "*I* just got the e-mail."

"Boy, you people are real wimps about snow,"

observed Casey. He gave Melanie a quick hug and added, "Gotta go, princess. Thanks for the pizza."

Melanie looked horrified. "But it's snowing really hard! You can't go home." She appealed to me. "He can't go home. Why can't he sleep over? We have lots of extra rooms."

"So do I," Casey replied, ruffling her hair. "At my house."

"But it's a snow day tomorrow," Melanie protested. "I can stay up late. We can play Monopoly and have waffles for breakfast. Please?"

I could tell Casey was about to protest again, but Miles surprised us both by saying, "She's right. We've got extra rooms, and Monopoly sounds fun. After all, it's a snow day."

After that, Casey could hardly refuse. He grinned at Melanie. "Waffles, huh? That might make it worth being pummeled by you and your dad at Monopoly."

"Oh, boy!" Melanie grabbed Casey's hand and tugged him after her, grinning like she'd just won the lottery. "Let's go set up the board! I'm the dog. I'm always the dog."

They left the room amidst a tangle of excited canines. Even Cisco, catching the mood, abandoned his quest for a crumb of chocolate and joined the pack. I turned to Miles with a lift of my eyebrow. "That was unexpectedly nice of you."

He shrugged. "I can be nice on occasion. Ask anyone." Then he smiled ruefully. "Don't you remember how excited you used to get about snow days? They were better than Christmas and birthdays put together. My daughter wants to have a party. And there's something about hanging by your fingernails over the side of a cliff that makes you want to say yes every chance you get. Also," he admitted, "I have a feeling I've got about six more months before the last thing my little girl wants to do is hang out with her old man, so I'm trying to enjoy it while I can."

I got up and came around the table to kiss him. "Thanks for not letting go on that cliff."

"You bet." He caressed my cheek. "Thanks for jumping off a cliff to rescue me."

"You bet." I straightened up. "But I'm showing no mercy on the Monopoly board."

He laughed. I had never won a game of Monopoly against Miles in my life.

CHAPTER SEVENTEEN

By a quarter to midnight, six inches of fine, powdery snow had coated Hanover County, turning it once again into a winter picture postcard. Already the accumulation surpassed expectations and showed no signs of stopping. The tires of the sheriff's office SUV crunched on the soft snowpack as it made its way slowly through the empty streets of Hansonville.

"Guess y'all don't see too much snow up in Raleigh," commented Sergeant Harvey as he made an easy right off of Main Street onto Maple.

"Enough," replied Dakota from the passenger seat. "Not as pretty as this, though."

Sergeant Jack Harvey was in his fifties, balding, and carrying the comfortable extra weight that was the result of riding a patrol car and eating fast food for twenty years. He was on his second marriage, with two teenagers at home that he loved to brag about. He'd been with the Hanover County Sheriff's Office for eight years, and before that had worked for various small town police departments in the surrounding area. He was Dakota Bradshaw's self-appointed guide to all things Hanover County for the next week of nights, and he loved to talk. That was fine with Dakota. The more he talked, the less she was required to.

"Yeah, something about the street lights on the snow when nobody's around makes the town look like something somebody would paint," Harvey said now. "We won't start plowing until the snow stops," he added. "Forecast says sometime before dawn. Main roads first, the hospital, fire station, utility substations. A lot of people hire private plows, or do it themselves with tractors. Sixty percent of the roads up here are private, you know. Meanwhile, we'll patrol as many roads as we can and report on conditions, keep an eye out for stranded travelers, that kind of thing. Good chance for you to get the layout of the county."

"Yes, sir," she replied. Technically, she was his superior since she would be coming on board as a lieutenant in the Hanover County Sheriff's Office. But that job didn't officially start until her two-week orientation was over, and for now she was a probie. She would give the man the respect he deserved. "I've been doing some of that already."

Dakota didn't see any reason to share the information, but she had left the Raleigh-Durham PD a little more abruptly than she'd planned and had been living in a motel just outside of town for the past two weeks. She'd spent the time looking for a more permanent—and secure—place to live, and in the process had seen much more of the county than she'd ever intended to. The little house on Farmstead Lane that the sheriff had referred her to was a god-send.

"Not too many folks'll be out this time of night," the sergeant went on, "so it should be a pretty quiet first shift for you. Of course, there's always a few jackasses that like to cut donuts in the snow in the McDonald's parking lot, that kind of thing. We try to catch them before anybody breaks a neck or crashes through a window or anything."

She smiled politely. "I don't mind a quiet shift."

"Me, I prefer to stay busy," he said. "Helps me stay awake."

"There's that," she agreed, watching the snow drift past the window.

"Most folks around here are pretty decent," he went on. "We've got a few trouble spots, a couple of bad seeds, but you'll get to know them pretty quick. Most of the calls we get are domestics, burglaries, petty theft. Drugs are getting to be more of a problem than they used to be, but I guess you've seen your share of that upstate."

She returned a noncommittal, "Hmm." Her gaze was fixed on the pattern of snowflakes whooshing past the window. Some people found the swirl of snowflakes as seen from a moving vehicle disorienting, even vertigo-inducing, but Dakota found it soothing. She was beginning to think, cautiously, that she might like it here.

He glanced at her. "I hear you moved into the old Lawson place."

"Yes, that's right."

"Quiet out there. Except for the dog kennel, of course. Getting settled in okay?"

"It'll take a while," she admitted. "My furniture just arrived this weekend." It occurred to her that Harvey's fondness for chatting might be useful, so she added, "I met my neighbor the other night, at the jail of all places. The dog kennel lady. What's her name?"

"Raine Stockton," he replied without hesitation. "She used to be married to Lawson, back when he was with the sheriff's office. The Stocktons go way back around here. One of the founding families, I think." He made a turn. "Her father was some kind of judge, her uncle the sheriff for a couple of generations, then her husband took over." He made a turn and resumed his narrative. "I worked under him for a while. Good man. I think he's down in Georgia somewhere now."

"She seemed nice," Dakota offered, trying to get him back on track.

"Raine? Oh, sure. A bit of a busybody, but she does a lot for the community with those dogs of hers. She used to be our go-to for search and rescue but now we mostly count on the surrounding counties. Shame, too. That retriever she's got was pretty good, and of course, them being local really helped. I guess she retired or something after she found herself that rich boyfriend."

Dakota was surprised. "Really? That kid I brought in for fighting at the Borderline? Casey something? "

He shot her a confused look. "Casey Macintosh? No, no, that's the guy I was telling you about before—the one that was some kind of informant for the Feds that the man that had your job before got fired over. Well, I guess he didn't exactly get fired, but he sure left in a hurry."

"Right," Dakota murmured. "Lot of history to keep up with here."

"Anyhow," Harvey went on easily, "Macintosh is not Stockton's boyfriend, he's her brother. Half-brother, I guess. Don't know much about him, but he's only lived here a year. The fiancé is Miles Young, some kind of big developer and investor out of Atlanta. He's the one that's putting in that fancy golf community up on Hawk Mountain. I heard it's supposed to have its own airstrip and everything. A lot of people don't like him coming in here and changing things up, but he seems like a regular guy to me. Gives a lot of money to charity, goes to church now and then, that kind of thing. But man, you should see his house. It's right up the road from you, but you probably can't see it, all tucked back on the mountain the way it is. I worked a call there once. Talk about your grand estates." He gave a low whistle of appreciation and added, "He's got a little girl, but she goes to that fancy private school over in Knightsville. Out of our jurisdiction," he explained. "But they have a nice Italian restaurant over there. Gino's. You ought to try it sometime."

She smiled vaguely. "Thanks. Maybe I will." Then, "What was the call?"

"What call?"

"At the millionaire's estate."

"Oh." He grew somber. "His wife was shot. Ex-wife, I guess. Bad scene. He was a suspect for a while —the spouses usually are—but it turned out to be a professional hit. I felt bad for the kid. Real bad."

Dakota couldn't help giving him an incredulous look, which he didn't notice. *A murdered woman, an orphaned child, a professional killer*, she thought, *and all you remember was the fancy house?*

Small town cops. This would take some getting used to.

They rode in silence for a while, accompanied only by the soft crackling of the radio in the background and the crunch of snow beneath the tires. A car passed them going south at a snail's pace through the snow, but otherwise Harvey was right—no one was out and about on a night like this.

After a time, the sergeant spoke again. "None of my business, of course," he said amiably, "but you got a fella up in Raleigh?"

Dakota stiffened. "No." She made her reply as pleasant as possible. "Just my mom and dad."

"Never been married?"

"No." This time, she didn't bother trying to sound pleasant.

"Well," said the sergeant, evidently not one to take a hint, "like I said, lotta nice folks around here. You'll make friends."

She said, because she did not want to get a reputation as a stick-in-the-mud, "I expect I will."

That seemed to make him happy, and an easy silence fell again. It was broken in another moment by the crackle of the radio. "Suspicious activity reported at Number Four Eagle Way. Any units in the vicinity respond."

At the address, Dakota was alert. That was near her house.

Harvey picked up the mic. "This is Unit 12-6. We've got it. Crossing Lee's Creek on Highway 11 now. Four minutes out."

Harvey replaced the mic and flipped on the lights, picking up speed. Blue shadows pulsed in the snow around them. "Speak of the devil," he said, grinning at her. "That's Miles Young's place. You get to see the house after all."

CHAPTER EIGHTEEN

The Monopoly game was brutal, but what did Casey and I expect, playing against the masters? As ruthless as Miles and Melanie were, being massacred on the game board was still better than the tribulations of the day I'd had. There was something about having the people I cared most about gathered around the game table by the fire with a pack of dogs sleeping at my feet while snow piled up outside that made the whole concept of missing and battered women seem very far away.

Melanie went to bed without her snowflake fractal, or whatever it was supposed to be, but Miles promised to have it ready for her by morning. Since remote learning often included a certain amount of creative classroom freedom, I suspected Miles and his snowflake would take over a good part of her lesson plan for the following day.

Casey and I made hot chocolate and brought it to the sunroom while Miles sent his drone out into the storm. Casey was still fascinated by the thing, and Miles was more than pleased to show off how it could maneuver in the dark and seek out roadways and houses by following their heat signatures. Cisco and I settled in on the sofa, watching the two boys at play. Since Cisco was never sure which sofa he was allowed on in Miles's house and which he was not, this was a particular treat for him. He panted happily as he watched the snowflakes drift down on the deck outside.

"What is a fractal, anyway?" I asked Miles, hoping to bring him back to task.

"It's a simple pattern, repeated infinitely, that forms a complex whole," he responded, his attention on the controls of the drone. "Fractals are found all around us in nature and mathematics."

Casey, who had drawn a chair up next to Miles's operating station so he could watch the drone's monitor screen, looked over his shoulder to exchange a blank look with me.

"Are you serious?" I demanded flatly. "She's eleven."

Miles grinned. "It's not that difficult a concept. Think about a fern. If you pick off a leaf, the leaf looks like a miniature version of the fern. Or an oak leaf—the veins in the leaf form a pattern similar to the branches of the tree. Simple, repeating patterns."

Like two women in trouble, I thought randomly, *and two abandoned dogs.* Was that a repeating pattern, too?

Casey, apparently bored with the subject of fractals, pointed to the screen. "I thought these things couldn't see at night. This picture is as clear as day."

"There's always some ambient light everywhere, and we're pretty close to town here," Miles replied. "This model amplifies reflected light to give you a fairly clear picture, even at night. And of course the snow helps." He glanced over his shoulder and explained to me, "Because snow reflects light."

I scowled at him, knowing he was just trying to annoy me. "Got it, professor. So what does any of this have to do with Melanie and her snowflake project?"

"Come here and I'll show you."

Reluctantly, I left my cozy sofa and took my mug of hot chocolate over to the work station in front of the window. Cisco opened one eye lazily but decided against following me and settled back to sleep again. I leaned over Miles's shoulder to watch the video from the drone. He had a whole network set up there, with two computer monitors, one reflecting the same video as the drone monitor and the other displaying a topographical map and coordinates that changed as the little red dot that represented the drone moved. I was pretty sure the sheriff's office didn't have anything this fancy.

On the other hand, I didn't see what was so fascinating about the whole thing. The video display looked like a staticky black-and-white film of snow-covered roads and treetops to me.

"We're pretty far out in the country now," Miles said. "Less interference from power lines and headlights, so we should be able to get a good shot. Here you go."

With dizzying speed, the computer monitor zoomed in and froze on a single, drastically magnified snowflake. Miles leaned over and pointed to a branch of the snowflake. "See how the basic hexagonal pattern branches out into arms at repeating intervals, and each arm sprouts a series of smaller, equilateral protrusions that can basically repeat to infinity. Zoom in on any branch…" he did so. "And you'll see a smaller version of the whole. Pretty cool, huh?"

One of the things I love about Miles is that he can find fascination in almost anything—a dog agility trial, a new recipe, an antique car, a well-engineered building, a snowflake. For most of these things I can share his admiration but this, I'm not ashamed to admit, was completely over my head and absolutely outside my spectrum of interest.

I sipped my chocolate and said, "That's nice, Miles." I couldn't help but notice my tone bore a remarkable resemblance to the one my mother used to use with me when I brought home a crayon scribbling and wanted her to display it on the fridge. "Really."

He grinned and returned the image to the live feed from the drone. "It is," he assured me. "Really."

"But I don't understand why you have to use a drone to find these snowflakes. Why can't you just take a picture with your phone through the window and enlarge it on the computer?"

"You could," Miles admitted. "But that wouldn't be as much fun."

I stared at him. "Are you kidding me? It's almost midnight! You're sitting here flying your ten-thousand-dollar toy in a snowstorm when you could have just taken a picture any time today?"

He shrugged, his eyes back on the controls. "I wanted to see how it would perform under these conditions. And this thing cost a lot more than ten grand, by the way."

"Otherwise we'd all have one," remarked Casey.

"Terrific," I muttered, exasperated. "So when it crashes, you'll be out multiple tens of thousands. Great example of fiscal responsibility for your daughter."

"I'm not going to crash it," Miles responded, sounding only mildly irritated.

"Say, what is that?" Casey said, pointing to the screen. "A car?"

"Looks like some kind of truck or SUV to me," Miles said.

"I'm going to bed," I said irritably. "You two children have fun."

"You know what else is interesting about fractals?" Miles said without looking around. "They always have jagged edges." And he glanced over his shoulder with a wink. "Like you."

"Ha, ha. Very clever."

I turned to leave, but he went on, "If you think

about it, that's really how the natural world is constructed. Humans are the ones who keep trying to round things out and smooth them down. But nature loves imperfection."

"Good night, professor." I pretended to smother a yawn as I headed toward the door. "And oh, by the way," I tossed over my shoulder, "you've got one or two jagged edges yourself. Come on, Cisco."

"That's why we fit together so well, sugar," Miles returned.

Cisco placed his forepaws on the floor, stretched out his spine, and took his time bringing his hindquarters down. He followed me across the room, tail swishing in a way that indicated he knew all the fun was over for the day.

Casey said, looking at the second monitor, "This thing says we're in the middle of the national forest. What's a car doing out there on a night like this?"

I was intrigued. "It might be a forest ranger vehicle," I suggested, coming over to them. "Maybe someone is lost or in trouble." At the thought, my heart started to beat a little faster; my attention quickened. This was my purview. This was where I, or someone like me, would typically be called in to stand by or report.

I looked at the map on the monitor. "That's Franklin Junction Road," I said. "Dirt road, not too steep. It should be passable in a four wheel drive or heavy truck. But nobody lives out there. Why would anybody be on that road unless they're lost or responding to some kind of emergency?"

"Maybe some kids joyriding," suggested Casey.

"Maybe," I agreed reluctantly. "But I hope not. That road narrows in another mile or so, and there are some steep drop-offs."

"Damn," said Miles. "They turned off their headlights."

I sat on the arm of Miles' chair while he pushed some buttons and flipped some switches on the console. The screen displayed a veil of white on black night.

"I thought you said this thing can see at night," I said.

"Can't get close enough," he said. "Too much tree cover. Wait. Here's something."

He made an adjustment, and a moderately sized greenish blur appeared on the screen. "It's the heat signature from the engine," he explained.

"Good-sized vehicle," Casey observed. "Probably a pickup."

"Like I said, forest service," I added, but I was trying to convince myself as much as them. What would a single forest service vehicle be doing in the middle of the woods in a snowstorm with no lights and no backup? If it were a rescue situation, they would have used ATVs or snowmobiles to gain access, and more than one truck for the rescue equipment. Could he be scouting roads? And if so, why?

One thing was certain: I now understood how watching this drone footage could become addictive, and I definitely owed Miles an apology.

"Look," Casey said suddenly, pointing to the

screen.

Another green blur had appeared beside the first, moving slowly around the vehicle. Miles made some more adjustments, and the blur took the shape of a human figure trudging through the snow to the back of the vehicle, which we could now see was shaped like a pickup truck. The figure appeared to lower the tailgate and then disappeared for a moment as it climbed inside. A moment later, something large and cumbersome tumbled out of the truck and onto the ground, making a large dark blotch against the snow. We watched, riveted, as the figure leapt down from the truck and bent to grasp the lower portion of the object, dragging it a few feet. Abruptly, the screen went black.

"Son of a …!" Miles exclaimed.

I demanded at the same moment, "What happened?"

A white message flashing on the screen answered my question: *Returning to base*. Miles sat back heavily in his chair and said, "It's programmed to stop recording and return to dock when the battery power hits 51%." He released a frustrated breath. "Damn it."

Casey's eyes were still fixed on the screen. He said, "What did that look like to you? What he pushed off the truck."

Neither of us answered for a moment. Cisco pressed against my leg, wondering why we weren't going to bed as promised, and I scratched his ear absently.

Miles said, "Could have been trash."

I objected, "It was too big for a regular trash bag."

"And why was he dragging it off into the woods?" Casey asked.

"We don't know that's what he was doing," Miles said.

"Can you replay the video?"

Miles typed a few keys on the computer keyboard and brought up the video. He fast-forwarded the footage until the headlights came into view, and we watched the scene play out again. When it got to the part in which the dark bundle was pushed to the ground, Miles stopped the replay and zoomed in.

In truth, there was nothing definitive about the picture. It was a digitally enhanced snippet of a black-and-white image created by a drone's thermal imaging night vision. A long, dark, loosely rectangular shape lying upon a carpet of snow. And yet we all knew what we were looking at. And no one was willing to say it.

Miles resumed the playback, and we watched until the screen went black. Still, no one spoke. I looked at Casey, but his eyes were still fixed on the blank monitor. I thought about Izzy. I thought about Tina, home with an abusive husband and bleeding from a wound she wouldn't let Casey see. Finally, I couldn't stand the silence anymore.

"We should call the police," I said.

Miles's lips tightened. "And tell them what? That someone was dumping trash in the woods? We don't know what we saw, Raine. Don't jump to conclusions."

I argued, "That's national forest land. Dumping trash there is a crime. Or," I added, thinking fast, "we don't know what happened to the person in the truck. The camera cut out before we saw where he went. Maybe he needs assistance."

"Raine..."

Casey turned in his chair to look at us, his eyes dark and his face still. "How about," he said levelly, "we tell them the truth? That a woman is missing and we just saw someone dump a body in the woods."

Miles did not reply. The three of us looked at each other for another long moment. Then Miles picked up his phone and dialed the police.

CHAPTER NINETEEN

Dakota Bradshaw had been in Hanover County for exactly two weeks, and she still wasn't used to how dark the mountains got after sunset. Back in Raleigh, even the quiet neighborhoods had a glow—streetlamps, traffic, the soft haze of a city that never fully slept. Up here, the night pressed in like something alive, thick and cold and absolute.

Snowflakes spiraled in the beams of the cruiser's headlights as she and Harvey wound their way up the long, curving drive toward Miles Young's house. "House" wasn't the right word, she thought. The place rose out of the hillside like a modernist fortress—glass, steel, and stone, all sharp angles and clean lines. It looked like it had been dropped here from another world.

"Whoa," she murmured. "You weren't kidding about

the house."

Harvey shot her a gratified look. "Something, huh? The man does this for a living, ends up with more money than God, this is what you get."

And it was also, she reflected, but didn't say, *why you answer a call after midnight in the middle of a snowstorm about something that might or might not have been seen from a drone that shouldn't even have been able to fly in these conditions. The rich are different.*

Dakota watched the way the snow drifted across the asphalt but didn't stick to it. The man had a heated driveway that was at least a half mile long. *Okay*, she thought, unwillingly impressed. Maybe she should have taken the Stockton woman up on that offer of pie the other night. Her boyfriend probably had it flown in from France for her.

"Got to admit," she said, "I didn't expect to see anything like this around here."

Harvey looked amused. "Not a bad way to spend your first shift, huh? Hanging out in a nice warm mansion, taking a report about something that probably didn't even happen. Better than standing out in the snow directing traffic around a wreck, am I right? I hope they have coffee on. I bet it's top shelf."

Harvey parked in the circular drive in front of the door behind a snow-covered pickup truck. He killed the flashers and they got out, boots crunching in the fresh snow as they climbed the steps. Before they reached the door, it swung open.

Raine Stockton stood there, framed by warm

light. She held the collar of a grinning golden retriever, its tail swishing happily in the way of golden retrievers everywhere. She seemed surprised to recognize Dakota.

"Oh," she said. "Hey. Thanks for coming." She stepped away from the door and gestured them inside. "I'm Raine Stockton. We met the other night."

She seemed reluctant to say more about exactly where they had met, which Dakota could understand.

Dakota nodded a cordial acknowledgment and smiled at the dog. "And this must be the famous Cisco."

The golden retriever wagged his tail harder at the sound of his name, and Harvey bent down to pet the dog. "Hey there, big fella," he said.

Raine let the dog's collar go and closed the door on the cold. Cisco wiggled a happy greeting to Harvey in acknowledgement of the petting, then turned to Dakota. Dakota obligingly tickled his chin.

Raine's mood did not seem nearly as ebullient as her golden retriever's, and there were worry lines between her brows. "Come on in," she said, leading the way into the tall, glass-walled main room. "They're in the sunroom."

Dakota brushed snow from her jacket and followed her inside. The house was warm, almost too warm, and smelled faintly of cedar and something homey from the kitchen. Chocolate, maybe. And pizza? Maybe the rich weren't as different as she thought.

Cisco trotted ahead, his claws clicking on the polished hardwood and echoing a little in the vast space. Every now and then he'd glance back as if to make sure they were keeping up. Dakota had to scold herself for being a little awestruck and quickened her step. But the room had a triangular glass wall that was at least thirty feet high, for Pete's sake. Who wouldn't stare at that?

The sunroom, as its name implied, was composed of three walls of glass and decorated in light colors and comfortable-looking sofas. There was what looked like a gaming station set up in front of the north-facing bank of windows, with a couple of computer monitors and a control console on a long glass table. Miles Young stood in the center of the room, leaning on a pair of crutches. He was a good-looking man in his early fifties with short-cropped hair and broad-shoulders. There was no mistaking who he was. A black brace encased his lower right leg, but even with that obvious disability, he had a kind of presence that filled a room even when he wasn't speaking. Tonight, though, he looked uneasy.

"Thanks for coming," he said. He balanced one crutch against his body and extended his hand. "I hope we're not wasting your time."

Harvey went forward quickly to shake the man's hand. "Not at all, Mr. Young. That's what we're here for. I'm Deputy Harvey and this is my colleague Dakota Bradshaw."

Dakota started to come forward but Young grimaced with apology and leaned again on the crutch.

"Sorry," he explained. "I'm still a little clumsy with these. Hiking accident," he added, and let it go at that. He nodded toward Raine. "You've met my fiancée, Raine. And this is her brother, Casey Macintosh."

Dakota had, of course, recognized him sitting at the gaming console even before he turned around. That curly blond ponytail, that lanky build, that almost-perfect profile. Most women would have found his kind of lazy good looks irresistible. But Dakota was not most women, and she knew trouble when she saw it.

Casey's frowning expression as he turned around was mitigated with a spark of surprise when he recognized Dakota. She thought he'd say something flip like "Fancy meeting you here" or "We meet again." But all he said was, "Come look at this." He turned back to the monitor.

Both deputies moved toward the display setup. "All we got from dispatch was that your drone had picked up some suspicious activity in the national forest," Harvey said.

Dakota added, "I didn't think drones could pick up anything in this kind of weather, and at night."

"This one is pretty advanced," Miles said. He made his way over to the chair next to Casey at the glass table and lowered himself into it. He gestured toward the screen "But this is probably nothing."

Raine shot him a look as she moved his crutches out of the way. "It's not nothing."

Dakota stepped closer to the screen. A grainy image was paused on the screen—night vision struggling against heavy snowfall—but she could make out the shape of a pickup truck on a narrow forest service road. The drone hovered above it, its camera tilted down.

"Play it," Casey said tensely.

Miles hesitated, then hit the space bar.

The footage rolled.

The truck door opened. A greenish blob of a figure climbed out—hooded, shoulders rounded, virtually indistinguishable as to size or shape. He moved to the back of the truck, lowered the tailgate, climbed in, and hauled something large and shapeless into view. A bundle wrapped in a tarp or blanket. Heavy. He struggled with it until it rolled to the ground.

Dakota felt her stomach tighten.

The figure reached down and grasped the end of the bundle. He started to drag it away, staticky snow swirling around him. Abruptly, the video cut to a black screen.

"That's it," Miles said. "Battery cut out."

Casey exhaled sharply. "Tell me that doesn't look like a body."

Sergeant Harvey rubbed his chin skeptically. "It could be anything. Old furniture. Trash. Hunters dump deer carcasses all the time."

"In a snowstorm?" Raine objected. "At night?"

Casey said, "A woman is missing, or have you forgotten that? Now we see somebody trying to dispose of a body in the woods in the middle of the night..."

Harvey gave a grunt of uneasy amusement and

raised a hand in protest. “Whoa, there, son, that’s a pretty big leap. What missing person are you talking about?”

“Isabelle Stedman,” Dakota replied before Casey could answer. “I remember the report. Maybe you could check on the progress of the case?” she suggested.

Harvey looked mildly disgruntled as he looked from one to the other of them. “Yeah, I will. Hold on.” He took out his phone and walked away to make the call.

Dakota turned to Miles, her voice neutral. “Do we know when this was recorded?”

“About an hour ago,” Miles said. “I was testing the drone’s thermal camera. Storm was coming in, figured it was a good time to see how it handled low visibility.”

“And you just happened to catch this?” she asked.

Miles bristled. “I wasn’t looking for anything. It was random.”

“Do you have the coordinates?”

Miles hit a couple of strokes on the keyboard and brought up the coordinates of the last frame. Dakota took out her notebook and jotted them down.

“Sergeant Harvey is right, you know,” she said. “This is national forest land and out of our jurisdiction. If it’s a misdemeanor improper disposal of refuse…”

“Oh, for heaven’s sake,” Raine said impatiently. “It’s right off Franklin Junction Road. Well within county limits. And you know as well as I do there’s something more than a little suspicious about what we just saw."

Harvey joined them, his brow creased thoughtfully. "It's still an open case, all right. No sign of foul play, but no leads either. The boys have interviewed her associates, people at work, that kind of thing. Nobody knows anything except that she just didn't show up at work one day. There's a report of her leaving the bar where she worked with some guy, but we haven't been able to interview him yet. Purse and phone are gone, but nothing else seems to be missing. One strange thing—her car is still at her house."

"And her dog," Raine put in. "She left her dog behind with no food or water."

"That is strange," Dakota admitted. And that explained why Raine Stockton was invested in the woman's disappearance. Dogs were apparently a thing with her.

Casey said, exasperated, "Izzy's been missing for two days. Two days, for God's sake. And now we have footage of someone dumping something big enough to be a person in the woods. Are you not connecting the dots?"

Dakota felt the weight of both Raine's and Casey's gazes. She looked at Miles Young, whose expression was neutral. She was usually pretty good at reading the dynamics in human interaction but she was on uncertain ground here. She wasn't even an official investigator yet, but for some reason, everyone was deferring to her. She suddenly found herself in charge.

Sensing her uneasiness, Harvey cleared his throat. "We can't assume it's her."

"No," Casey said sharply. "But we can't assume it isn't."

Cisco whined softly, nudging Raine's hand. She absently stroked his head, eyes never leaving the screen.

Dakota replayed the footage in her mind. The way the figure moved. The weight of the bundle. The urgency. The snow.

"Do you have the raw file?" she asked.

Miles nodded and handed her a flash drive. "It's all there."

Dakota slipped it into her pocket. "We'll take it back to the station, enhance what we can. But with the snow coming down like this, any tracks out there are going to disappear fast."

"That's why we need to go now," Raine said.

Dakota turned to her. "I don't think—"

"Cisco can track in snow," Raine said. "He's done it before."

Harvey shook his head. "It's dark. The storm's getting worse. Even if we can get to the location, we're not going to be able to see anything." He looked at her narrowly. "Anyhow, I didn't think you did that kind of thing anymore. Tracking, I mean."

Raine swallowed visibly, then lifted her chin. "Well, I do."

Casey said. "We're wasting time. Whoever we saw on that video might still be out there. But the longer we stand around here, the less likely we are to find him."

Raine stepped closer, Cisco at her side. "Look, you've seen the footage. You know what it looks like."

Dakota hesitated. She did know. And she hated that she knew.

Raine continued, "Whatever happened out there left tracks. And those tracks are disappearing in the snow as we speak. Every minute we stand here arguing is a minute we lose."

Cisco barked once, sharp and insistent, as if punctuating her words.

Harvey muttered, "Damn dog's got timing."

Dakota looked at the screen again. The figure dragging the bundle. The darkness swallowing them. The snow a white, frozen blur.

She looked at Raine. At Casey. At Miles, who was staring at the screen with a tight expression, no doubt wishing he hadn't launched the drone at all.

Dakota sighed. "Fine. But we do this by the book. Raine, you and Cisco stay behind us until we assess the scene. If it's safe, we let Cisco track. If it's not, we pull back. Understood?"

Raine nodded. "Understood."

Casey grabbed his coat. "Let's go."

Dakota held up a hand. "Not you."

Casey stared at her. "What? Why not?"

"Because you're not trained for this," Dakota said. "You're a civilian. And the fewer people out there trampling all over the trail, the better."

Casey drew in a sharp breath and looked as

though he would protest before assessing the wisdom of her words. "Fine," he said. "I'll stay out of the way. But I've got the coordinates and I've got snow tires on the truck. I'll drive Raine and Cisco."

Before anyone could argue, Raine said, "Come on, then. We need to stop by my house to get my gear."

The two of them didn't hesitate another moment. They hurried for the door, Cisco racing ahead. "We'll meet you there," Raine called over her shoulder.

Harvey frowned at Dakota. "You sure about this?"

"No," Dakota said, sighing. "But she's right. If someone dumped a body out there, we're already behind."

Harvey grunted. "Hell of a first shift for you."

Dakota managed a thin smile. "Welcome to the mountains, I guess."

CHAPTER TWENTY

The wind hit us the moment we stepped out of Casey's truck. Snowflakes stung my face like needles, and the wind shoved at us hard enough to make me brace my legs. Cisco pressed against my thigh, vibrating with tension. He wasn't afraid. He was focused.

Casey pointed down the narrow forest service road. "This is where the drone picked up the truck."

Dakota nodded, her flashlight already sweeping the ground. Harvey followed her, shoulders hunched against the cold. I stayed close, Cisco's lead wrapped around my wrist, though he didn't need it. He wasn't going anywhere without me.

The snow was falling fast, but not fast enough to hide everything. Dakota crouched near the shoulder of the road.

"Here," she said. "Tire impressions."

I stepped closer. Two faint parallel lines cut across the fresh snow, barely visible but unmistakable.

My stomach tightened. "That's the truck."

Harvey grunted. "Looks like it."

Casey looked around, squinting through the snow, then back down at the ground. "Well, he's gone now." He pointed. "Look at the mud where he backed up."

Dakota frowned at him. "You're supposed to wait in the truck."

"I'm twenty feet from it," he replied impatiently.

Dakota stood and turned a slow, full circle, her flashlight beam sweeping the ground. "There should be tracks," she said, "or drag marks."

"Not as fast as the snow is falling," I pointed out. "Not with this wind." I walked a few feet away, following the fast-disappearing tire tracks, and pointed to the ground. "Look," I said. "There's a shadow beneath the snow. This is where he pushed the bundle out of the truck."

She looked at me. "Do you think your dog can track this?"

Instead of answering, I bent down and brushed the snow around the depression with my fingers. "Track." I told Cisco.

Cisco sniffed the snow enthusiastically, and then the air. His nose returned to the ground and then, tail waving, he lunged ahead. I gave him the line.

"Stay behind me," I told the deputies, struggling to keep up with Cisco.

Dakota told Casey sharply, “You! Stay here!”

I did not look around to see if he obeyed. I heard the deputies crunching through the snow and breathing hard several yards behind me, but my focus was on Cisco.

We descended the embankment, boots sinking into the snow. The trees closed around us quickly, their branches heavy with ice. The wind was muffled here, but the cold was worse—thick, biting, the kind that seeped into your bones.

Cisco moved with purpose, nose low, tail straight. I could no longer see the drag mark, but Cisco followed the invisible trail determinedly. He wove between trees, dipped into hollows, climbed small rises. Sometimes he wandered off, doubled back. I wondered if the person we were tracking had become disoriented in the snow, perhaps after he had left his heavy burden behind, and wandered off his own trail trying to return to his truck.

Snow has a way of swallowing sound, but tonight it felt like it was swallowing light too. My headlamp carved a narrow tunnel through the darkness, flakes drifting across the beam like ash. Cisco moved ahead of me, golden fur turned silver under the glare, tail low, nose working the wind. He was all business—no hesitation, no wasted motion. I wished I could borrow even a fraction of his certainty.

“Come on, Cisco ,” I whispered into the cold, “you can do this.” But he hadn’t done it at Izzy’s house this afternoon. He hadn’t worked a trail in months. What if all he was tracking now was a rabbit?

I added, "Please." The word hung in the air like frost vapor and I wasn't even sure why I said it. Did I really want to be right about what we had seen? Didn't I really hope that this long, frozen trek into the woods would ultimately lead to absolutely nothing?

It's just that I didn't really think that was going to happen. At all.

Cisco stopped suddenly, head lifting, nostrils flaring. His body tightened like a bowstring.

"What is it, buddy?" My voice came out thinner than I intended.

He didn't look back. He surged forward, pulling the line through my gloves. I stumbled after him, snow dragging at my boots, branches clawing at my jacket. The wind shifted, carrying a faint, metallic scent that made my stomach clench.

Cisco veered off the trail, plunging into deeper drifts. I followed, heart hammering. The forest pressed close around us—black trunks, white ground, the world reduced to contrast and breath and fear. Somewhere far behind us, the radio crackled with distant voices, but out here it was just me and my dog and the cold truth waiting to be found.

Cisco barked once—sharp, urgent. Then again.

"I'm coming," I called, pushing harder. My legs burned. My lungs burned. That was Cisco's alert bark. He had found something.

The ground dropped away without warning. I skidded to a halt at the edge of a ravine, snow crumbling under my boots. Cisco sat stiffly a few feet ahead in his alert position, front paws planted, staring down into the shadows.

I edged closer, sweeping my headlamp beam into the gully below.

At first I saw nothing but swirling snow. Then the wind shifted, and the beam of my light cut through the shadows.

A dark shape lay at the bottom of the ravine. It was long and heavy and still, wrapped in black plastic that glinted through a thin layer of snow.

My breath froze in my throat. "Oh, God."

Footsteps crunched behind me. Dakota and Harvey appeared at my side, flashlights sweeping the ravine.

Harvey swore softly. "That's it. Has to be."

Dakota didn't speak. She didn't need to. The shape was unmistakable.

My breath caught. For a moment, I couldn't move, couldn't think. The world narrowed to the shape in the snow and the pounding of my own pulse.

"Is it ... do you think it's ...a body?" I managed.

But from this distance, in this light, she could be no more certain than I was. We all knew what it probably was. But we would have to wait to find out for sure.

Dakota stepped back from the edge. "We need to call this in. No one goes down there until we get some help."

Harvey keyed his radio. "Dispatch, this is Unit

12-6. We've located a possible body. Send a recovery team to our coordinates."

Static crackled, then a voice answered, "Copy that, Unit 12-6. Team en route."

I knelt beside Cisco, burying my fingers in his fur. "Good boy," I whispered. "Good, good boy. Everything's okay now."

He leaned into me, panting heavily. Neither of us ever wanted a search to end this way, and both of us knew nothing was okay.

CHAPTER TWENTY-ONE

The descent into the ravine took the better part of twenty minutes, though it felt longer. Casey left the truck and came to wait with us, sharing the grim, awful silence. Of course, the deputies tried to get us to wait in the truck, out of the cold, out of the way. And of course we wouldn't. We had come this far. We would see it through.

It was Casey who called Miles and informed him briefly of the situation. I could sense Miles's frustration through the phone, across the distance. He wanted to be here. If it hadn't been for him, none of us would be here. And if it hadn't been for him, no one would have ever known what lay at the bottom of the ravine.

By the time the first officer reached the body, my fingers were numb inside my gloves and Cisco was pacing at the edge of the drop, whining in frustration. He hated waiting. So did I. Every few minutes I would stop him to dry his fur with a chamois I kept in my pack. The snow kept falling.

Casey said quietly, "You guys did good work."

I smiled at him briefly, gratefully, with lips that were half frozen. The truth was—and maybe Casey knew this—I hadn't been at all confident in our abilities after all this time. But we had to try. "A good dog never forgets his training," I said. But I had to wonder if somehow Cisco's search tonight had been aided by his search for Izzy at her house. Had he remembered her scent? Had he somehow followed it through the snow? Even if she was… even if she was deceased?

Casey stood with his hands in the pockets of his coat, his gaze locked on the floodlit snowscape in front of the ravine, his expression fixed. I couldn't imagine what he was thinking. This had all started when he wondered idly why a waitress he had been flirting with hadn't shown up for work. Now he was about to identify her body. I had to look away from him.

A cluster of headlamps bobbed below as the team worked, their voices low and clipped. Snow kept falling, soft and relentless, settling on my shoulders, on Cisco's fur, on the rope line stretched taut between trees. The cold had a way of sharpening everything —every sound, every fear.

I kept my eyes on the figures below, trying to read their movements. Trying not to imagine a woman's face uncovered beneath its plastic shroud. Still.

Frozen. Lifeless.

Cisco pressed against my leg, leaning his warmth into me. I rested a hand on his head, grateful for the warmth, the steadiness. "Easy, boy. They've got it."

A shout rose from the ravine, brief and indistinct. Then another. They'd made contact.

My breath caught. I didn't realize I'd stopped breathing until Cisco nudged me sharply, as if reminding me to stay present.

The team began the slow, careful process of bringing the stretcher up the incline. Casey and I stepped back to give them room, Cisco glued to my side. The black plastic had torn in places, and the body was wrapped in sheet for its ascent. But it wasn't fully covered. A sleeve showed. A boot. Snow clung to the fabric like frost on old bark.

"Raine," one of the deputies called softly as they reached level ground. "You'll want to see this."

I looked at Casey. I could see his breath fogging the night air. I could see my own. I touched his elbow. We stepped forward together.

The deputy pulled back the edge of the sheet just enough to reveal the face.

Not Izzy. Not a woman at all.

A rush of relief hit me so hard my knees nearly buckled, and I heard the gush of Casey's breath as he released it, felt the slackness of his muscles. Yet the relief was followed immediately by a different kind of dread—because the man lying on the stretcher with a neat round bullet hole in the center of forehead was someone I recognized.

My eyes met Casey's, and I saw there the same shock and confusion I felt. I looked back at the corpse, and the name tasted like cold metal in my mouth even before I spoke it.

"Rooster Hoggins," I said.

CHAPTER TWENTY -TWO

Casey and I sat in his truck with the heater running full blast and the windows cracked for ventilation, warming our hands in front of the vents. Cisco was stretched out on a blanket on the narrow back cabin seat, panting to regulate his own body temperature. Blue and red lights flashed all around us and radios crackled as the people in charge of death moved back and forth importantly.

I called Miles and told him what had happened. "We might be here awhile," I said. "The police told us to wait."

"Baby, I'm sorry." I could hear the frustration in his voice. He wasn't used to being on the periphery of the action. And he most definitely wasn't used to being wrong. "I should have listened to you. Maybe if we'd called the police sooner..."

"It wouldn't have made a bit of difference," I told

him. "The man has been dead at least six hours, and whoever dumped the body would have been long gone before the police could get out here. We did the best we could."

"I don't suppose there are any leads."

"Not that I know of." I rubbed a tired hand over my face. "You should go to bed. I'll see you in the morning. And so," I added, "will the police, probably."

We said goodnight, and I put my phone away. I looked at Casey, who looked as drained and unsettled as I felt. "I know you think Rooster Hoggins was the only clue you had in finding Izzy," I said, "but the good news is that, you know, it wasn't her in the ravine."

Casey nodded absently. "Actually, that's not what I was thinking." He glanced at me in the dimness, blue shadows flashing across his face from the police car parked half a dozen yards away. "You know this afternoon when I went to his house, and his wife had blood on her hand? I was thinking—what if it wasn't hers?"

I nodded solemnly. I had thought the same thing. The spouse is always the first suspect in a homicide, and in this case, this particular spouse had more than just cause. I thought about Riley the pointer, sleeping peacefully—I hoped—in his warm kennel at Dog Daze, who would very likely never see his mom again. She had loved him enough to make sure he was safe, and then she had gone home to face the unthinkable. Had she known it would end this way?

Or had she being trying, once again, to escape, and things went terribly wrong?

There was a tap on the driver's side window, and Dakota Bradshaw's face appeared there. She motioned to Casey to open the door. "I hate to bring y'all out in the cold again," she said when he did, "but I have just a few more questions for you. Could you step out for just a minute?"

I zipped up my jacket, pulled my hat and gloves back on, and waded through the snow to meet her and Casey on the other side of the truck. Cisco stood up in back, watching me, his breath fogging up the window. The snow had lightened to a frozen mist that was easily more miserable than the big powdery flakes had been. It was like being wrapped in a cold soggy blanket.

Dakota pulled the hood of her county-issued jacket over her head and stamped her feet in the snow to warm them, giving us a rueful smile. "Is this weather typical around here?"

"You'll get used to it," I told her, shivering. Some of the snow I'd kicked up was beginning to melt around the tops of my boots, and just when my pants were starting to dry.

She glanced down at the notebook in her hand. "So I just need to know a few more things. How is it that you knew the victim, again?"

Casey replied impatiently, "I already told you that. We saw him at the thrift store, drunker than a skunk at closing time, yelling for his wife, Tina. He thought he was at the women's shelter."

"And that was what time?"

Casey looked at me and I shrugged, my hands in my pockets. "Maybe 10:00 Monday? The store had just opened."

"So you were there during this encounter?" she asked.

"That's the only time I saw him," I said. "But he made an impression. Casey calmed him down, and he left."

She turned back to Casey. "So you calmed him down that morning, but a few hours later you were fighting him in a bar."

"He threw first punch," Casey reminded her. "And do we really have to go through that whole thing again? It's all in your report."

Dakota gave him a flat, overly patient look. "This is a murder investigation, sir, not an assault complaint. It's late, I'm freezing, and I know you want to get home. So could you work with me here?"

One corner of Casey's lips quirked briefly. "Sir, huh? In that case, what do you want to know?"

"Why did you seek Mr. Hoggins out at the Borderline Bar?"

His amusement, however faint it had been, faded abruptly. "I told you, I just came in for a beer. I didn't know he was going to be there. The bartender pointed him out and said he might know the whereabouts of a friend of mine, Izzy. So I asked him about it, and that's when he punched me."

"This is Isabelle Stedman, who you reported missing?"

Casey nodded, his jawline tensing with impatience.

"What was your relationship with her?"

"None," he replied shortly. "She was a waitress at the Borderline. We talked. I saw her two or three times a week at the bar. I drove her home one night. We weren't dating or anything. I got worried when the bartender said she hadn't been at work all week, and the last time he saw her, she was leaving the bar with Rooster. So I asked him about her. Seriously, we've been over this."

"And that was the last time you saw Rooster Hoggins. At the bar?"

Casey didn't hesitate. "Right."

I thought she would close her notebook and thank us for our time, but that's when I remembered: she was an investigator. Sure enough, she glanced at her notes and looked back at Casey.

"So just check my facts here," she said. "After the fight with Rooster..."

"Assault," Casey corrected her, and I could tell he was just being difficult now. "After he assaulted me."

She held his gaze for a moment and went on, "You then picked up your vehicle at the Borderline and went to Izzy Stedman's house."

"It was on my way home," he said, which it was not.

"Why did you do that?"

"I told you, I was worried."

"And she wasn't home?"

"No. She wasn't there, but her car was. I was

about to leave when I heard a crying sound from inside."

Which he hadn't.

Dakota said, "What did you do then?"

"I went inside and found her dog. It had pooped all over the place and had no food or water. It had even drunk the toilet bowl almost dry."

"The vet said the dog was dehydrated and severely malnourished," I put in. "He guessed she hadn't eaten in close to a week."

Dakota turned back to Casey. "So her door was unlocked?"

Casey managed a blank look and she clarified. "When you went in to find the dog. Was the door unlocked?"

He replied, "It wasn't secure. It was one of those cheap sliders. I didn't have any trouble opening it."

She made a note completely without expression.

Casey said impatiently, "I told all this to the deputies who said they were investigating Izzy's disappearance. Don't you guys ever read each other's reports?"

Dakota replied mildly, "It's hard to keep up with all the reports your name appears in, Mr. Macintosh. But we do our best. What about Mrs. Hoggins?" She glanced at her notebook again and specified, "Tina, you said her name was. Did you ever talk to her?"

I could tell Casey was surprised. So was I. This Dakota Bradshaw was a much better investigator than I had expected.

Casey said, stalling, "Why would you ask that?"

"You were concerned after your fight in the bar. You asked us to check on her. When we did, we found she was no longer at the shelter. It seems logical you might have wanted to check on her yourself."

Casey glanced at me, but he knew what I was thinking. There was no way he could lie about this without being found out later and looking even guiltier than the truth would make him appear now. He said with a huff of breath, "Yeah, okay, I went by there today. I spoke with her for a minute. She said Rooster wasn't there, but she seemed scared, and..." he added reluctantly, "it looked like she was bleeding. I asked her if she was okay, and she told me to leave, so I did. But I noticed Rooster's truck was in the carport."

Dakota seemed very interested in this, as naturally she would. "And what time was this?"

"I don't know. Mid-afternoon. Maybe 3:00."

"And you didn't see Rooster then, or after you left?"

"No." I could see his jaw knot in annoyance.

"You said you had dinner with your sister. What time did you arrive?"

"I don't know. After dark. Maybe five or six."

"Did you leave there any time between then and when we arrived?"

"Oh, for heaven's sake," I interrupted, exasperated. "You've got five witnesses, including two cops, and about 60 security cameras to prove Casey was at home watching the drone record in real time while

Rooster Hoggins' body was being dragged into that ravine. You can't seriously think..."

She ignored me. "Do you own a gun, Mr. Macintosh?"

"I do," he replied. "It's a Ruger .44, and it's in the glove compartment of my truck. Completely legal. And I didn't shoot Rooster. He was killed with a .38, execution-style. My gun would have blown his face off."

She stared at him for a moment. "When was the last time your weapon was fired?"

"I killed the hell out of a row of tin cans last month. Not since then."

"Do you mind if I have a look?"

Casey scowled at her. "Take it, keep it, test it for residue, and give it back to me in the morning. Knock yourself out."

Dakota walked around to the passenger side of the truck to open the glove compartment, and I dug my hands deeper into my coat pockets, hunching my shoulders with both cold and annoyance. "Do you still think she's hot?"

He pretended to think this over for a minute, then gave me one of his signature half-grins and a one-shouldered shrug. "Hot is hot."

My phone rang, its chime muffled in the depths of one of my upper zippered pockets. I unzipped the pocket and took out the phone, expecting the call to be from Miles. Instead, I saw Corny's face on the screen. I pulled off my glove with my teeth and answered it with some urgency. "Corny, what's wrong?"

His voice was hushed and tense. I could hear barking in the background. "Miss Stockton, I don't know what to do. There's a woman here, very upset, saying we stole her dog. She's demanding I give her Riley. I asked her for ID, and her birthdate or phone number like you said, I have the brochure right here where you wrote it down, but she just keeps crying and yelling at me. Miss Stockton, what do you want me to do?"

I said, astonished, "She came out in the middle of the night in a snowstorm to get her dog?" Casey looked at me sharply, and I gave a small shake of my head, assuring him it wasn't Izzy. "Is her name Tina Hoggins?"

"She didn't say. She won't tell me anything. Should I…" he lowered his voice to a whisper. "Do you think I should call the police?"

At that moment, Dakota came back around the truck toward us. I said, "That won't be necessary. Just keep her there, will you? Tell her I'm on my way."

Dakota was saying to Casey, "We don't need to examine your gun at the moment, but I might have more questions for you tomorrow. In the meantime…"

"In the meantime," I interrupted her, "Rooster Hoggins' wife is at my house threatening my kennel manager. I have to go. Should I tell her you want to talk to her?"

She stared at me. "What does she want?"

"Her dog," I explained. "The women's shelter turned him over to me after she left him there."

"She came out in the middle of the night in a snowstorm to get her dog?" she said, echoing my words exactly.

I simply nodded.

Dakota said, "Keep her there. We'll be right behind you."

CHAPTER TWENTY-THREE

The lights at Dog Daze were blazing when we pulled into the gravel lot, too bright for this time of night, glaring off the fallen snow so harshly it practically hurt my eyes. "Great," I muttered, unbuckling my seatbelt. "Will this night never end?" I knew what was waiting inside for me and, honestly, I didn't know if I had the strength to see it through.

Cisco was on his feet in the back before the engine even cut off, nails scrabbling against the liner, ears pricked, sensing distress the way he always did. Casey swung out of the truck and slammed the door, scanning the building and the surrounding area. He pointed toward a shadowy area toward the side of the building, where the driveway to my house veered off from the parking lot of Dog Daze. People often make that mistake, parking in my driveway instead of the Dog Daze lot.

"Rooster's truck," he said.

I opened the back door and snapped on Cisco's leash, pushing out a breath as he leapt to the ground. "Yeah," I said, looking over my shoulder for the sheriff's office SUV that was supposed to be following us.

Casey unlocked the gate, and we started up the path, Cisco leading the way while we trudged as fast as we could through snow that covered our boots. All five kennel dogs were awake and barking frantically, and little wonder. Dogs are incredibly sensitive to emotions, not to mention raised voices. The words were indistinct, but I could hear the woman's voice even through the closed door and windows, high, frantic, ragged at the edges, cutting through the cold like a serrated knife.

As I pushed open the door Corny's voice became clear, strained but steady, like someone trying to dam a flood with his bare hands.

"Miss, please, you're upsetting the dogs—"

"Then give me my dog! Give me my dog and I'll go!"

Tina Hoggins stood in the middle of the lobby, coat unzipped, hair hanging loose around her face, cheeks blotchy and wet. Snow clung to her shoulders and boots, melting into muddy puddles on the bright yellow mats. Her hands were clenched into fists at her sides, shaking so hard her whole body seemed to vibrate.

Corny looked like he'd been dragged out of a fire

drill in the middle of the night—which, in a way, he had. He was once again in his fire-truck pajamas and cocker spaniel slippers, bright orange curls mashed flat on one side of his head, eyes wide behind his glasses. One hand hovered helplessly in the air, the other pressed to his chest as if reminding himself to breathe.

I stepped forward quickly, "Are you Tina?"

She spun toward me, eyes wild, chest heaving. "Are you the owner? Can you get my dog?"

"I'm Raine Stockton," I said, as calmly as I could. "And it's the middle of the night. We're not exactly open. What makes you think we have your dog?"

Tina ran a shaking hand through her damp hair and drew a hitching breath. She looked like she hadn't slept or eaten in days. Her eyes were dark and sunken, her skin sallow. The coat she wore was stained with mud and other, unidentifiable things. She was clearly a woman on the edge of a breakdown.

She said, "That woman—there's always somebody at the shelter, even at night. I banged on the door until she came and she told me they'd—they'd given Riley away. They weren't supposed to do that!" Her voice rose to a high, shrill pitch. "I didn't tell them they could do that! I was coming back for him! I *did* come back for him, only he wasn't there! You can't keep him! You can't!"

Some people might think her reaction, bordering on hysteria, was over the top. Those people do not understand how much emotion women—some men, too, but mostly women—invest in their dogs. It's the same protective instinct they might feel for a child, only I sometimes think it might be stronger. I've seen a woman threaten to sue an agility club because her dog got a splinter on the A-frame. Another burst into tears in my puppy class when I told her she was ruining her relationship with her dog by refusing to correct bad behavior. And let's not even talk about the woman I read about at a dog park who pulled a gun on a man whose Doberman attacked her Yorkie. While I certainly don't recommend going that far, I have to confess I could understand how she felt. By the same token, I was entirely sympathetic to Tina.

At her obviously growing agitation, Casey took an instinctive, protective step closer to me, and he said, "Maybe you could try to calm down. It looks to me like this is all just a misunderstanding, but my sister is right—it's awfully late and..."

"I don't care how late it is!" she cried.

That was when Cisco, who had seen and heard enough, did what therapy dogs do: comfort the grieving, heal the sick and the broken-hearted. A lot is made of Cisco's tracking ability, and he had proven his worth in that arena tonight. But this is where he really shines. Moments like these are where Cisco comes into his own.

He pushed forward, crossing the distance between Tina and me when I dropped his leash, and nudged his nose against her hand. She looked down, startled out of her near hysteria, and caught a small breath. "Oh," she said softly. She lifted an unsteady hand and stroked Cisco's head. She started to cry. "I'm... I'm so sorry," she said. "I just...I'm so tired and I just... I just want Riley back. He's all I have."

I felt a twist of sympathy in my chest for her, and it was easy to forget for a moment that she had tried to break into my kennel and had threatened Corny and had –possibly—done worse to her husband. An almost visible wave of relief went around the room as Tina dropped to one knee beside Cisco, pressing her face against his furry neck, her tears dampening his fur. I could see her muscles relax, her breathing grow steadier as she held on to my dog.

There is this thing called neural mirroring. It's a built-in protective device the human nervous system has developed to imitate, or mirror, the emotional and physical reactions of others close to him. It's why yawns are contagious, and can even account for mass hysteria in some cases. It helps humans empathize with other humans and pick up on social cues before they are recognized by the conscious mind. When a dog brings his calm, even temperament to an agitated human, those mirror neurons in the human brain pick up on the dog's demeanor. The human's blood pressure lowers, her heartbeat slows, her breathing regulates. This is what therapy dogs do. This is what I saw happening as Tina rested her face against Cisco's fur, letting the distress seep out of her body drop by drop.

My own tight and aching muscles relaxed a fraction as I glanced at Corny.

"Maybe," I suggested quietly, "some tea?"

"Yes, ma'am." Corny made no attempt to disguise his relief as he turned to leave the room. "Right away."

"And Corny?"

He looked back and I said, "After that, maybe you could bring out Riley."

I wasn't entirely sure why I said that, except for the fact that my heart ached for the woman who had, up to this moment, lost everything but her dog. And I had a very bad feeling she was about to lose him too.

There was a moment of puzzlement on Corny's face, but then he nodded. He, too, had noticed what I had seen: a flash of blue lights through the window.

Tina looked up at me with helpless gratitude on her wet face. "Thank you," she said, choking. "Thank you."

That was when I knew I had done the right thing.

I unzipped my jacket and removed my gloves. "Come sit down," I said, indicating the well-worn green sofa against the wall. "It will take Corny a minute."

She gave Cisco a final hug, wiped her face with her sleeve, and stood. "I shouldn't have made such a fuss," she said in a small voice. "It's just—I didn't think anyone would be here this time of night and I could hear Riley barking and I thought I could just take him… But then that man came out and I was scared. He wanted to see my ID but I didn't have it, and then he wanted my birthdate, but I couldn't see why he'd want that..." She blew out a shaky breath as she sank onto the sofa. "I just...I'm sorry. It's late and I shouldn't have..." She trailed off.

Casey agreed kindly, "It might have been better to wait until morning."

She seemed to notice him for the first time. "You were at my house today," she said slowly.

He nodded. "Yes, ma'am. I was looking for your husband. You said he wasn't there."

She dropped her eyes and swallowed hard. "I remember." She took a breath and looked up again. "I couldn't wait until morning to get Riley," she said in a rush. "I heard my husband was in jail and I knew I didn't have long before he got out... he always gets out. But my car was parked across the street at the impound, and I couldn't get it out until nine, so I called my mother to come get me early this morning. I just wanted to pack some things and leave, you know?"

I nodded sympathetically, and Casey said, "But Rooster was already out of jail."

She looked away again and pressed her lips together. When she looked back at Casey, it was with suspicion. "Are you a friend of his?"

"No," Casey assured her. "I'm not. I'm the one who put him in jail."

She didn't seem to know how to react to this, and before she could say anything, Corny returned with a mug of tea and some packets of sugar on a small tray. "It's chamomile and lavender," he told

Tina, setting it on the coffee table in front of her. "Very soothing. You should let it steep. I have honey, if you'd rather."

"Thank you, this is fine." She reached for the mug shakily.

I thought we were getting somewhere then, that maybe she was finally starting to trust me.

And then the police arrived.

CHAPTER TWENTY-FOUR

The door opened with a blast of cold and the sharp smell of snow. Deputy Dakota Bradshaw stepped inside, snow dusting the shoulders of her jacket, her hair frizzing out of its tight bun from the dampness. Tina saw her and the mug clattered against the saucer. She stiffened.

"You called the police?" she accused me. "I told you, all I wanted was my dog and you..."

Dakota raised a staying hand and surprised me with the gentleness of her tone. "No one called me, Mrs. Hoggins. I'm here on another matter. You are Mrs. Hoggins, aren't you?"

Tina gave a single, uncertain nod, her eyes wide. She sat back and twisted her fingers together in her lap.

Corny looked from Dakota to me to Tina and back to me again, unsure about this new development. "Should I, um, get..." He left the question unfinished and instead nodded his head back toward the kennel area.

I said, "Maybe hold off on that for a minute."

Dakota said, still in that very gentle, unthreatening tone I rarely heard from a law officer, "Mrs. Hoggins, my name is Deputy Bradshaw and I'm afraid I have some very bad news. We found your husband's body tonight in the woods. I'm sorry to tell you he has been fatally shot."

The last of the color drained from Tina's face leaving her eyes a dark, unblinking smudge across a parchment background. But she did not flinch, or make a sound.

I felt the room hold its breath.

Tina remained stiff and silent, shoulders hunched, fingers locked together so tightly her knuckles were white. No gasp. No sob. No questions.

Just stillness.

Dakota didn't rush to fill it. She let the silence stretch until it felt almost loud, until I was sure someone would break it just to make it stop.

No one did.

Behind Dakota, the door opened again. Deputy Harvey slipped inside, stamping snow from his boots, then paused when he saw the scene. His eyes flicked to Dakota, and she turned smoothly, meeting him halfway across the room.

He leaned in and spoke quietly, but not quietly enough.

"There's blood in the pickup parked in the side

driveway," he murmured. "Bed and tailgate. And a scrap of that black plastic like the body was wrapped in, caught on the latch of the tailgate."

Dakota nodded once, silently, and turned back to us. Her expression remained unchanged, professional and calm, but in her eyes was something I didn't expect to see. Compassion. "Mrs. Hoggins," she said, and then, "May I call you Tina?"

Tina said nothing.

Dakota said, "Tina, we need to talk about what happened tonight. About what brought you here. Can we do that?"

Finally, Tina raised her eyes to Dakota. They were filled with shock and confusion. She said in a small voice, "You... found him? How... how did you find him?"

I felt something sink inside me and my eyes met Casey's. His gaze reflected what I was thinking. That was just about as close to a confession as I had ever heard.

Instinctively, my heart breaking for her, I reached over and covered Tina's cold hand with mine. Cisco jumped up on the sofa on the other side of her and sank down, putting his chin on her knee. He always knows when he's needed, and he was badly needed now.

Tina lifted a pale, fluttery hand, and let it drop to Cisco's fur. Dakota's gaze went from Tina and me to the three onlookers, and she said, "Gentlemen, if you don't mind, could you leave us alone for a minute?"

Harvey looked as though he was about to protest, and so did Casey, but Corny said quickly, "I have a pot of coffee going in the back."

I cast him a grateful look, and Casey said after a moment, "Yeah, I could go for that."

Deputy Harvey gave Dakota one more look and then conceded, however reluctantly, "Sounds good. Thanks."

The three men left the room and Dakota looked around until she noticed a box of tissues on the reception desk. She retrieved them, as well as the rolling chair behind the desk. She offered a tissue to Tina, then set the box on the table in front of her. I felt bad about that. I should have gotten Tina a tissue before.

Dakota pulled the chair up in front of the sofa across from Tina and sat down. She didn't say anything, she just waited in patient silence while Tina wiped her nose and her eyes and then balled the tissue up in her fist, looking down at Cisco, stroking his fur with her free hand. The dogs had quieted down in the back, and I knew that was because Corny had been back there to reassure them. The overhead lights hummed. Snow tapped faintly against the windows. Still, Dakota respected the other woman's suffering and did not press. She just let the moment breathe.

Finally, Tina whispered, "I just wanted my dog." She dabbed at her eyes. "I didn't mean to cause any trouble."

Dakota glanced at me. I squeezed Tina's hand

briefly. It should go without saying that I'm on the side of anyone who is devoted enough to her dog to come out in the middle of the night in a snowstorm to reclaim him. But there was something else about Tina that touched me deeply. Her vulnerability, maybe, or her determination in the face of what she must surely have known was defeat. She had made up her mind to leave. She had almost made it. Not many women can claim that.

"Riley is fine," I assured her. "You can see him in a minute. You were about to tell us why you left him at Welcoming Arms."

Tina leaned forward and retrieved her tea. She took a sip without removing the teabag or adding sugar, and then set it down on the saucer with a clank. She cleared her throat. "I heard Rooster was in jail," she said in a voice that was almost steady, "and I wouldn't have another chance to leave him as good as this. I knew I didn't have much time before he got out. He always gets out. But my car was in the lot across the street and I couldn't get it until the gate opened at nine, so I called my mama to come pick me up before work and drop me off at the house. I was just going to pack a few things and then Mama would take me back to pick up Riley and my car as soon as she got off work. She only works half a day on Mondays and Wednesdays. I would have been back for Riley before lunch. Only..."

"Only Rooster was already out of jail," I supplied quietly.

She looked down at her hands, still twisted in

her lap. "You don't understand," she said softly. "You don't know what it was like."

She was right. I couldn't possibly understand. I had been married to two men, both of them stubborn, opinionated, incredibly frustrating and undeniably flawed. But they were kind men. Gentle men. Honorable men, each in his own way. And they loved me. I had never felt anything but safe in their presence. When I tried to imagine the kind of terror Tina must have endured every single day in her own home, my mind literally balked.

She looked up at Dakota now with a sudden fierceness in her expression. "But I didn't kill him. I know that's what you're thinking, but you're wrong. He deserved killing, but it wasn't me."

Dakota nodded her quiet understanding. Her gentle expression didn't change. "Why don't you tell me what happened, then?"

"He was mad..." There was a hitch in her breath as she tightened her fingers. "Mad at Riley about something. Said he was going to shoot him if he was still there when he got back. And then he got in his truck and roared off. That's when I knew I had to get Riley out of there. So I put some clothes and dog food and stuff in a grocery sack and drove to the shelter. I'd been there before. They were real good to me. I knew they'd let me stay." Her exhaled breath was choppy, and she dropped her gaze again. "I never should have left. You know, that first time. But they don't let you live there, you know. You can only stay for a few days. And I thought when I came back that

Rooster'd be better. He was for a while. But not long."

Silence fell. She lifted a hand to stroke Cisco's head. His eyes closed in contentment.

Dakota prompted, "When you went back to the shelter this last time, what day was that?"

"Friday," Tina said. "It's so quiet there. Peaceful, like. And Riley liked it there. There's a big yard out back with a high fence. It was nice. I wanted that for him. For us. I knew I had to get away from Rooster, this time for good. So when I heard he was in jail, I took my chance."

"So your mother picked you up early this morning," Dakota said, "and dropped you off at your house. What happened then?"

She tightened her fingers on Cisco's collar. Sensing her tension, he opened his eyes, but didn't protest. She said, "I didn't see his truck at first. It was dark, and the truck was pulled up under the shed. If I had, I wouldn't have got out of Mama's car. But I didn't see the truck until after Mama drove off and there was nothing I could do but sneak in the house real quiet like, hoping maybe he was drunk and passed out and wouldn't notice me. And sure enough, when I opened the door, there he was laying on the living room floor."

She stopped talking and instead stroked Cisco's fur, maybe reliving the scene, maybe trying not to.

Dakota said, "What did you do then?"

Tina just shook her head.

Dakota sat back in her chair. She said conversationally, "I think sometimes we give men too much power. More than they can handle, really. My mother used to say it's because we feel sorry for them. They don't understand us, so we play dumb. They want to feel important, so we let them protect us." She smiled a little. "Silly stuff like that. But the problem is we spend so much time giving our power away we forget how strong we really are. I think you're a strong woman, Tina. I've read Rooster Hoggins' record and I know what it must have been like, living with him. But you survived it. You did what you had to to survive. I can understand that. You don't have anything to be ashamed of."

Tina shook her head again, not meeting Dakota's eyes. "You don't understand at all. I didn't kill him. I didn't."

Dakota sat quietly for a while, gazing at Tina. Then she said, "When I lived in Raleigh, I made the mistake of getting involved with a coworker. It was great at first. He was fun, adventurous, always up for new things. Cool. But then we were both up for the same promotion. I could tell how badly he wanted it, but I didn't realize that the truth was he *needed* it to feel like a man. Anyway, I backed off, and he got the promotion."

I was riveted on Dakota's face, my chest tight. I had a feeling I knew where this was going, and it was nowhere good.

She went on, "Afterwards, he changed. He became more demanding, controlling. He wanted to tell me who my friends could be, what I could wear off duty, when I could talk to my family, that kind of thing. And I fell for it, at first. I was in love with him, you know, I wanted him to be happy. You can relate to that, right, Tina?"

My heart was beating in my chest, hard.

"But then one night," Dakota said, "I came home after a long shift. He wanted to have sex. I didn't. He tried to rape me. I broke his nose. He gave me a black eye. And I packed my things and got out of there that very night." She gave Tina a brave, tight smile. "The truth is, Tina, I wanted to kill him. If I could have gotten to my service weapon in that moment, I would have. I was so hurt, so betrayed, so *battered* in every sense of the word. I want you to know that I do understand. And nothing you can tell me will shock me."

She leaned forward and took Tina's hand. "It's okay," she said softly. "I'm on your side."

I believed her. I only hoped Tina did, too.

Tina said shakily, "I didn't kill him."

Dakota sat back. "We have surveillance footage of you dragging a body into the woods. We found blood in the back of the truck you parked outside. Rooster's truck."

Tina had started shaking her head from Dakota's first word. Her voice was high and tight. "He was dead, there on the floor, when I got there. I knew you'd think I'd killed him. I tried to call my mama but my phone was dead. I knew the police would blame me. They always blame me. I got one of those orders—you know, to keep him from hitting me again, but they said because I went back home that time it didn't apply anymore. But it was my home!" She looked at Dakota with helplessness and hopelessness in her eyes. "It was my home!" she repeated. "What was I supposed to do? And the deputies, they just said there was nothing they could do. And they looked at me like I should've known better. Like it was my fault."

I thought if I could find out who the officers were who had made her feel like that, I might break a few noses myself.

Tina started to cry again, and her voice became thick with mucous and tears. "I knew you would blame me. I just wanted to get away. I just wanted to get my dog and leave. So I cleaned up the mess and I waited until dark and I dragged his body out to the truck. I had to use a ramp to get it in. Then I drove out as far as I could and I dragged him into the woods and pushed him over the hill and I thought maybe nobody would find him until spring when all the snow was melted and I would be long gone by then.... Riley and I would be long gone, in a house with a big yard and a tall fence..."

Her words dissolved into tears, and it was all I could do not to cry, too. I took out my phone and texted Corny. *Bring Riley*. This woman had been lied to and betrayed so many times. I told her she would get to see Riley. And I was going to keep my word.

Dakota's eyes were brimming with sympathy. I thought it was genuine. "Okay, Tina. I understand. But I want you to know that if you did shoot your husband, it will likely be viewed as self-defense.

There's a good chance you and Riley could go on to live a happy life in a house with a big yard. But if you lie to me, that's a different matter. There's nothing I can do to help you. So I want you to think about it for a minute. Is there anything else you want to tell me?"

"No," she said, her voice breaking. "No I told you the truth." She plucked a tissue from the box and buried her face in it. "I told you. I told you everything. I didn't kill him."

The door from the kennels opened with a scrabbling of claws and Riley entered at the end of a leash, tugging Corny behind him. Corny did not try to correct the dog for pulling, but simply dropped the leash and let him gallop to the woman whose whole world was wrapped up in him, and his in her. Cisco looked up alertly, and Tina gave a small cry, leaping to her feet with her arms open for her dog.

I hooked my fingers around Cisco's collar so he wouldn't spoil their reunion, and I couldn't stop a small smile as Tina dropped to her knees, hugging her dog. Riley put his paws on her shoulders and licked her face, his tail wagging so hard it threatened to throw him off balance.

I got up and walked over to Corny with Cisco, giving Tina and Riley their moment. I said quietly, "Thanks, Corny. Would you take Cisco back and give him a treat? We're okay here for now."

At the word "treat" Cisco's ears pricked up and he looked from me to Corny. I scratched his head affectionately. "You did good today, buddy. Real good."

Corny took his leash, looking worriedly at Tina and Riley. "Is she going to be okay?"

I answered honestly, "I don't know."

Dakota stood beside us. "Would you ask Sergeant Harvey to join us when you go back?"

"Yes, ma'am." Corny cast one more anxious glance toward Tina and Riley, then said, "Come along, Mr. Cisco. Let's see what's in the cookie jar."

Cisco trotted after him happily, and I turned to Dakota. She looked weary, as worn out as I felt, and it was the kind of exhaustion that comes from the inside out. I glanced at Tina, who sat on the floor with Riley mostly in her lap, her face close to his as she murmured reassurances. I turned back to Dakota.

"You were really good with her," I said quietly. "Most cops aren't that patient. Or kind."

Dakota replied, "Psychology major. I specialized in conflict resolution back in Raleigh. And I was on the hostage negotiation team."

I asked curiously, even though it was definitely none of my business, "What happened to the guy? Your ex, I mean."

She didn't seem to mind answering. "Nothing. I got two weeks suspension without pay for assaulting a superior officer. When I went back, it was pretty bad around the station. So..." She lifted a shoulder. "I left. And ended up here."

I was stunned. "That's not right!"

"No," she agreed. "It's not." Her expression changed, became mitigated with a trace of uneasiness. "Listen, I'd appreciate it if that story didn't get around. Cops can be funny about stuff like that, and I've already got one strike against me, being an outsider." She added after a beat, "Two. I'm also a woman."

"No one will hear the story from me," I assured her firmly.

Harvey and Casey entered just then, and Dakota glanced over her shoulder at them, then back at me. "You'll keep her dog, right?"

I stared at her. "You're not taking her in?"

Rather than answer me, Dakota turned to Harvey. "No cuffs, okay?" she said, nodding toward Tina. "We need to search her house and do some more questioning before we bring charges. It would be good if we could find the murder weapon. And the bullet. There's a clean exit wound, so the bullet should be in the house if he was killed there."

Harvey said, "You got it." He went over to Tina.

I turned to Dakota urgently. "I don't think she killed him. I think she's telling the truth."

Dakota's look told me what I already knew: it didn't matter what I thought. She replied, "She's our primary suspect." Her gaze moved to Casey. "Aside from your brother, here, and it looks like he's alibied out." Casey raised an eyebrow in acknowledgement. Dakota went on, "She had motive, opportunity, and she's obviously a high flight risk. We have to take her in."

I heard Tina cry, "No!" and the sound went through me like a knife. "I didn't kill him, I told her I didn't!"

I turned to see Harvey pulling her too her feet, not entirely ungently, and Riley looking at her uncertainly, his tail tucked, his eyes big. I hurried to take Riley's leash.

"It's okay," I told her. "We'll take care of Riley for you. As long as it takes. He's going to be fine, I promise."

She dropped her head, and her hair fell forward to hide the tears that wet her face. She did not fight the deputy as he turned her toward the door. I don't think she had any fight left in her.

Riley dragged his feet, his head turned toward Tina, as I led him back over to where Dakota stood. I felt sick and angry and tired and hurt all at the same time. "She's the victim," I said tightly, "and she's the one going to jail. It's not fair."

Dakota replied quietly, "Life is hardly ever fair. Especially..." Her head turned to watch the door close behind Tina and Harvey. "For women like her." She turned back to me. "Thanks for your help tonight. You did good work." She handed me her card. "My cell's on back. I'll be in touch."

When they were gone, Corny took Riley back to the kennel and Casey went to the kitchen to get his coat. I sat wearily behind the reception desk, aching with defeat. Tina was never going to see her dog again. Dakota was right. Life was never fair for women like her.

Cisco put his paws up on the desk, possibly trying to comfort me, more likely looking for treats.

In the process, he knocked to the floor the brochure from Sheltering Arms on which Millie had written Tina's information. I bent to pick it up and the open page caught my eye.

If you need help but feel unsafe asking for it, it read, *use this hand signal*:

Below was a bold black and white illustration of an open hand, palm up, followed by that of a closed fist. I stared at it blearily. Was there something familiar there? Had I seen that hand sign before?

Casey returned, pulling on his jacket, and I put the brochure back on the desk. "Don't hit on Dakota anymore," I said, gathering up Cisco's leash.

"What? Why? What are you talking about?"

"Just don't. And," I told him grimly, standing, "we are building Hope Acres. I don't care if I have to stand on the street with a bucket and a bell to collect money for it."

As we left, my gaze fell one more time on the brochure and the illustration. Where had I seen that hand signal before? I was too tired to try to figure it out. I was probably just imagining it anyway.

But in the middle of the night, I woke with a start, my heart pounding, perfectly alert. I was not imagining it.

I remembered.

CHAPTER TWENTY-FIVE

Only it wasn't the middle of the night. It was ten o'clock in the morning, as my gritty eyes told me when I fought my way out of the cloud of downy pillows and comforters enough to see the numbers on the bedside clock. I was at home—my second home, as it were—in the familiar master suite of Miles's house. The blackout curtains were drawn on the glare of daylight bouncing off the snow, but enough light filtered through the gloom to allow me to see Melanie, standing at the foot of the bed with her hands on her hips and a disapproving look on her face. She was wearing the chef's apron I had given her for Christmas, the one featuring a grinning golden retriever in a toque holding a spatula and the caption, Chow's on!

"You're late," she announced. "Cisco had his breakfast hours ago. Uncle Casey is in the shower and Dad is on the phone with Chicago. Waffles in ten minutes."

"Right," I managed hoarsely, pushing my tangled curls out of my eyes. Snow day. Waffles. Had it really been less than twelve hours ago that we made those plans? "Sounds great."

"What do you want in yours?" she demanded. "Bacon or pecans?"

"Um...both."

"Well, hurry up, then!"

She strode off, and I climbed out of bed, still disoriented and unfocused and unable to get that illustration from the brochure out of my mind. But by the time I'd splashed water on my face and pulled on a sweater and jeans, I was sure. I knew exactly where I'd seen that sign before.

"Amber," I said as I came into the kitchen.

All four dogs were there because when Rita wasn't present the kitchen rules didn't apply. Casey, his hair still damp from the shower, leaned against the breakfast bar, helping himself to bacon from the platter there while Melanie presided over the waffle iron. The kitchen was redolent with warm breakfast smells, which on any other morning I would have reveled in, but today I barely noticed.

The two Aussies wiggled their way toward me with happy greetings; the two goldens, Cisco and Pepper, glanced over their shoulders at me and returned their fixed gazes to the platter of bacon on the counter. That didn't mean that they loved me any less, only that someone had been sneaking them bacon. I dipped to plant kisses on the heads of Mischief and Magic and ruffled their silky curls, and they bounded back over the breakfast bar, resuming their perfect sits next to Pepper and Cisco, their eyes fixed on Casey.

Casey looked at me curiously as he crunched down on the bacon. "Amber who?" Sure enough, he tossed a bit of bacon to each one of the four waiting dogs.

"That girl that was with Booker," I reminded him impatiently. "The one with the butterfly earring. She was doing this hand signal." I showed him —open fist, closed fist. "I'm sure of it. She was trying to tell us she was in trouble."

Melanie paused with the pitcher of waffle batter in her hand, watching as I repeated the signal. "Oh, sure," she said. "That's the international signal for help. She was definitely in trouble."

Casey looked at her skeptically. "Who says?"

She rolled her eyes. "Everybody knows that. We learned it in Health and Safety class way last year. And there are only posters of it in, like, every airport bathroom everywhere. You know, along with that number you're supposed to call if you or someone you know is being trafficked."

I stared at her as she opened the steaming waffle iron and poured a measure of batter into it. Clearly, I did not visit enough airport bathrooms. Secondly, were eleven-year-old girls really supposed to know so much about human trafficking?

As though in answer to my question, Miles entered the room on crutches behind me, and I could see he barely had time to erase the frown from his face as I turned. "What's all this?" he said.

"Raine knows someone who's being trafficked," Melanie replied easily. "Do you want bacon or pecans in your waffle?"

"Both," Miles said, even as he lifted an inquiring eyebrow at me.

"That girl who was with Booker," I explained somewhat reluctantly. "I think she was trying to signal me for help."

The curiosity sharpened into a scowl, which he once again quickly disguised. He made his way over to the breakfast bar, addressing Melanie. "You know, I've been looking into that project of yours. I think I have just the right piece of property. Four acres within walking distance of town, and—good news—I already own it. We'll have to request a few zoning variances, but it just might be doable."

Her face lit up. "Hey, that's great! And Raine, I was thinking, maybe Corny would like to come out once a month or so and do like a mobile dog grooming clinic, wouldn't that be cool?"

"It certainly would," I agreed, and decided now was not the time to go into how extremely complicated the logistics of operating a mobile dog grooming salon like that would be. "And I know Corny would be on board."

Casey looked from me to Miles, took his cue from both of us, and said to Melanie, "You know what you and Raine should think about doing? Organizing some kind of dog show this summer to help raise money for the thing."

"Dad has plenty of money," she replied dismissively.

"Which I didn't get by giving it away without due diligence," he reminded her sternly. "And if you're going to be project manager, the first thing you should do is sit down and work out a budget."

She wrinkled her nose. "I was going to go sledding today."

We all shared a glance of amusement at how ephemeral her attention span could be. "After sledding, then," Miles agreed. "Which will be after your class session, which starts in exactly..." He glanced at his watch. "One and a half hours."

"Dad!" she protested. "It's going to be forty-six degrees today! All the snow will be gone by then !"

"Interesting thesis," mused Miles. "How long will it take for six inches of snow spread over two acres of hillside to melt at 46 degrees Fahrenheit?"

Casey reached for another slice of bacon, murmuring, "Why do I feel like I just wandered into the wrong classroom?"

Before Miles could assign Melanie the melting-snow math problem, and because I thought the adults in the room really needed some private time to talk, and because I could see a perfectly good snow day—not to mention breakfast— was about to ruined by a temper tantrum, I said, "An hour and a half sounds like plenty of time for a couple of sledding runs down to grandma's house after breakfast."

Melanie, spatula in hand, looked thunderously at her father, who replied thoughtfully, "I tend to agree. But only because you're my favorite daughter and a hell of a cook, and if you burn those waffles, all bets are off."

Melanie grinned and turned quickly to retrieve the waffles. "You know, Dad, one of these days your jokes aren't going to be that funny anymore."

"And you know I wouldn't tease you if you weren't such an easy target. And say." He helped himself to a piece of bacon and added, "Have I told you lately how proud I am of you?"

She smiled and started scooping waffles onto the waiting plates. "Hurry up and eat, everyone. I've got sledding to do."

It was such a sweet moment, such a perfect scene with the sunshine bouncing off the snow outside the windows and the smell of waffles and maple syrup inside, four gorgeous dogs and three of the people I loved best the world all gathered together around the breakfast bar…it was all so calm and lovely and normal that it was hard to believe last night had ever happened. Hard to focus on the pretty young Amber, who may or may not be in trouble, and easy to believe I had imagined it all. And then I thought about Tina, sitting alone in a jail cell with a microwaved breakfast grown cold and coffee that tasted like dishwater, and I had to call Corny to check on Riley. He reported that the dog was depressed and had barely touched his breakfast. It was hard to enjoy my own breakfast after that.

Melanie finished her breakfast in record time and was quickly excused from the table. She raced upstairs to change into her snowsuit and sledding helmet. The dogs galloped after her—all but Cisco, of course, who maintained his position beneath the table, holding out hope as ever for a dropped crumb.

As soon as she was out of earshot, Miles's expression sobered, and he said, keeping his voice low, "I was on the phone with Parker earlier."

Parker was Miles's second in command, in charge of the Chicago office and, more and more since Miles's injury, Atlanta. He had been the best man at our hospital wedding and was, it was safe to say, one of the few people Miles trusted enough to rely on completely.

Miles went on, "I asked him to look into what Booker's interest in the land around here might be. He says that Booker's boss, a man by the name of Reid Compton, has a strong lobby in several state legislatures for legalized gambling in certain restricted areas. He, of course, defines those areas, usually with widespread resort potential—mountains, lakes, beachfront, that kind of thing. His plan is to build a resort destination around a luxury casino in each of the places he's investing in. North Carolina is one of the states he's lobbying, and he's confident enough of success to start buying up land in his target locations. That's what Booker is doing here. His job is to acquire the property so slowly and so quietly that no one will suspect a coordinated plan. And he likes to do it in small, rural communities because the people in charge—commissioners, city councilmen, zoning boards—are relatively easy to buy off."

I stared at him. "A casino in Hanover County? Are you kidding me? It'll never happen. The people won't stand for it, I don't care what you say about 'buying off' the commissioners."

He looked at me levelly. "Baby, you know that helipad that's going in above the country club two miles from here? How do you think I got the permits for it? The county could have held me up for years, but for under a hundred grand, I'm fast-tracked. And I wasn't even trying to do anything illegal."

I sank back heavily, trying to digest this.

Casey added, "It's the cost of doing business, sis. My dad used to talk about it all the time when he had his construction company. Some people—like this Compton fellow, I'm guessing—just do it on a bigger scale than others."

"But..." I hesitated, still struggling with the concept. "Didn't you say Booker's boss, Compton, had been indicted for fraud and racketeering and other stuff?"

Miles shook his head, raising his coffee cup to his lips. "I said he hadn't been indicted, which is worse. It shows you how much power he has. But there's more. This is what I didn't want to talk about in front of Melanie."

He paused and took a sip of coffee. "Parker said he knew a guy who went to this private art auction at one of Compton's estates. Very exclusive, invitation only, A-list kind of thing. Apparently, he gives these parties once or twice a year in various places around the world. People fly in from all over." He sipped his coffee, almost as though clearing his palate for what he was about to say. "Anyway, when Parker's friend got there, it turned out it wasn't art Compton was auctioning off at all, but young women. Some of them really young. So when I heard what you said about Booker's girlfriend, Amber..." He took another sip of coffee, and didn't finish.

Casey said, "Jesus." He looked at me. "We need to call the police."

The sweet taste of maple syrup clung to the back of my throat and made me feel sick. Amber had been trying to signal me for help, and I had been too stupid to notice. That was days ago. I remembered the shadow behind the curtain when I had been at her house, and Booker telling me she wasn't home. Lying.

And I also remembered Tina, the victim, being dragged away to jail, sobbing for her dog.

I said hoarsely, "No. No police. Not yet."

Miles agreed somberly, "Raine is right. This could turn out to be bigger than just Booker and we have to be really careful before we start accusing him of things we can't prove." When he saw Casey start to object, he raised a staying hand. "I'm not saying we let this slide. I just need to do some more research, that's all."

Casey looked back at me sharply. "That girl

Amber was at Izzy's house. What was she doing there? If she knows what happened to Izzy, there may not be time to do more research." The last was pointed at Miles, and not in a very nice tone, either.

I stepped in quickly. "I need to talk to Amber. I tried yesterday, but Booker wouldn't let me see her. We need to get her away from him."

Casey grunted and stirred sugar into his coffee. "Good luck with that. What, do you think he's just going to let her go have lunch with you? You just said he wouldn't even let you see her."

Miles was thoughtful. "I might have an idea."

He took out his phone and punched in a number. He put the phone on the breakfast bar and put it on speaker. We heard the ring, and in a moment a man answered.

"Lance Booker."

Casey and I looked at each other.

Miles said, "Mr. Booker, this is Miles Young. We haven't met, but..."

"I know who you are," interrupted Booker. He sounded completely congenial, just as he had been when he handed over a thousand dollars to Casey to persuade him not to report the accident with his truck to the police. "What can I do for you?"

"I hope I can do something for you," replied Miles, leaning back in his chair. "Or maybe we can help each other. I understand you're interested in acquiring property in Hanover County. I happen to have a few parcels that I think would suit your needs."

"My needs are pretty specific," replied Booker cautiously.

"So I hear," replied Miles. "But I'm not known to waste people's time. I think it would be worth your while to talk to me."

Booker was silent for a moment. "I'm intrigued."

"Unfortunately," Miles went on, "I'm a little mobility-impaired at the moment. I was hoping you wouldn't mind coming to my house. The roads are cleared up this way, and it's not hard to find. When is good for you?"

Now the silence was longer. I tensed, waiting. Then Booker said, "I'm not going to be able to get out today, but I have a man coming to plow the access road tomorrow morning, and then I have some business in town. How's around noon?"

"Sounds good," said Miles. "I'll text you the address."

Booker replied, "I have it."

I lifted an eyebrow, but Miles looked unfazed. "Good. Looking forward to meeting you."

"Same, Mr. Young. Same."

Miles disconnected. For a moment, no one spoke.

Outside, sunlight flashed off the snow so brightly it hurt my eyes. Inside, the kitchen was warm and ordinary and full of the smell of bacon and maple syrup, and it looked like just another snow day. The sense of incipient evil that man's voice had brought into our pleasant little world was jarring.

Casey looked at Miles with a flicker of respect. "All

right, then," he said.

I frowned. "How did you get his number?" That, of course, was the least of my questions.

"Rich guy directory," returned Miles, and my frown sharpened.

He shrugged and explained. "My investigator. I thought I might need to make contact with him sooner or later."

"So you get him out of the house for an hour or two," I said. "But that's *tomorrow*, Miles. A lot can happen between now and then, if it hasn't already."

He shook his head. "Nobody's going anywhere on those lake roads today. That's why I had him come here and let him pick the time."

Casey said, "So the plan is to wait for him to leave, then Raine and I go to his house and talk to the girl."

I was shaking my head before he finished. "She won't talk to you. Someone who's been through what she has— if I'm right—won't talk to any man. That's why Dakota had you all leave the room last night when she was interviewing Tina."

"Well, you're not going alone," Miles said.

Just to be clear, I adore Miles. I trust his judgement, most of the time. And I know he always has my best interests at heart. But the last thing I needed right now was some man, any man, telling me what to do. The memory of Tina was too fresh in my mind, and I felt the flare of defensive anger like a match-strike in my soul.

He must have seen it in my eyes because he said sternly, "I mean it, Raine. I will call off the meeting with Booker right now unless I have your word." The set of his jaw was as stubborn as mine, and there was no doubt in my mind that he would do it.

Casey stepped in. "Maybe I just wait in the car." He added wryly, "I seem to be good at that."

I looked from one to the other of them. "Just because you're male," I said coolly, "doesn't mean you always know best. And in this case, it pretty much proves you don't."

Miles put on his most patient expression, the one he always resorted to when he thought I was being especially difficult, and he said gently, "Look, babe. I know you want to do something, and do it now. But believe me when I tell you, you don't mess with a man like Booker. We need to go about this thing the right way, or we're only going to make things worse."

Okay. I could agree with that. "I'm not even sure she'll talk to me," I said. "Or that she'll tell the truth if she does. But I know she won't talk if she thinks she's being set up. And that's exactly what she'll think if she sees Casey."

"Then I'll make sure she doesn't see me," Casey said. He spread his hands. "Hey, it's the best we can do. Either this, or get the police involved. And we all know if we do that, we get nowhere."

I paced to the window, staring out at the untouched snow. Cisco followed, having given up on any more breakfast treats, and put his paws on the windowsill, searching for whatever it was that held my attention. I dropped my hand to his head absently. Images kept replaying in my mind: Amber's nervous smile. How enchanted she had been by Cisco. The butterfly earring. Her fingers folding into that signal I should have recognized sooner.

I glanced down at Cisco, rubbing his velvety ear between my fingers. Slowly, my shoulders relaxed. I even smiled a little. Sometimes things weren't nearly as hard as we tried to make them.

"All right," I said at last.

Both men looked at me as I turned.

I said, "Let's hear the plan."

Miles nodded, as though never having doubted I'd come around. He said, "I'll text you when Booker gets here. I'll keep him at least an hour, which should give you plenty of time to get to his place and talk to the girl before he gets back there."

Casey added, "We should probably leave from my house. It's closer to the lake."

I nodded. "Sounds like a good plan," I said, stroking Cisco's head.

But mine was better.

CHAPTER TWENTY-SIX

Sheriff Marshall Becker was a neat man, composed and organized. He wore a long-sleeved uniform shirt and tie, gold badge, starched khaki uniform pants. He had a well-groomed mustache and immaculate nails. Dakota had always thought you could tell a lot about a man by the way he kept his nails. Miles Young, for example, had perfectly manicured nails, probably professionally done. His hands spoke of money. By contrast, Casey of the curly blond hair and the wicked smile had a working man's nails, short but rough-cut. Pragmatic. Marshall Becker's nails were somewhere in between as, she suspected, was his personality.

He took the file folder she offered him and opened it, glancing over the contents. "Looks like we threw you into the deep end of the pool on your first day," he said, not looking up. "Not the way I like to do things, but I appreciate you jumping in like this. Have a seat." He gestured toward the chair in front of his desk as he took his own seat. "Did you get any sleep? I don't like my deputies working a double unless it's an emergency."

Dakota said, "Yes, sir. I'm fine. I wanted to follow through with the case while it was fresh in my mind."

She hadn't bothered to go home after arresting Tina Hoggins, since, by the time she had finished the paperwork, it was almost daylight anyway. She spent most of the following day supervising the search of the Hoggins house and dogging the powers-that-be to get preliminary forensics and medical examiner's reports. By the time she had finished up and made her way home along the slushy, newly plowed roads last night, she had been tired enough to sleep like a log on the mattress on the floor of the living room—where it had been since she'd moved in and where it would remain until she had time to actually put her bed together.

She gestured to the report in the sheriff's hand. "It's not complete, but I thought you'd want to see what we have so far. A search of the Hoggins' house and the pickup truck turned up several long guns, a .22, and a large caliber revolver, all of which I assume belonged to Rooster Hoggins. The .38 was found in the glove compartment of the truck, along with a mixed bag of narcotics and a baggie full of fentanyl patches. Nothing in the house. It looks like the drugs were a side hustle, not his main business."

Marshall grunted. "Hoggins had his hand in a little bit of everything around here, as long as it was crooked. We've got a few like him. Might as well put their names on a cell door, they're in and out of here so much. I'm not surprised he ended up at the bottom of a ditch, to tell you the truth."

"Yes, sir. It's just that..."

He glanced up. "That what?"

She said, "We found the bullet that killed Hoggins embedded in a bookcase in the living room. Tina Hoggins is 5'3". Her husband was 5'9". I did a quick trajectory test, and unless she held the gun over her head or stood on a chair, there's no way she could have shot him."

Marshall frowned and flipped back a page. "What about the gun? The .38. Is that the murder weapon or not?"

Dakota shook her head. "I don't think so. We're waiting for the ballistics report, but I ran a quick-prints and the only fingerprints on the gun are Rooster Hoggins'. And, just eyeballing it, it didn't look like that gun had been fired in a while. Of course, we'll know more when we get the report back."

"That's good work," murmured the sheriff, turning a page. "The last guy we had in your job would have signed off the minute he brought in the wife."

She cleared her throat self- consciously. "Yes, sir. I read that file. I thought it best we try not to make a similar mistake."

He smiled wryly. "I agree. If Miles Young weren't a

friend of mine, this department would be bankrupt from the lawsuits. Speaking of which…" He glanced down at the folder again. "I see you interviewed Casey Macintosh."

"Just due diligence, sir, after the bar fight with Hoggins. He was at the victim's home on the afternoon of the incident. Since we don't have an exact time of death, we have to consider that to be opportunity. Other than that, we don't have anything concrete to tie him to the crime."

"So." Marshall looked up. "What about the wife? Are you going to cut her loose?"

Dakota hesitated. "She's charged with illegal disposal of remains, a misdemeanor, and attempted obstruction in a homicide case. The judge set bail at $2500, but I don't see how she can make it. I think she might know more than she's saying." She shook her head slightly. "I don't know, maybe she has some kind of misguided loyalty to her late husband, or maybe she doesn't even realize what she knows. But she's holding back."

Marshall said, "The man beat her and terrorized her for years, she called 911 on multiple occasions, she had a restraining order, and now that he's dead she's still protecting him? That I don't understand."

Dakota flinched inside. She smiled thinly, but she couldn't stop herself from saying, "No, sir. You wouldn't."

Marshall gave her a sharp, questioning look, and Dakota said quickly, "I'd like to interview her one more time. She's waiting for me in the interview room now, in fact."

"All right, then." He stood and offered his hand across the desk. "Good job, Lieutenant, and good to have you on board. Keep me informed."

"Yes, sir. Thank you." She shook his hand. "I will."

CHAPTER TWENTY-SEVEN

At 11:59 AM Miles, watching the security monitor of his driveway, sent a group text to Raine and Casey: He's here.

Only Casey replied. *Raine's not here. Not answering texts. Leaving for the lake. Drop me a pin.*

Miles muttered, "Damn it, Raine. Once, just once, could you stick with the plan?"

He texted Casey, *Are you surprised?* Then, quickly, he searched Booker's address and sent the location to Casey. He turned, balancing on his crutches, just as his housekeeper escorted Lance Booker into the room.

"Mr. Booker," he said. "Good of you to come. Pardon me if I don't shake hands. Still a little unsteady on these things." He smiled dryly and indicated the crutches.

"Not at all, not at all." Booker waved his apology

away as he came forward, smiling warmly.

He was a big man, dressed in an Alpine sweater, western boots, and the kind of gold jewelry that was designed to draw attention, if not admiration. "Looks like you did yourself some damage there." He added, indicating the injured leg.

"I've done worse," Miles replied genially. He nodded toward one of the two white sofas that flanked a glass coffee table where a luncheon tray had been set up. "Have a seat. I asked my housekeeper to make us some sandwiches and coffee. I figured we might as well have a bite to eat while we talk a little business."

"Well, that's mighty hospitable of you. Can I give you a hand with those crutches?"

Miles assured him he was fine and lowered himself onto the opposite sofa. They made small talk about the condition of the roads and the unpredictable mountain weather while his housekeeper poured coffee and served sandwiches on porcelain plates. Miles had decided to hold the meeting in his home office, an oasis of white carpets, glass tabletops, and modern art, partly because it was the only room in the house he could be sure was completely free of dog hair, and partly because of its excellent surveillance system. He did not expect to need the latter, but it was good to have it, nevertheless.

Booker finished off a couple of chicken salad sandwiches while Miles told him about his plans for Eagle Landing—the helipad and eventual airstrip, the luxury condos, the three-acre estate plots, the golf course. "We hope to have the golf course operational this summer," he said, "but the country club is open now. You ought to come check it out as my guest. Nice restaurant and spa, two pools, a gym."

"Well, I just might do that," conceded Booker, settling back on the sofa with his cup of coffee. "Golf course, eh? Airstrip? I've got to say, I sure didn't expect anything like this way up here in the hills."

Miles knew, of course, that Booker knew all about Eagle's Landing. He would be a fool not to have done his research. He said, "A lot of people look at a place like this and see God's country. I look at it and see opportunity." He smiled. "I understand you do, too."

"I might have a few plans," agreed Booker modestly. "But that's why we're here, isn't it?"

"It is," Miles agreed pleasantly, picking up his own coffee cup. "But before we get into that, let me ask you a question, if I may."

Booker inclined his head politely.

"The other day," Miles said, "when you met my fiancée and her brother, Casey, did you ram their truck intentionally?"

Booker showed no surprise, only the mildest of amusement. "Why in the world would I do that?"

"To get my attention, maybe," suggested Miles, sipping his coffee. "To send a message."

Booker's smile was stiff and did not reach his eyes. "And what would that message be?"

"Why don't you tell me?"

Booker regarded him steadily for a moment, took a final sip of his coffee, and put the cup down. "You promised not to waste my time, Mr. Young," he said, starting to rise. "I'm disappointed, and I have places to be."

Miles said, "Sit down, Mr. Booker." His voice was mild, but his expression was cold, and brooked no argument. "This conversation has just begun, and I promise you won't be disappointed."

With his gaze never leaving that of Miles Young, Booker slowly sat back down on the sofa. "I'm listening," he said.

CHAPTER TWENTY-EIGHT

Tina Hoggins was sitting at the small table in the interview room, her fingers twisted together on the table surface, knuckles raw from the constant friction. Thirty-six hours in jail had done her no favors. The jailhouse khakis sagged on her, her face was gray with fatigue, her dishwater colored hair hung in lank strands around her throat. Her eyes were weary with pleading as she looked up at Dakota.

"Can't I go home now?" she said. "Rooster never spent this long in jail and he did real crimes."

"Mrs. Hoggins," Dakota explained patiently, pulling out a chair, "you're charged with trying to conceal a death in a homicide case. That's a pretty serious crime. The judge has set bail, and if you pay it you can go home to wait for your trial. Otherwise, you have to stay in jail."

She shook her head. "I don't have any money. When is the trial?"

Dakota checked the papers in her folder as she sat down. "It says here March 25. Didn't you talk to your public defender?"

"Do you mean that lawyer that was here yesterday? He just asked me some questions and then he left. I told him," she added a little desperately, "that I didn't do anything, but that didn't seem to make any difference. "

Dakota nodded. She had been told, over and over again, not to get emotionally involved with the situations she ran into while enforcing the law, but she had never been sure that was good advice. And in this case, she didn't see how it was possible. She suggested, "What about your mother? Maybe she could raise your bail money?"

"Maybe." Tina looked bleak. "But she don't have much herself and, well…" She sighed. "She drinks."

Right, thought Dakota. *Don't get involved.*

"Mrs. Hoggins," she said, and then added more gently, "Tina. I know this is hard. I don't believe you killed your husband, and I don't want you to stay in here any longer than you have to. But I think you may know more than you realize about who did kill him. If you can help me figure that out, there's a good chance the prosecutor will talk to the judge and try to get your charges reduced. Then you could go home."

Tina's fingers wound together so tightly that Dakota was afraid they might crack. "I'm worried about

Riley. Who will take care of him?"

"The lady you met at the boarding kennel said she would keep him," Dakota assured her. "It looked like a really nice place, and I hear a lot of good things about it."

Tina wiped at her eyes with the back of her wrist. "He doesn't like to be alone. Sometimes he doesn't eat when he's upset."

Dakota said, "I'm sure the people at the kennel won't let that happen." Then, impulsively, she volunteered, "I could go check on him if you like."

For the first time, Tina looked hopeful. "Will you? And could you maybe...He has this toy horse he likes. A stuffed horse. I have to hide it in my underwear drawer at home because Rooster doesn't think dogs should have toys. But Riley loves it." Her expression grew wistful. "He carries it around for hours, even sleeps with. It breaks my heart every time I have to take it away and hide it. But if you could go by my house and pick it up, maybe take it to him...is that too much? Could you do that?"

There was no way Dakota was saying no. "I can do that," she told Tina. "I'll even take a picture of him with his toy for you."

Tina sank back in her chair, the worry lines on her face relaxing fractionally, her fingers unwinding. "Oh." Her voice was barely a breath. "Thank you."

Dakota said, "Tina, tell me about Casey Macintosh."

The other woman looked blank, and Dakota

prompted, "He came to your house two days ago looking for your husband. Young man, blond hair, good looking. Had a cut on his lip. He had been in a fight with Rooster the night before. What did he want with Rooster, do you know?"

Tina shook her head. "He didn't say. I'd never seen him before. He was at the kennel the other night when I went to get Riley. He said he put my husband in jail. Is he a cop?"

Dakota's lips quirked with a half-smile. "No. Do you have any idea what his relationship with your husband might have been?"

Again, she shook her head. "He seemed nice. Not the kind of person Rooster usually hung out with."

"Okay," said Dakota, "Let's talk about the people your husband usually hung out with. Is there anyone who stands out to you? Somebody he might have had an argument with recently? Somebody besides Casey Macintosh, I mean."

She said, "He didn't like me being around when he was doing business. I usually tried to make myself scarce when people came over. Me and Riley."

"What kind of business?" Dakota asked.

Tina gave another uncomfortable little shake of her head. "I don't know exactly. Nothing good, I figured that. You know he only brought home a part-time check at the excavating company. The rest of the time he did deals."

"What kind of deals?"

"Hauling stuff, selling stuff, odd jobs. There was this one guy out on the lake, some rich guy, he cleared out his driveway a year or so back. Every now and then he'd come around with another job for him."

"More excavating work?"

"No. Whatever it was, Rooster'd take the van and be gone a couple of days. I figured he was delivering something somewhere." She looked at Dakota with tired eyes that held neither shame nor regret. "Probably drugs. I didn't care. When he took off, Riley and me would have a few days peace. That's all that mattered."

Dakota nodded her understanding. "We didn't see a van when we searched your place."

She said, "It's a minivan. He took all the back seats out for some reason, so maybe it wasn't drugs he was hauling. Maybe it was guns. He's done it before. Got arrested for it too, but something went wrong. They had to let him go."

Dakota had read that case file. It turned out the stop was illegal. The guns were confiscated, but a drug runner and wife abuser had walked free.

"Anyway," Tina said, "I don't think he works for that man anymore. I heard him yelling at Rooster about something on the phone the other night after Rooster got in, and Rooster saying something about it being 'the last damn time.'"

"When was this, do you remember?"

Tina thought for a moment. "Maybe the middle of last week? A couple of days before, you know, he got arrested, and Riley and me ran away."

"It would really help to know who he was working for," Dakota said, "and who he was arguing with on the phone. Are you sure you don't know what happened to his phone, Tina?"

"Maybe," suggested Tina wearily, "whoever shot him took it."

Dakota thought that was not a bad theory.

She said, "Where is the van?"

"Oh," she said. "I drove it when I, you know, left. I had to leave it in the lot, remember?"

Dakota opened her mouth to question further, but just then there was a knock on the door and one of the day-shift deputies entered. He leaned close to her and murmured, "Tina Hoggins just made bail. We're gonna have to let her go."

Dakota looked at him in surprise. "Thank you, Deputy…" She was embarrassed to admit she didn't know his name, and she had to read his name tag. "Deputy Roarke." He nodded and went back to stand by the door. Dakota smiled at Tina.

"It looks like your mother managed to raise your bail after all," she said. "You can go home and see Riley."

The relief that swept Tina's face—mixed with a generous amount of joyous disbelief—was heart-wrenching to see. "Do you mean it? I can leave? I can go home?"

Dakota raised a cautious hand as Tina started to rise. "It'll take an hour or so to finish the paperwork. You can wait in your cell until then. But you still have to appear at trial, and we may want to talk to you again, so you can't leave town."

She nodded energetically. "I'll just get my things and pick up Riley and then I'll go stay with my mama. She just lives down the road a piece. I don't want to stay in the house where, you know, it all happened. Not for a while, anyhow."

Dakota stood. "I understand. Just let us know where to reach you before you leave." She gestured to the door. "The deputy will walk you back to your cell."

The smile that Tina Hoggins gave her as she got to her feet was the best thing that had happened to Dakota all day.

She was filling out the warrant for a search of Tina Hoggins' van when Roarke, the deputy who had escorted Tina to her cell, stopped by Dakota's desk. "It probably doesn't make any difference," he said, "but I thought you might like to know it wasn't her mother who bailed Tina Hoggins out."

"Yeah?" Dakota looked up curiously. "Who was it?"

He glanced through the papers on his clipboard. "The same guy who bailed her husband out a couple of days ago. Seemed a little odd to me."

Dakota sat up alertly, a theory beginning to form. "Have you got a name?" she demanded.

CHAPTER TWENTY-NINE

When Lance Booker left for his appointment with Miles in his fancy Ford King Ranch pickup, I was standing at the pump in front of the clapboard country store five miles from his house, putting two gallons of gas in my car even though I had filled it up before the snowstorm, so that I would have a good view of passing traffic. I didn't think he would recognize me in my hooded coat and snow boots, but he was easy to spot. Aside from the truck, there was no other traffic in this isolated spot. Only one paved road led away from his house. And he was the only one using it.

Typical of our mountain weather, the temperature had been in the forties all day yesterday, and was already forty-two before noon today. Some of the lesser used roads would remain impassable for days, especially in the higher elevations, but for the most part, what remained of the snow had turned to slush on the roads and was piled up in dirty banks and patches on the shoulders. People like Booker, who could afford to pay someone to clear their private access, made it easy for me to navigate my way back to the lake.

As soon as Booker made the turn at the corner, I got back in my car and turned in the opposite direction. Cisco, excited to be on an outing, panted happily in the back seat. I had three texts from Casey demanding to know where I was, since the plan was to meet at his house between 11:00 and 12:00. I stalled him with "on the way" for a while but knew that wouldn't work for long. Finally, as I parked in Lance Booker's newly plowed driveway shortly before noon, I typed, *Sorry. Change of plans.*

I hit Send and was surprised to realize I had less than 10 % left on my battery. I'd made a point to plug it into the car charger on my way over, but when I examined the charging cord I found it wasn't even plugged into the charger. "Great," I muttered, annoyed with myself. Of all times to be betrayed by technology. I plugged the cord firmly into the charger and reminded myself to connect the phone on the way home. For now, I turned the phone off to save the battery and tossed it into my purse. I unbuckled Cisco from the backseat, and the two of us started up the steps that led to front lawn.

No one answered the doorbell, which surprised me because I remembered the big, silent man who had let me in previously. I'd thought he was household security, but if he was a bodyguard, maybe he had gone with Booker to his meeting with Miles. I rang again, waited, and then knocked. I saw a shadow pass in front of the stained glass door inset. Cisco, sensing someone's presence, pricked up his ears. I knocked again. "Hello!" I called. "Amber? It's Raine Stockton, from the other day." I was not at all sure I had introduced myself at the accident site, or that she would remember if I had, but I thought giving a name might put her at ease. Then, on inspiration, I added, "I returned your earring, remember? I just wanted to make sure you got it."

I waited, and the shadow moved again. After a moment, the door opened just enough to show one eye and about a quarter of her face. I smiled. "Hey," I said. "Remember me?"

That one eye remained completely expressionless, and I thought she was getting ready to close the door in my face when Cisco nosed at the opening. "Oh!" she exclaimed softly, and relaxed her grip on the door a little. "You brought your dog!"

I dropped the leash and Cisco, taking advantage of the moment, pushed his way through the door, tail wagging excitedly, eager to explore. *Good boy*, I thought, even as I exclaimed, "Oh, dear! I'm so sorry!" and rushed in after him.

Amber stepped back from the door, looking helpless and confused, as I pretended to chase Cisco across the black marble foyer while he sniffed and play-bowed and playfully danced away. A single command would have brought him instantly to my side—most likely—but Amber didn't know that. And I couldn't help noticing her consternation faded into a smile as he wagged his way over to her.

She closed the door on the cold and dropped to her knees to pet him. "Pretty boy," she exclaimed softly. "What a good dog!"

I said, "Sorry about that. He gets excited to meet new people."

Proving my point, Cisco tried to wiggle his way into her lap. She laughed and hugged him, abruptly sitting on the floor when she lost her balance. I couldn't help smiling as I picked up Cisco's leash. I knew I could count on him.

"Okay, Cisco, that's enough," I said.

He nudged her chin one last time and, still grinning happily, came over to me. I petted him enthusiastically, and he leaned against my leg, tongue lolling.

Amber got up from the floor, brushing off her clothes. She was wearing a slim cotton maxi skirt and a tee shirt with a big-pocketed summer-weight cardigan, which I thought was odd attire for this time of year. Even odder, her feet were bare. They must be freezing on the marble floor.

"I used to have a dog like that," she said, still smiling at Cisco, "when I was growing up."

"Oh?" The great thing about golden retrievers is that almost everyone used to have a dog like that.

"Where did you grow up?"

The smile left her eyes before it left her lips. "Not far from here," she answered vaguely. The smile was completely gone now, replaced with a nervous anxiety that caused her to dart her eyes around as though she was afraid of being caught at something illegal. "You should go. I'm not supposed to let anyone in."

I was inside now, and I had no intention of leaving unless it was either with her or some very good answers. "I understand," I said. "I think we'll be okay for a little while. Where's that man who answered the door the other day? The security guard?"

She swallowed visibly, looking uncertain. "Sean. Sean Wilkins. He, um, went with Lance. I don't know where."

I nodded. "The other day, when we first met, you tried to signal me for help." I spoke to her in her in the same tone I would use to soothe a frightened dog, maintaining eye contact, keeping my voice gentle but certain. "I'm sorry I didn't understand. "

Her eyes went big, and she crossed her arms over her chest defensively. As she did, her sleeves rode up a little, and I saw an angry red stripe around each wrist. Ligature marks.

"I don't know what you're talking about," she said. "You need to go."

Now it was my turn to swallow back the tightness in my throat. "Okay," I said. "But first, I want to ask you about Izzy."

At the name, the wariness in Amber's eyes was

overtaken by a flare of hope, or perhaps desperation. "Have you seen her? Is she all right?"

I glanced around. "Can we sit down for a little while?"

She shook her head, a series of short, fierce movements that caused her blonde hair to ripple around her shoulders. "I can't. I'll get in trouble. You shouldn't be here. Only..." She looked at me, pleading. "Tell me about Izzy. Please. Tell me she's okay. I've been so scared..."

I said regretfully, "I don't know anything, Amber. I was hoping you could help us find out what happened to her. She's been missing since last week."

Amber's fingers fluttered to her lips, and her whole body seemed to sag. I took an alarmed step toward her, afraid she was about to fall. "Oh, God." Her voice was high, thin, and shaky. "Oh, God, it's all my fault. I knew it. It's all my fault."

I spotted a doorway opening off the black marble hallway to my right. I took Amber's elbow and led her toward it. I could feel her thin frame shaking as we walked, and tears were wetting her cheeks.

The room turned out to be a tall-ceilinged living room done in deep blues and black with arched gothic windows overlooking the lake. There was a gas fire in the fireplace that did nothing to make the room cozier, and lamps in the corners cast feeble yellow circles on the walls behind them. Amber sank onto the first sofa we came to, a black leather number that felt as cold as it looked. I sat down beside her.

"Tell me how you know Izzy," I invited somberly.

Amber gulped and wiped her streaked face with her fingers. I looked around for tissues but didn't see any. She pulled down the sleeve of her shirt and blotted her runny nose with the back of her wrist like a child. She said, "She was...is...my best friend. We did everything together, told all our secrets, always had each other's backs. We were like sisters, only closer. We were going to strike out and see the world together as soon as we graduated, just me and her. Only there was this guy."

There's always a guy, I thought.

"Izzy told me he was bad news, and she was right. We fought about it, and I got mad and stopped speaking to her. Things were bad at home anyhow, and Izzy was mad at me, so I ran off with the guy. He dumped me in Atlanta." The last was said in the flat, emotionless tone of inevitability. "I was sixteen."

She took a bracing breath. "Anyway, when we moved here last year, Lance and I stopped by that bar where Izzy works. It was really crowded, and I don't think she saw me—or maybe she didn't recognize me. I look a lot different now. But I recognized her and I kept thinking about her, thinking maybe if I could get to her, she would help me. We always had each other's backs." She looked down at her hands, lying limply in her lap. "It took months to work up the courage, but I finally looked her up on my phone —I'm only allowed to use it twenty minutes a day and Lance always checks my calls—and I found out where she lives. I told Lance I wanted to do some

Christmas shopping, and I went to see her. I told her everything. About the woman in Atlanta who picked me up off the streets and took me home to live with her in a nice apartment with a bunch of other girls and gave us nice clothes and makeovers and took us clubbing and acted like our best friend. There were drugs," she admitted, "and guys, but nobody wanted to leave because we knew what it was like on the street. Then one night we went to a party with a bunch of rich men and an awful lot of drugs, I think they were bidding on us because at the end of the night Lance Booker put me in his car and said something like, 'you're mine, little darlin', bought and paid for, free and clear.' And I've been with him ever since."

She pushed back a fall of her hair with an unsteady hand. "So anyway, when Izzy heard the story, she was real mad and said it wasn't right and we should call the police, but that scared me so much. I'd seen what Lance was capable of. What his friends could do. I tried to leave one time and he locked me in this storage box with nothing to eat or drink for days. I couldn't take the chance. I begged Izzy not to tell, not to do anything that would get me in trouble, and finally she agreed we had to have a plan."

She looked at me with hopeless, helpless eyes. "People think I stay because of the pretty dresses and the jewelry and the parties." She gave a small shake of her head. "That's not it. None of those things make up for being scared every single minute. I stay because..." She hesitated, finding the words but ashamed to say them. When she spoke again, her voice was small. "I don't know how to leave."

I reached for her hand and grasped it firmly. Cisco put his head on her knee and looked up at her with those big, brown, golden retriever eyes. "I know how to leave, Amber," I said. "I can help you."

Again, she gave a single short shake of her head. "Izzy had a plan," she said. "I was supposed to come to her house that day. She had a bus ticket and money and a wig and old clothes for disguise. At least that's what she said. She said she had it all figured out. A friend in San Antonio that I could stay with. A job cleaning houses. Lance would never look for me there. He'd never know. And I thought it would work. He had been in a good mood since we moved here. He let me drive by myself, go shopping, get my hair done in town. It was almost like he was a regular person." She shook her head. "But I knew it wouldn't last long. It never does. I thought maybe Izzy was right. There would never be a better time to get away."

There was an eerie echo of those words in my head. Where had I heard them before?

She went on in a tired, flat tone, "So I told Lance I was going shopping, but when I got to Izzy's trailer, she was gone. She didn't answer my knock, my calls. Her car was there. I could hear her dog barking. But she didn't come to the door. I knew something was wrong. And…" Amber pressed her lips together tightly. "I was scared. I ran away. I think that's when I lost the earring. It was that day. The day of the accident in the truck. Because when I got back to the house, and I looked at Lance, the way he smiled at me, I knew. I knew he'd done something to Izzy."

I said softly, "What do you think he did?"

She looked at me with eyes that were too old, too weary, too broken for her age. "I think he sold her," she said.

CHAPTER THIRTY

"I've done my research," Miles said. "I know that your company specializes in buying up property in protected and uniquely underutilized areas like this one, making sure the zoning restrictions and protected status slowly and quietly disappear, then turning them into profitable commercial resort areas. Harbor Falls, Montana, population 815 in 2016, is now a four-billion-dollar ski resort and casino. Crestview Island, Texas, a protected wetlands research station reachable only by boat, uninhabited and restricted from residential or commercial construction. Now the sole beneficiary of a 30-million-dollar government funded bridge, no more wetlands, no more research, and very much under construction. I've seen the plans. Impressive."

Booker said, "Your point?"

"I appreciate a man with vision," Miles said. "I appreciate even more a man who knows how to get things done. You probably realize I'm one of the primary investors in property in this area. I don't think I'd be wrong in assuming you're planning to do something here similar to what you did in Montana."

"Or," pointed out Booker, "similar to what you've done here with Eagle's Landing."

Miles inclined his head in agreement. "Similar. Of course, in order to do that, you're going to need some major infrastructure changes around the lake, road expansions and the like. Not to mention a lot more property than you currently own."

Booker smiled. "Which is where you come in."

"As of 10:00 A.M. this morning," Miles informed him, "I own 84 acres around the lake—virtually all of it— and 200 acres on either side of County Road 17, which, as the only access point, you'll need to widen considerably before you even try to bring heavy equipment in to build. It's a long-term investment, I understand, but I'm a patient man."

Booker's expression showed neither surprise nor rancor. "You realize, of course, that we anticipated something like this."

"You should have, yes."

"I must say, I'm surprised you were able to get it done this quickly."

Miles picked up his coffee cup and replied modestly, "I have a few connections, myself."

Booker murmured, "I see that." His phone buzzed in his pocket and he said, "Excuse me one moment." He took out his phone and read the message briefly, pocketed it and returned his attention to Miles. "I'm afraid something has come up. We're going to have to cut this meeting short. So let me get right to the point. We are prepared to offer you a twelve percent profit on all the property you own, and a two percent equity stake in the development as we proceed. We can close in thirty days."

Miles nodded his head thoughtfully. "All the acreage? Twelve percent?"

"That's right."

"I assume there's room for negotiation."

Booker smiled. "There's always room for negotiation. Where would you like to start?"

"With the closing date," Miles replied.

If Booker was surprised by that, he didn't show it. He was, in fact, an excellent negotiator. "What date did you have in mind?"

Miles replied, unblinking, "When hell freezes over." Then he smiled and once again indicated his crutches. "Please show yourself out. I'm a little indisposed."

Booker held his gaze for another long moment, and then he returned the smile and stood. "Well," he said, "as they say, this is a start. When you're ready to talk business..." He took out his card and held it out to Miles. When Miles did not take it, he placed it on the coffee table. "Give me a call."

Miles said, "Good day, Mr. Booker."

He waited until he heard the door close behind Booker to send the text: *On his way*.

Then Miles leaned back against the sofa, frustrated, and closed his eyes. He waited.

CHAPTER THIRTY-ONE

I said, "Why do you think Lance sold Izzy?"

I worked hard to keep my voice even and my expression neutral. Inside, I was shaking, and I tasted the disgust that lodged in the back of my throat. Cisco, sensing my unease, lifted his head from Amber's lap and looked at me. Her hand, which had been stroking his ears, stopped.

She darted her eyes away briefly, as though debating whether to answer. Then she looked me straight in the eye, and she said steadily, "Because that's what he did in Arkansas. When we lived there before this."

I just nodded. My heart was pounding. "Okay."

She said, "Mexican girls, mostly, who didn't speak English or have papers or anything. The kind nobody was looking for. I don't think Lance knew I figured out what was going on. Or he didn't care. But he had these guys working for him, and I saw the girls all chained up in the back of a cargo truck, and the satchel of cash they would bring back and afterwards Lance was always in a good mood and he'd take a roll of it and toss it to me and tell me to go buy myself something pretty." She paused for a hitching breath. She wasn't looking at me anymore. "And I did. Because when it came right down to it, I was no better off than they were, was I?"

I said gently, "Didn't you ever try to call your parents? Or… or the police?" I knew it was a stupid question as soon as I asked it.

She said tiredly, "I tried to call my folks once. He broke my arm. I saw a poster in an airport bathroom and I wrote the number you were supposed to call for help on my palm. That was stupid. He found it and broke two of my teeth. He had them replaced, but it hurt a lot." She pulled back her lip and showed me the canine and molar on the upper right side. They looked to be a slightly different color than the rest of her teeth. She dropped her hand again to Cisco's head. The look in her eyes was utterly defeated. "The police won't help me. They won't even believe me. He's friends with all of them. "

"Not here, he's not," I told her firmly. "And the police are already looking for Izzy. If you can tell me anything that might help find her, we can not only save Izzy but stop Booker for good."

Amber's lips pressed together, and her fingers closed on a tuft of Cisco's fur. I could see in her eyes she was struggling to believe me, struggling to hope.

Finally she said, "There was this man. He worked for Lance. A couple of times, he came with a toolbox full of cash. He always had on muddy boots and jeans that were dirty and too big. He had a funny name. Reminded me of a chicken, because that's what he looked like."

My heart skipped a beat. "Rooster? Was his name Rooster?

She nodded, unimpressed, "That's it. He had a face like a rooster, too. Red hair. Anyhow, one time Lance asked if they gave him any trouble, and he said, 'No, didn't hear a peep out of them when I put them in my shed. Moved them out the next day.' Or something like that. They used to talk like I wasn't even here. That's how I heard Lance on the phone, telling him about Izzy. He told him to pick her up at the bar and keep her knocked out until he made arrangements. He said she was too valuable to go in with the next batch on account of her being white. He told the man to deliver the others like they planned but hold Izzy out. That's what he said. The man—the chicken man, I used to call him, but I guess his name was Rooster, like you said—he was supposed to bring money in a few days, like he always did. But I never saw him again."

"That's because he was dead," I said, barely on a breath.

She stared at me.

Quickly, I checked my pockets for the card Dakota had given me, then rummaged around in my purse. Nothing. I grabbed my phone and turned it back on.

The first thing that popped up was Miles's text message: *On his way*. It had been sent twenty minutes ago.

"Crap!" I whispered. I quickly texted Miles, *Leaving now. I have Amber.* I pocketed the phone and got to my feet. Cisco, immediately alert, came to stand beside me. "Amber," I said urgently, "we've got to go. Booker is on the way back here."

Terror flashed in her eyes, and she shrank back. "You have to get out of here!" she said hoarsely. "If he finds you here…"

"I'm not leaving without you," I said firmly. "But we have to hurry. "

She shook her head frantically. "He'll find me! He always does, and when he does …"

I interrupted sharply, "Do you know who my husband is?" That was the first time I had said that word out loud to anyone except Miles. I was surprised how natural it sounded.

She just looked at me with deer-in-the-headlights eyes.

"His name is Miles Young," I told her, "and he's one of the richest men in the country. Maybe the world." Miles would have laughed at that, but I felt a little exaggeration could be forgiven here. "Everybody worth knowing in this part of the country owes him a favor, and he will crush Lance Booker like a bug. He sent me to help you. We can protect you, but we have to leave *now*."

I closed my hand around her wrist and tried to tug her to her feet, but she refused to budge. "Why?"

She looked as though she desperately wanted to believe me but was just too afraid. "Why would he... why would you..."

"Just come with me, please, Amber," I begged. "I can explain later. Please, trust me."

She looked at me helplessly for a moment and then said simply, "I can't." She gestured wanly to her bare feet. "I don't have any shoes."

For a moment, I just stared at her, nonplussed.

"After Izzy," she explained, "he took my shoes and socks and locked them up. My coats too."

"So you couldn't run away," I said softly, and she merely nodded.

I sat down abruptly and began to unlace my boots. It wasn't that cold outside, so frostbite wasn't an issue, but the trek across the lawn and down the steps to the parking lot could be treacherous—not to mention dangerously slow—in bare feet. I, on the other hand, was wearing double-insulated wool socks, and I was confident in my ability to make it to the car without breaking stride. I kept a pair of galoshes in the back that I could put on when I got there.

I passed the boots to Amber. "Put these on," I commanded. "Let's go."

To my surprise, she actually took the boots and began to push her feet into them. "Wh-where? Where are we going?"

"Some place safe," I assured her.

She got to her feet, the laces of my boots tied loosely around her ankles, and looked at me with a defiance I would not have thought possible of her. “Not without Izzy,” she said.

I stared at her. “What?”

“It’s my fault he took her,” Amber said. “I’m not leaving her behind.”

“But we don’t know where she is!”

“We do,” she insisted. “The chicken man took her and hid her in his shed. We have to find her.”

“But…” I did not know where Rooster Hoggins lived, and the chances of there being a shed on his property, and that Izzy was there—that she was even still alive—were beyond slim. I glanced again at my phone. Twenty-five minutes had passed since Booker had left Miles’s house. It had taken me thirty-five minutes to get here, but I had been driving slowly, waiting for Booker to leave. We couldn’t afford to waste any more time.

“Okay,” I promised rashly, reaching for her hand. “Okay, we’ll find her, but we have to go *now*.”

This time, when I tugged at Amber’s hand, she followed quickly and willingly. We hurried out of the house and down the steps, Cisco bounding ahead of us, and all the while I was wondering desperately how I was going to keep my promise.

CHAPTER THIRTY-TWO

Miles would never have activated the drone if Raine had answered his text. He had no qualms whatsoever about turning the tracking app on his phone back on and narrowing in on her location. When he saw she was still at Booker's house, he made his way to the station in the sunroom and launched the drone. He called Casey.

"Where are you?" he demanded.

"Almost to the lake," Casey replied. "Some of the roads between my house and Booker's were still closed. I had to go around."

"Raine is still there," Miles replied, "and Booker just left here."

"Damn," Casey said. "I can still get there before he does and get Raine out of there."

"I'm trying to track his vehicle with the drone," Miles said. "I'm not spotting him on the highway. Let me know if you see him. I don't want him walking in on Raine and Amber."

"Yeah, will do," replied Casey grimly. "That truck of his is hard to miss."

Miles said abruptly, "Hold on. I have a text. She's leaving Booker's place. She's got Amber with her."

"Is she headed home?"

"Don't know." Miles quickly sent the text, *Come home.* No reply. No bubbles indicated she was typing. "Damn it. She's not answering."

"I am going to wring her neck," Casey muttered. "Turning around now."

"She'll probably take Amber to the women's shelter," Miles said. "I'll let you know when I hear from her."

But even as he said it, he knew that the women's shelter was a bad idea. It was not secure against a man like Booker, and Raine knew that. She wouldn't make that mistake. He texted again, *It's safe here.* But Raine knew that, too.

Didn't she?

Casey said, "Don't hang up. She's calling me. I'm pulling over."

"Put me on." Miles's voice was clipped, and he tried without much success to hide his frustration.

In another moment, he heard Casey say, "Raine, Miles is on. Where the hell are you?"

Raine replied, "Don't yell at me, either of you. My phone's almost dead, and I don't have time. I have Amber with me. She says Booker and Rooster Hoggins were working together and that Izzy might be hidden somewhere on Rooster's property. A shed or something. I promised her we'd look, but I don't know where the house is. Casey, you've been there. Give me the address."

Casey said, "What? What are you talking about? How does Amber know where Izzy is?"

Miles did not waste time with questions. "Raine, that's a bad idea. Bring Amber here before Booker finds out she's gone. She can tell the police what she knows, and they can search the Hoggins place."

"They already searched," Casey added impatiently. "Don't you think if there was anything to be found, they would have found it?"

"They didn't know what they were looking for," she insisted. "And they didn't have Cisco."

Casey said, "His place is way out on Lookout Road, and there's not another soul around for miles. You've got no business out there alone. Miles is right. You need to..."

"Where on Lookout Road?" she interrupted.

Miles said, "Raine, listen to me."

"I promised," Raine said. "I promised we'd look." She lowered her voice a fraction. "It'll only take ten minutes, but..."

Her voice was cut off by a series of mechanical beeps.

"Raine?" Miles said, and Casey echoed, "Raine, are you there?"

Silence.

"Damn it," Miles said. "Her phone died." He switched apps on his own phone. "Last location was about six miles from Booker's house. County Road 17. Out of range of the drone and I can't track her phone if it's dead." Then he added in a low half-growl, "Plug in your damn phone, Raine."

Casey said, "She's going to try to find Hoggins' place. I'll head that way."

"Good idea. I'll give Deputy Bradshaw a call, just to be on the safe side."

Casey said, "Is she always this much trouble?"

Miles smiled wryly and replied only, "Keep me updated." He disconnected the phone.

That was when he spotted Booker's distinctive King Ranch truck through the drone camera. And it was not headed in the direction of Booker's home.

CHAPTER THIRTY-THREE

The thing about men is they are so busy being right, they hardly ever take the time to really try to understand the other person's point of view. Of course, Miles and Casey were both right. I had seen for myself what Booker was capable of, and the important thing was to get Amber as far away from him as possible. But why couldn't they understand I had let Amber down once when I was her only hope? That I had let Tina down when I knew her drunken, violent husband was looking for her, and I hadn't tried to stop him? And if there was any chance at all Amber was right about Izzy...well, I had promised her, hadn't I? I had promised her we would try.

I could not fail her again.

Having grown up in Hanover County and spent most of my life roaming the woods, hills and backroads that comprise it, there aren't too many places that are unfamiliar to me. I had a general idea where Lookout Road was, and after plugging it into the car's nav system, I had no trouble going straight there. The only mailbox on the road bore the name "Hoggins" in sloppy white paint.

There are many such places around the county, chopped-up farms and homesteads that sit at the end of what used to be a cow path or a tractor trail, passed down through the generations to sons and daughters who were less and less able to maintain them. The Hoggins place was a rambling piece of hilly, rocky, winter- barren acreage cut through with criss- crossing dirt roads and dotted with outbuildings in various states of disrepair. There were a couple of pieces of construction equipment in the front yard, a rusted-out tractor near the tree line at the side of the house, and an old trailer with two flat tires. Rooster's familiar truck sat beneath a carport roofed in three different colors of tin. Behind it was a brown minivan with the back cargo door open and all of the back seats removed. This gave me pause, because no one was supposed to be here. Tina was in jail, wasn't she? Then who had left the door open to the van? And whose van was it, anyway? Hadn't Tina said she had left her car parked in the impound lot when her mother picked her up from the shelter?

I sat there for a moment, looking around cautiously. Everything seemed quiet. Muddy snow hugged the banks that surrounded the single-story house with peeling paint and worn shingles. Curtains were drawn, door closed. A scrap of yellow crime scene tape fluttered by the door. The police must have released the crime scene, otherwise the tape would still have been across the door.

Amber unfastened her seatbelt, but I put out a hand to stop her.

"Stay here," I said. "I'll look around."

"See, there are sheds," she protested. "Izzy could be in any of them. I'll go with you."

She reached for the door handle, but again I shook my head. I hated to disillusion her but I had to be honest. "Rooster has a wife. Had a wife. She would have noticed something, heard something..."

"I told you," Amber replied impatiently, "he kept them drugged. He did everything at night. Izzy could be here. She *could*."

"I'll look," I assured her. "I'll look everywhere. But you need to stay here. Cisco is a tracking dog, and there's a chance he could pick up a scent. But he can't do it if too many people get in the way."

She seemed to understand this. "Okay," she said, rubbing hands together nervously. "Okay, I'll wait. I'll stay out of the way."

I opened my car door, then turned back, remembering to plug in my phone and double-check that it was actually connected. I turned the car engine on to auxiliary functions so it would continue to charge, taking no chances this time. On the off-chance that I did locate Izzy, we might need the phone to call for help.

I unbuckled Cisco from the backseat and he leapt

down. He immediately began sniffing the ground in the way all dogs do in a strange place. I went around to the cargo area to retrieve his tracking lead, although what, exactly, I expected him to track with no scent object and the ground covered with a mish-mash of scents from the police search, I wasn't sure. As I turned with his tracking harness and lead in hand, Cisco abruptly spun around and took off toward the back of the house.

"Cisco!" I ran after him, my galoshes squishing and sliding in the mud. He dashed this way and that, distracted by the melee of fresh scents that littered the ground—first to an old falling-down chicken house, then to a well pump cover, then to a rusty garden shed, then across the yard again. By the time I caught up with him, he had reached the big metal barn at the back of the property, and he was pawing and sniffing at the ground around the door. I thought he might have caught scent of a rat or a possum trapped inside until, abruptly, he sat and gave a single bark. That was his alert signal. He had found his target.

He had found Izzy.

Most people don't believe this, but retrievers have amazing memories. In field trials, they are asked to spot three or four targets in the sky, watch where they fall, one after another when they're shot, and then, when the signal is given, race across an enormous field and retrieve each target in the order in which it was felled. Sometimes, even I don't believe what these dogs can do, and I've seen them in action.

The last scent target Cisco had been given was Izzy's glove, and the search had ended in frustration. But he hadn't forgotten his target. When he caught the scent again, he zeroed in on it.

If I'd had the breath, I would have cursed myself for doubting Amber. Instead, I gave Cisco a hearty hug around the neck and a gasping, "Good boy!" as I dug a handful of liver treats out of my pocket and fed them to him one by one. In most cases, he is rewarded for a find with his favorite tug toy, but he's never turned down a liver treat, and I thought he would overlook my transgression this once.

There was a padlock on the door, and it didn't even budge when I shook it. I needed a crowbar or something to pry it loose. I started to turn to look for one when Cisco gave a surprised bark of greeting to someone behind me. I thought it was Amber, because no one ever stays put when they are told to, and I said without looking around, "Amber, see if you can find..."

That was when I felt the cold press of a steel barrel against the back of my neck.

CHAPTER THIRTY-FOUR

Miles brought up the street map showing the drone's location on the computer and tried once again to text Raine. The good news was that Booker was nowhere near any of the roads that Raine might use to return home. The bad news was that Miles didn't know where, exactly, he was headed. And the text, of course, did not go through. He pulled the drone back and higher, taking no chances of being spotted as the King Ranch made a left on Turkey Trot Road and moved deeper into the hilly countryside. He checked the location on the map and swore softly. Turkey Trot Road dead-ended into Lookout Road. And Casey had said there was only one house on that road: the exact house where Raine was headed now.

He texted Casey: *Looks like Booker is headed to Hoggins' house. Be careful.*

Casey replied, *How close?*

Miles zoomed the screen out to show both locations and made a rough guess. *Maybe 5 minutes.*

Any sign of Raine?

No. But the single word conveyed more confidence than he felt. The drone's maximum camera scope was only 500 yards, even at this height, so if Raine was further than a quarter of a mile away from Booker in any direction, Miles would not have seen her. He could only hope that if they passed each other along the route, surely she would recognize the truck and keep going. Surely.

But as the tiny farmhouse came into view, looking like a matchstick replica at this distance, Miles began to understand how unlikely that was. The house was impossible to see from the road; the scraggly lot littered with outbuildings and heavy equipment. There was a car parked in the yard, a brown van of some kind. Another car, a gray sedan, squatted behind a broken-down chicken house, invisible from the road and looking oddly out of place there. As he watched, a woman got out of the van and started toward the front door. He lost sight of her in the shadow of the porch. At that moment, Booker's truck came up the drive, circled behind the house, and parked there.

Raine would not be able to see the truck when she arrived.

"Damn it." He tried her phone again. Nothing.

Booker got out of his truck and came around the house. He went directly to the brown van and opened the cargo door. He rummaged around inside for a minute, then pulled out a dark colored toolbox. He paused to open it, then went back around the house to his truck and put the toolbox inside the passenger door.

That was when Raine turned in the driveway.

"No," Miles whispered. His hands tightened impotently on the drone's control console. *No, no, no, no...*

Raine got out of her car, then let Cisco out of the back. While she was leaning inside to get something, Cisco bounded off toward the metal building at the back of the property. Raine turned and ran after him.

Miles could no longer see Booker. Had he gone inside the house? He thought about dipping the drone down to try to warn Raine but he suspected he would only succeed in warning Booker. He zoomed in on Raine. She had almost reached Cisco, who was pawing at the door of the metal building. When Raine ran up to him, Cisco sat abruptly and barked. Raine knelt to give him treats. In the periphery of the drone's camera, something moved. Miles zoomed out. A man, not Booker, was crossing the yard behind Raine. He had a gun in his hand, and it was pointed at her.

Instinctively, Miles started to lunge out of his chair. He fell back down again heavily, his leg throbbing, and grabbed his phone. Not daring to take his eyes off the drone screen, he dialed 911. It rang. And rang. The man reached Raine. He pressed the gun to the back of her neck. She froze.

"Hanover County 911. What is your emergency?"

Miles said hoarsely, "This is Miles Young. A man is holding a woman at gunpoint at 21 Lookout Road. Send help *now*."

"Sir, are you safe?"

In the time he had been waiting for an answer, the man had twisted Raine's arms behind her back and started marching her toward the house, the gun now at her temple. Cisco was in a restless down-stay near the building. Miles watched helplessly as Raine and her captor disappeared beneath the porch roof.

"I'm not there," he ground out tightly. "I'm watching through a drone. There are two men, both of them in the house. At least one of them is armed. There are two women. All of them are in the house."

Except for the sound of typing in the background, there was silence. Miles's fingers tightened on the phone as he guided the drone to a new position. "I think there's another woman in the SUV. I can't tell for sure."

The dispatcher said, "Sir, did you say you were watching with a drone?"

"That's right."

"Are you certain of what you saw? Perhaps—"

He said, "Just send officers to their location! Can you do that?"

She replied a little frostily, "Units have been dispatched to the address you gave me. But they are at least twenty minutes away and I need more information..."

Miles disconnected the call and fumbled for his crutches. Where had Raine put the card that Deputy Bradshaw had given her the other night? Where did she put anything? On the kitchen counter, when she came in from the mudroom. He hadn't seen it since. The housekeeper would have put it somewhere logical, somewhere safe. He reached the kitchen, scanned the spotless kitchen island, navigated around it to the counter, which was also spotless.

Years of disciplined thinking had trained Miles to maintain calm under pressure, but he had never felt quite so helpless before. He had to force himself to stop and think rationally. He looked around the room one more time. The desk where Melanie sometimes did her homework. The basket at the entrance from the mudroom that held nothing but keys. The chalkboard above it, where Raine and Melanie and his mother occasionally wrote funny notes to each other and to him. And on the console table below it, next to the basket with the keys, a day calendar and a small memo book with a list of important numbers. On top of the memo book was a business card.

He made his way over to the table and snatched up the card, dialing the number with one hand while holding on to his crutch with the other. She answered on the second ring.

"Bradshaw."

"This is Miles Young." He started back toward the sunroom. "There's trouble at Rooster Hoggins' place. A man named Lance Booker is holding Raine at gunpoint, and possibly another woman, too. I've been monitoring them with the drone. I called 911, but they're twenty minutes out."

The silence on the other end was brief and startled, but at least it wasn't followed by a series of inane, time-wasting questions. "I'm headed that way now," she said. "My GPS shows ten minutes."

Miles released a breath he didn't know he was holding.

Dakota said, "Tina Hoggins was released from jail this morning. Her bail was paid by a man named Sean Wilkins. He's the same man who paid Rooster Hoggins' bail. It turns out he works for Lance Booker. I was on my way to ask Tina about that."

"Christ," muttered Miles. He should have known. "I don't know how the two are connected, but Booker is into some very bad business. I saw him take something from Tina Hoggins' car."

Dakota said. "You said you can see them on the drone?" He heard sirens switch on. "What are they doing?"

Miles reached the drone station in the sunroom and sank into his chair, letting the crutches clatter to the floor. He picked up the drone control, and he felt his heart stop.

The monitor showed a scene that was still and lifeless except for Cisco, who spun to bark silently up at the sky in the direction of the drone as Miles swooped it in closer. The mini-van that Tina had gotten out of was still there, cargo door open. The sedan parked behind the house was still there. Raine's car was there, passenger door open. The front door of the house was open. But the King Ranch pickup was nowhere to be seen. Cisco continued to bark, almost as though calling for help.

Miles said numbly, "They're gone."

CHAPTER THIRTY-FIVE

I thought the worst was when Cisco, confused by the gunman's aggressive move, bounded toward me, and the gunman spun around and pointed the gun at Cisco.

"No!" I gasped. The man had pinned me with an arm around my throat, and I clawed at it. There was hardly enough air for me to choke the command, "Cisco, down!"

Cisco stopped and sank into a down. We had worked on that one command all his life, knowing that it might one day *save* his life. A rattlesnake on the trail, a speeding car, an aggressive dog racing toward him... that one command, practiced to 100 percent compliance, can save a dog's life in an instant. I had never imagined, although perhaps I should have, that it could also save him from a man with a gun.

“Keep that dog away from me,” the gunman growled in my ear, “or I’ll blow his head off.”

“Okay,” I gasped. “Okay, don’t hurt him. Stay!” I managed to catch Cisco’s eyes long enough to issue the command just as he was starting to wiggle and crawl his way out of the down.

There is a famous story about the woman who was packing her car for a dog show and put her two border collies in a down-stay on the porch while she finished. She got in her car and drove away, forgetting her dogs in her rush. When she realized what she had done an hour later and returned to her house, her two good dogs were still on the porch in a down-stay.

Cisco is not that kind of dog. All I could do was pray that once, just once, he would hold his command, at least until the gunman was out of sight.

The man twisted my arms behind me and shoved me toward the house. My knees were shaking so hard that I couldn’t have resisted if I’d tried. I didn’t try.

Lance Booker was inside the house, standing over Tina with a gun in his hand. She sat on the faded brown sofa with her hands duct-taped behind her back and tears streaming down her cheeks. “I didn’t know the money was in the car, I swear,” she said. “Rooster never told me anything. I don’t even want it. You can have it all. Just let me go, please.”

To which Booker replied, “I believe you, sweetheart. That husband of yours was a piece of work. I did you a favor by getting rid of him, but you can thank me later. None of this is your fault, but I'm sure you understand I can't just let you go on with your life like you don't know anything."

"But I don't," she sobbed. "I don't know anything!"

Booker ignored her, turning to look at me. He smiled. "You, on the other hand," he said, "seem to go out of your way to interfere in other people's business."

"People know where I am," I said hoarsely. "The police are already on their way."

He lifted an eyebrow. "We'd better hurry then."

He tucked his gun back inside his jacket and picked up the duct tape as he strode toward me. The pressure of the gun barrel abruptly disappeared and Booker grabbed my wrists with one hand and wrapped them in duct tape with the other. The gunman who had held me went quickly back outside and I thought, *Oh, God, Cisco, stay, please, please stay...* I hardly even felt the pain of my wrists being bound, so focused was I on trying to send Cisco that silent message, on listening for the gunshot that would mean he hadn't received it, until Booker shoved me roughly down on the sofa beside Tina.

My thoughts were whirling like liquid in a blender, and some of them slipped through into speech, almost without my volition. "That's why Rooster was so upset about his car that day we first saw him," I said. "There was money inside. I thought he was looking for his wife. But all he really wanted was the car. And Tina had parked it in the one place he couldn't get to it—in the police impound lot."

"You must appreciate the irony," Booker observed.

"And you killed him for it," I said.

The look he gave me was a cross between pity and amusement. "My dear girl, it wasn't the three hundred thousand. Money comes and goes. It was the idea. The man thought he could outwit me. He thought he could steal what was mine. No one does that. And those who try…" He shrugged. "They only try once." He looked at me steadily. "You'd do well to remember that. As would your boyfriend."

The door opened again, and the gunman shoved Amber inside. At the look on her face, I felt a little part of me die. Beyond the fear, beyond the despair, there was simple resignation. I had promised to keep her safe, and I had instead delivered her straight into the hands of her tormentor. And she wasn't even surprised.

I thought that had to be the worst part.

Booker smiled as he came over to Amber. "Welcome back, little bird," he said softly. He grabbed her arms, twisted them roughly behind her back, and taped her wrists together. She didn't so much as flinch. He leaned close to her ear and said, "We're going to have a long talk about this later. But now…" He pushed her toward the door. "We have more important things to do."

"What about these two?" His henchman nodded toward Tina and me. "Shoot them?"

Booker gave him a sharp look. "Don't be absurd.

They're prime merchandise. Put them all in the back of the truck."

"And the girl? The other one?"

A small frown creased Booker's brow. "We'll come back for her tonight. She's no good to us dead, and we can't leave her in there much longer."

I realized then that he was talking about Izzy.

The two of them pulled us outside and around to the back, where Booker's big truck was parked. I stretched my neck to look for Cisco, and there he was, still in his down-stay outside the metal building, his eyes alert, his ears pricked for the sound of the command that would release him. My eyes went hot with tears. "Good dog," I whispered out loud.

If those were the last words I'd ever say, they were enough.

Booker grabbed Amber and literally threw her into the bed of the pickup truck. She landed hard and rolled to the back. The other man picked up Tina and shoved her in after Amber.

"Are you crazy?" I cried. "We'll freeze back here!"

Neither man seemed particularly interested. Booker seized my shoulders, but I twisted away, got one knee on the tailgate, and hoisted myself inside. "Where are you taking us?" I demanded. "You can't keep us back here like—like sacks of grain!"

Booker said, "Heads down."

He pushed a button on a remote control, and I heard a whirring sound. The other women were already lying on the floor, but I was sitting up. I barely ducked down in time to avoid being struck in the back of the head by the advancing bed cover.

Darkness descended, and I heard a click as the heavy plastic cover locked into place. My cheek was pressed against the cold metal floor, my arms pinned uncomfortably beneath me. The metal reverberated as two doors slammed, one after another. The truck roared to life.

I heard a bark. I went cold. "Cisco, no," I whispered.

I squeezed my eyes shut as the truck started to move, expecting at any moment to feel the fatal thump, hear the final yelp. But instead, all I heard was barking, close at first, then farther away as Cisco tried and failed to keep up with the truck that was taking us away. I could see him in my mind's eye, racing after us, barking, running, barking until I couldn't hear him anymore. Until he couldn't run any more.

That was the worst part.

CHAPTER THIRTY-SIX

Casey saw Raine's car with both doors open. He saw the minivan with the back cargo door open. Rooster's truck in the carport. Muddy tire tracks crisscrossing the yard. The front door of the shabby little house left open to the wind. He took his pistol out of the glove compartment and tucked it carefully into the waistband of his jeans before he even got out of the truck. And then he saw Cisco.

The golden retriever came bounding around the corner of the house, spattered with mud, tongue lolling, panting hard. Casey felt his gut tighten. Raine would never willingly leave Cisco behind. The big dog raced toward him, and Casey met him half-way, giving his fur a reassuring ruffle when Cisco jumped up to place his front paws on Casey's sweat-shirt.

"Hey, buddy," he said, sweeping the area with his

gaze. He was a little breathless himself, but from anxiety, not exertion. "Where's Raine?" He raised his voice and called, "Raine! Hello! Is anybody here?"

Cisco dropped his front paws to the ground and trotted off toward the back of the property. Casey started toward the front steps, and then he saw what Cisco was doing. The dog had stopped at the big metal building and was digging at the door.

"Shit!" Casey exclaimed softly, and ran toward the building.

The door was secured with a padlock. Casey slammed his hand against it in frustration. "Raine!" he called. "I'm here! Hold on!"

He ran back to his truck and got a crowbar from his toolbox. Cisco had managed to dig a good-sized hole in the mud under the door by the time Casey returned. He worked the crowbar beneath the hasp and pried the latch loose. He dragged the door open, and Cisco raced inside.

The building was windowless and cold, with a dirt floor and unfinished walls. Casey could see the shadow of crates and a few pieces of broken machinery, but nothing else. He called, "Raine!"

He heard Cisco's panting, but he couldn't see him. He took out his phone and activated the flashlight. The beam caught a glimpse of golden fur near the back of the building. Once again, he was pawing at the ground, whining. Casey hurried to him, and as he got closer, he realized the sound he heard was not whining. It was faint and muffled and high-pitched, but it was not coming from Cisco. It sounded human.

"Raine!" Casey shouted again.

He swept his beam across the ground where Cisco was digging. There was a wooden panel there, a trap door in the floor with a rope loop for a handle. Casey moved Cisco aside and pulled the door open. His flashlight beam revealed a short set of earthen steps and a cave-like room at the bottom of them. In a corner of that small room was what looked like a bundle of rags. That's where the whimpering sounds were coming from.

"Raine," he said, starting down the steps, "It's okay. I'm coming for you."

Cisco stood at the top of the steps, his ears flopping forward, his big eyes alert, watching as Casey moved toward the shivering, sobbing woman in the corner. "Hey," he said softly. "It's okay. I've got you. Come on, let's go."

He reached out to touch her shoulder, and she turned her face toward him. It wasn't Raine.

It was Izzy.

CHAPTER THIRTY-SEVEN

I rolled over on my back and flexed my knees, trying to get enough momentum to kick the overhead canopy that trapped us. All I could manage was a pathetic tap. There wasn't enough room to get any leverage, not that it mattered. The canopy was solid and had a mechanical lock. Even with my hands free and a set of tools, I doubted I could break it.

An icy wind cut through the infinitesimal gaps where the canopy met the metal of the truck bed, creating a high-pitched whistle that added to the roar of the road noise that reverberated through our metal coffin. Every bump or turn sent us careening into one another, adding another bruise to the canvas of my body. Amber, in her thin skirt and cardigan, must be freezing. Tina was wearing the same jacket and jeans in which I had last seen her, which, of course, she would be, having been taken directly to jail from Dog Daze.

I had already tried to find a sharp edge, a protruding screw or piece of metal with which to cut the tape that bound our hands, but the search was futile. This truck was nothing if not well built. It was impossible to sit up with the heavy canopy only inches from my head, impossible to keep my balance even when I did manage to leverage myself up a few inches. We were like sardines in a well-sealed can.

I tried to make a plan. I tried to think this through. But I couldn't think about anything except how it never should have come to this, how I should have been smarter, or acted sooner, or known, somehow, what Rooster Hoggins and Lance Booker were really up to. I had let these women down, and now there was nothing, absolutely nothing, I could do to save them.

Tina's voice, wet and husky, reached me beneath the rumble of the road. "I should have gone straight to get Riley. This would never have happened if... What will happen to him now? I should have taken better care of him. I should have."

I should have taken better care of all of them.

The motion of the truck had rolled me close to Amber, and I turned, with some difficulty, to look at her. "I'm sorry," I said, raising my voice to be heard over the sound of the wind. "This is my fault. I'm so sorry."

I could barely make out her shape in the darkness. I only knew it was her because of the light hair and clothing. For a moment, she didn't say anything, but I hadn't expected her to. Then she spoke.

"I have your phone," she said.

I thought I had misheard. "What?"

"Your phone." Her voice, small and uncertain, was closer to my ear now. "I took it from the car charger when I saw Sean coming for me. It's in my sweater pocket. I don't know if it works."

My heart started pounding, hard. "Which pocket?"

"This one. Close to you."

I twisted around by inches until my bound hands were facing Amber, scooting down until I thought I was on level with her sweater pocket. My fingertip touched the cotton weave, fumbled for the pocket opening. "Lift up," I gasped. "You're lying on it."

She wiggled around, lifting her weight but moving further away from me. I inched closer, straining to get my hands inside the pocket. I felt the shape of the phone. I couldn't get enough distance between my fingers to grasp it. I pushed back against the tape that bound my wrists. Casey had told me one time that duct tape was an ineffective binder if you ever wanted to tie someone up because it stretched. How he knew that, or why he thought I would want to know it, I can't say. But I remembered it now.

I strained and stretched my wrists apart until I gained an infinitesimal amount of distance between my two hands. I closed the fingers of both hands around the phone and dragged it from Amber's pocket.

The phone had only had a few minutes to charge in the car. It probably didn't have enough juice to even turn on. But all I needed was a few seconds, just enough to find the emergency button...

I couldn't see the face of the phone, but I slid my fingers along the side until I found the button that turned it on. A faint glow illuminated the bed of the truck, and I gasped with gratitude. "Amber," I said, "Can you see the phone? Can you dial 911?"

"I can't reach it," she said, her voice shaking with repressed sobs. "I can see it, but my hands..."

"I can," Tina said. She belly crawled her way toward us. "Tell me where to put my fingers. Which button to push."

"There's a red emergency button," I said urgently. "All you have to do is hold the two side buttons down until it comes up. Then just tap it, and it sends a message to 911."

"I see it," Amber said. "It's at the bottom of the screen. Can you..."

But just then the truck took a sharp turn, flinging me away from Amber. The phone skittered out of my hand and clanged against a far corner of the truck bed. The light went out.

CHAPTER THIRTY-EIGHT

The battery on the drone registered 52%. Miles had searched the road leading to Rooster's house, the cross-road and the highway within a radius of five miles in every direction, and had found no sign of the big pickup. Without knowing when they had left, their speed, or their direction, any guess as to where they might be now was just that: a guess. But he had to keep trying.

The sheriff's office had a BOLO out on Booker's vehicle. Officers had been dispatched to his house. Deputy Bradshaw was minutes away from Rooster Hoggins' place, with more units on the way. Everyone was doing everything they could and it wasn't nearly enough.

Miles had never felt so frustrated, so utterly useless, in his life.

His phone buzzed. It was Casey.

"Raine is gone," he said, breathing hard. "Cisco is here running around loose. I think she was taken. I found Izzy in an underground room beneath the barn. She's in bad shape. She looks like she's been drugged, and I don't think she's had anything to eat or drink in a while. An ambulance is on the way."

"So are the police," Miles said. His eyes were still searching, desperately scanning the hilly, winding stretch of highway that led away from the Hoggins house. "I was watching Raine on the drone. Lance Booker took her and Tina, and maybe Amber. I didn't see which way they went."

Casey said, "A sheriff's car just pulled up. It looks like Deputy Bradshaw. I'll call you back."

"Hold on." Miles could hardly believe his eyes as the brief notification from his message app flashed across the screen. "I just got a ping on Raine's phone."

In the background, he heard a woman's voice, "Mr. Macintosh? What's going on here?"

The rest Miles tuned out as he quickly brought up the app. The signal had been on less than thirty seconds, and was now gone. He programmed the coordinates of the last known location of the phone and sent the drone in that direction. The battery was almost at the turnaround point. If he pushed it to maximum speed, the battery would drain even faster. He pushed it to maximum anyway.

Casey was saying, "I didn't find her; Cisco did. I've already called an ambulance. No one else is here. I went inside to—"

"Put Deputy Bradshaw on the phone," Miles interrupted tersely.

Casey said, "Miles Young wants to talk to you."

In a moment, the deputy's voice came on the phone. "Mr. Young."

"I got a location on Raine's phone less than a minute ago." He watched the highway unfolding beneath the drone, his gaze intense. "County Road 17, about …" He turned to the map on the computer screen, manipulating the direction keys with one hand. "Three miles north of Danny's Country Store. The signal faded before I could tell whether they were going north or south."

"Okay. I'll send units out that way."

The battery indicator started to flash. The camera would disengage, and the drone would turn back in a matter of seconds unless he switched to manual override. If he did that, the drone would very likely crash and burn before it made it home. Miles switched to manual override and pushed to maximum speed.

In the distance, a black pickup was visible. Miles zoomed in the camera and, as the truck rounded a curve, the distinctive silver wings on the side panel came into view. Miles closed his eyes with a brief suspended breath, then released it. "I've got them," he said.

CHAPTER THIRTY-NINE

The truck lurched violently, fishtailing on a patch of black ice, and the three of us slammed sideways in the dark. Tina cried out. Amber's breath came in short, panicked gasps. My wrists burned where the duct tape bit into them and my fingers were growing numb, but I kept my arms braced, trying to keep us from toppling over each other.

The bed cover sealed us in tight. No light. No air. Just the smell of cold metal, gasoline, and fear.

"Hold on," I whispered, though my voice trembled. I was freezing. "I'll find the phone. We'll try again." I strained my eyes in the dark, looking for the phone. Maybe it wasn't completely dead. Maybe...

The truck slowed.

Then slowed more.

Then—stopped.

Car doors slammed. Boots crunched on frozen gravel outside. A man barked something. Another answered. The truck door opened and slammed shut, vibrating through the cargo bed. I strained to make sense of the sounds. Strained to see in the dark. My heart hammered so hard it hurt.

More footsteps. He was coming for us. Wherever Booker had planned to take us, whoever he had planned to turn us over to, we had arrived. I tried frantically to make a plan. The only weapons I had were my feet, my legs, my head...

There was the beep of a key fob, and the bed cover began to roll back. A blast of frigid air hit us like a slap. Daylight poured in, blinding after the darkness. I tensed my muscles to fight, to run, and blinked hard. Shapes swam into focus.

Dakota Bradshaw stood there, framed by the winter day and the pulsing red-blue lights of patrol cars. I struggled to my knees and twisted around to see the front of the vehicle, where two cruisers blocked the narrow mountain road. They were angled across the asphalt, tires half-buried in slush, steam rising from their hoods. Beyond them, the forest was a cathedral of black pines still dusted white, lifting their branches to the sky.

Tina started to sob when she saw Dakota, and Amber huddled into a ball in the corner of the truck bed. Suddenly, my teeth were chattering, and I was shaking so hard I couldn't move.

"Is anyone hurt?" Dakota asked. "Can you climb out?"

She reached for me, and I staggered toward her on my knees, unable to stand.

"I demand an explanation!" Booker barked, swaggering around the truck toward her like he still owned the world. That genial, over-polite manner he had exercised every time I'd met him previously was nowhere to be seen now. "This is outrageous. You have no right to search my vehicle. This was an illegal stop—"

"Was it, now?" Dakota cut him off, not even bothering to look around at him. "Then perhaps you'd like to offer an explanation for how these three women came to be bound in the back of your pickup truck."

Dakota sliced through the tape that bound my wrists and helped me to the ground. My legs cramped and almost buckled, and I rubbed my aching wrists against the sudden, painful flow of blood to them. The wind cut through my clothes like knives. Amber stumbled after me, assisted by another officer. Tina followed, her face blotchy with cold and terror, her breath coming in ragged bursts.

Dakota turned to face Booker, who had been stopped by one of the deputies and now stood on the side of the road beside the man who had held a gun to my head. Sean Wilkins. He had already been disarmed, and a deputy was searching Booker as we spoke. He found Booker's gun and retrieved it.

"Anytime you're ready," Dakota said to Booker. "You know, with that explanation."

He glared at her, his face like stone. "You can talk

to my lawyer."

I finally got my shaking under control long enough to speak. "He—he kidnapped us. We're not the first ones. He and Rooster Coggins were... t-trafficking women, getting m-money for them. He was holding Amber prisoner, beating and torturing her when she tried to get away."

"He, he bought me," Amber said in a small voice, rubbing her wrists. She pressed back against the tailgate of the truck, her eyes big and terrified and also defiant. She looked from one to the other of the men who surrounded her—the cops, her captors, not trusting any of them. But she spoke up anyway. "He bought me at a party and said I belonged to him."

"You lying little bitch," Booker spat at her.

I could tell that Dakota was having a very hard time keeping her expression neutral, but her tone was even as she said, "Shut up, Mr. Booker. Believe me when I tell you that's your best option right now."

"He shot Rooster," Tina said shakily, emboldened by Amber. "He told me so. Rooster was helping him, hiding the women and taking them to wherever they were supposed to go, and then bringing the money back to Mr. Booker. But he tried to keep the money from that last trip. He hid it in my car. I didn't know what he was doing, I swear. I knew it was something bad, but I thought it was drugs. Not... this."

Dakota was silent, looking at the three of us, and for a moment, I thought she didn't believe us. In a way, I wouldn't have blamed her. Then she turned to Booker and said, "Mr. Booker, you are under arrest for abduction, unlawful imprisonment, and God knows what else. You have the right to remain silent. If you choose to forfeit that right, anything you say can and will be used against you in a court of law. You have the right to an attorney. If you cannot afford an attorney, one will be provided for you. Do you understand these rights as I have recited them to you?"

He glared at her, and she began again, calmly, "You have the right remain silent. If you choose to forfeit that right..."

"Oh, for God's sake," he snapped at her. "I understand."

She nodded and turned to Sean, repeating the Miranda warning. When he grudgingly acknowledged his understanding, she nodded at the surrounding deputies and said, "Cuff them both."

Deputies swarmed Booker and his henchman, and it gave me unspeakable satisfaction to see their hands wrenched behind their backs, just as they had done to me, and snapped into handcuffs.

Booker twisted his head toward me, lips curling into a poisonous smile.

"Tell your boyfriend," he hissed, "he has no idea what a hornet's nest he's stirred up. The people I work for don't forget something like this."

A cold deeper than winter slid down my spine, but I didn't look away. "Good," I said. "Neither do I."

The officer holding his arm gave him a small

push toward the waiting patrol car, and I turned back to Dakota. "There's something else," I said, but Amber took over for me.

"My friend Izzy," she said, her voice high and tight. "He did something to her. I think he took her, and was going to sell her..."

With each word, her voice grew higher, her face tightening with mounting hysteria. Dakota raised a calming hand.

"We have her," she said. "She's okay. A young man and a very smart golden retriever found her, and last I saw her, she was on her way to being checked out at the hospital. Which," she added with a smile, sweeping her gaze around the three of us, "is where you all are going, just to be on the safe side."

I started to shake my head. "I'm fine. I have to get Cisco. And call Miles. He'll be so worried. I want to go home."

Dakota's smile deepened, and she gave a small shake of her head. "Cisco is fine. And Miles Young knows exactly where you are. In fact, we never would have found you without him."

She glanced upward, and, as if summoned by her words, a faint buzzing sounded overhead. We all looked up.

Miles's drone wobbled in the gray sky, dipped once, twice—then spiraled down and crashed into a snowbank with a sad little *whump*.

Something inside me finally gave way. Relief, exhaustion, and the weight of everything we'd survived washed over me all at once. My knees nearly folded.

Tina wrapped her arms around herself, shivering. “All I want is to see my dog.”

I swallowed hard, my throat tight, and turned my aching eyes toward home. “Me, too,” I said.

CHAPTER FORTY

Tina came to take Riley home the very next morning. I've never seen a reunion that made me happier. I thought the skinny little pointer was going to shake his tail off, he wagged it so hard. And when Tina dropped to her knees to hug him, he covered her face with kisses. She started crying, and so, I confess, did I.

Corny loaded up her car with a gift basket of dog food, treats, chew toys, a brand new leash and collar, vitamins, shampoo and shiny new stainless steel food bowls. "It's something we do," he assured her, "for our favorite clients."

It wasn't, but I thought maybe it would be from now on.

Tina looked at us gratefully. Riley was pressed so close to her leg you couldn't have gotten a piece of tissue between them. His tail was still wagging. "Thank you," she said sincerely. She looked from Corny to me. "For everything."

I smiled. "I'm just glad everything turned out all

right."

Dakota had interviewed me for three hours yesterday, and I was sure she had done the same with both Amber and Tina. Tina looked exhausted, but, oddly, calmer and healthier than I had ever seen her. Even the ordeal in the back of Lance Booker's truck had not been enough to erase the relief of no longer having Rooster in her life.

I said, "What will you do now?"

She said, "The deputy lady said I could go back to my house, but I don't feel good about staying there after, you know, everything. I was thinking maybe I'd fix it up and sell it."

"I know a good carpenter," I volunteered. "And he works cheap."

"Thanks," she said. She reached down to stroke Riley's ear. He looked up at her adoringly. "Meantime, I'm gonna try to get a job where my mama works. I'll be staying with her for a while, and that'll help pay the bills. The important thing is for me and Riley to be together, you know?"

"I know," I assured her. I dropped my hand to Cisco's silky head, and he waved his tail reciprocally. "I hope everything works out for you, Tina. Please let me know if you or Riley need anything."

"Grooming is free for our favorite clients," Corny volunteered cheerfully.

Tina was smiling as she drove off in the brown minivan, Riley by her side.

Three days later, the doctors released Izzy, and

Casey picked her up from the hospital and drove her home. She didn't even go in her house, but insisted on getting in her car and following Casey back to Dog Daze to pick up Gigi. We were all waiting for her.

Miles was celebrating his first full day in the weight-bearing boot and cane, and had come down to Dog Daze to see Gigi off, simply because he could. Melanie was not due home from school for another half hour, but she was celebrating an A-Plus on her science essay about the Koch snowflake. And Dakota Bradshaw had promised to stop by to give us an update on the case. Melanie had baked her an apple pie.

Afterwards, Miles and I, along with Casey, Corny, Melanie, Rita and Aunt Mart were all going to the fancy restaurant outside of Asheville that was catering the wedding reception for a two-hour tasting of all those dishes I couldn't pronounce. I wanted to thank Corny for sticking by me during the lean times, and for taking on almost full responsibility for Gigi and Riley. And I had a lot to thank Casey for, too. The whole thing was an event of sorts, a way of putting the entire miserable episode behind us… for the most part.

But the best news was that for the second time that week, I got the chance to see the joyful reunion between a woman and the dog who meant the world to her.

I had never met Izzy, of course, but I could see why, under different circumstances, Casey might find her attractive. She had a cute figure and a funny blond bob that went in all different directions and was tinted bright pink on the ends. Very punk. Her face was probably pretty when it wasn't lined with the stress of dehydration, malnutrition and sleeplessness, and haunted by the memories of a terror she would never forget. Her hazel eyes looked cloudy when I first met her, but were quickly lit by a brief and brilliant joy when Corny brought in Gigi and the little poodle raced toward her mom.

Izzy dropped to embrace her baby, burying her face in her freshly shampooed curly hair, murmuring indecipherable exclamations of delight and relief and endearment. I leaned against Miles, enjoying the moment.

When Izzy stood, wiping the tears from her cheeks, her eyes were no longer cloudy and her face didn't look quite so haunted. "I don't know how to thank you," she said, "for taking care of her. When I think of her, locked up all alone and running out of food and water… when I was in that place, that's all I could think about. What was happening to Gigi." The clouds were back. "But you saved her. You took her in and…" Her voice grew thick and she cleared her throat, forcing a tight smile. "Anyway, how much do I owe you?"

I waved it away as she started to open her purse. "No charge. It's what we do."

"And we have a parting gift for you," Corny announced cheerfully, presenting the big gift basket. "It's just a little something we do for our favorite clients. I'll put it in your car."

She looked a little stunned. "I, um, I don't know

what to say."

"I'm just glad you're all right," I said. "Everyone was so worried about you."

She smiled wanly. "Now I feel a little bad that I'm leaving town. But after everything... well, I thought I could use some time back home in Texas, near my family. Amber is going to be staying with her folks for a while, but as soon as we both get back on our feet, we're going to get a place together. She wants to go to night school and study cosmetology, and I thought I'd take some business courses. Maybe we'll open a salon together, I don't know. But it's good to have something to look forward to after... well, everything."

I said, "I think that sounds great."

"Of course," she added, "we'll both have to come back here for the trial, but I guess that won't be for a while. And I won't mind the trip at all. I look forward to seeing that guy fry," she added grimly.

There was really nothing to say to that.

Izzy forced another quick smile and turned to Casey. Without preamble, she took his face between her hands and looked somberly into his eyes. "I can never thank you enough," she said, and kissed him on the cheek.

Casey smiled. "That's a start."

She gathered up Gigi's leash, and we watched from the door as the two of them walked to her car: woman and dog, survivors together. I felt a sudden need to hug Cisco, and I did. "Best dog in the world," I murmured into his neck.

"I say we bring him back a pork chop from dinner," Miles said. "He went above and beyond on this one. And you thought he'd lost his touch."

"I never thought that," I objected, standing. Then I admitted, "I thought maybe I had." I looked up at him and said sincerely, for what must have been the fourth time, "I'm really sorry about your drone, Miles."

He hugged my shoulders with one arm. "You were worth it. And the sheriff's office was able to recover the video, which will go a long way toward seeing that Booker gets the sentence he deserves."

Casey said, "Well, that's good, of course, but that drone was something else, man. Are you sure it can't be repaired?"

Miles shrugged. "Nah, I've got other things to do. And it served its purpose."

We all turned at the sound of tires on the gravel, and Cisco gave an anticipatory bark. Dakota Bradshaw got out of the patrol car and came up the walkway.

There was a flurry of greetings all around, and she spent some time giving Cisco the attention he was demanding and so richly deserved. Then she straightened up and turned to us. "I just dropped by to give you an update," she said. "Between the video from the drone and the affidavits from Tina Hoggins, Amber Pritchett, yourself, and Isabelle Stedman, the DA has decided to press charges against Lance Booker and his associate, Sean Wilkins, for abduction, unlawful restraint, sexual and physical abuse, and human trafficking. Not to mention the first-degree murder of Rooster Hoggins. The ballistics report came back on the bullet that killed Rooster," she explained, "and it matches the gun we took from Lance Booker. It's going to be a long time before that man sees the light of day again."

"Good," Casey said briefly, his lips tight. "I hope he spends every day of the rest of his life in prison thinking about Izzy locked in that dark hole in the ground."

We all allowed a moment of silent agreement for that, and then Miles said, "Booker is a powerful man with nearly unlimited resources." He sounded worried, which made me a little worried, myself. "I wouldn't get too confident. Putting him behind bars might not be as easy as it sounds."

"Maybe not," Dakota agreed. "But the human trafficking makes this a federal case, and the FBI will probably be taking over. It turns out they've been looking to nail Booker's boss for some time now, and this case just might give them the leverage they need. When the federal government prosecutes a case, they don't often lose."

She looked from one to the other of us with a smile. "I just wanted to thank you all for your help. It means a lot to know I'm living – and working— in a place where people aren't afraid to do the right thing."

Miles returned her smile. "Welcome to the neighborhood."

"Oh," I exclaimed, remembering. "I promised you

a pie."

I hurried behind the reception desk and brought the pie back. "I didn't make it," I explained. "I don't really cook. But Melanie—she's Miles's daughter—she's a great cook. She made this. So is Miles. A great cook, I mean. You'll have to come to dinner sometime."

Why did I always end up babbling around her? Maybe it was because the last two female deputies I'd tried to make friends with had ended up marrying my ex-husband… one at a time, of course. And even though there was literally no chance of that happening here, it was hard to believe that this time my overtures of friendship might actually be received in the spirit they were offered.

Dakota took the pie with a grateful nod. "Thanks. That's real nice of you. And by the way…" She looked down at Cisco with a wink. "You and your dog live up to every bit of your reputation."

I couldn't help wondering, with just a smidge of consternation, what, exactly, our reputation was, and who had given it to us.

"Well," she said, lifting the pie in a small salute. "I'd better get back to work. Thanks again."

She started toward the door, and Casey hurried to open it for her. "Say, do you need any help moving in? Glad to offer my services."

"No, thank you. Got it covered."

"Really," he insisted, "I'm great at unpacking boxes, building bookshelves…"

She stopped to give him a dry look. "I almost

made you for murder, you know."

He put on a look of studious innocence. "I'm hurt. I've done a few crimes in my life, but I don't kill people." He pretended to think that over. "Anymore."

Dakota looked at him, unamused, then pushed through the door. "Have a good day, everyone."

"I'll be there tomorrow with beer and pizza," Casey called after her.

Dakota gave him a backwards wave over her shoulder and called back, "No, you won't!"

The bell over the door jingled as Casey let it close behind him, grinning.

"You are incorrigible," I told him.

"Thank you," he responded easily. He glanced at the big clock behind the counter. "I'd better run home and get a shower if we're leaving at 5:00. How fancy is this place, anyway?"

"A shirt with buttons," I told him, and he made a face.

"I guess I can do that."

As he left, Corny said briskly, "Well, I'd best get busy myself if I'm going to get all the pups fed and tucked in for the night before we leave." He paused on his way out and looked back at me, head tilted thoughtfully. "I have a red cowboy hat. Do you think that would be appropriate?"

I grinned. "I think it would be perfect."

Miles and I were alone, with Cisco stretched out contentedly at our feet. I wrapped my arms around Miles and rested my cheek against his heartbeat. It was so good to have him standing upright again, strong and healthy and by my side where he belonged. Finally, now that it was over, I could say to him what I had been trying to say for days now. "Since everybody is thanking everybody else, I guess I should probably..."

"Thank me for saving your ass?" he suggested. "Once again? My pleasure, sugar."

I glanced up at him dryly. "Did anyone ever tell you you have a superhero complex? But," I admitted, "just in case you had any doubts, you are not and never will be useless. Even on one leg and with no weapons but a drone controller, you saved the day. That guy in the old movie would be proud."

"Jimmy Stewart," he reminded me. "*Rear Window*."

"Right. Whatever." I rested my cheek against his chest again. "Anyway, what I was going to say is I'm not sorry that I married you. And I can't wait to do it again."

He kissed my hair. "Same."

We stood there for a time, just holding each other, and then I said, "You don't really think Booker can squirm his way out of this, do you?"

Miles took so long in answering that I looked up at him, concerned.

"It's not him I'm worried about," he said, "but the people he works for. There are some bad guys out there that even a superhero can't win against. The best thing to do is just stay out of their way."

"Then it's a good thing that's exactly what I intend to do," I said. I turned and slipped my arm through his. "Come on. We have a wedding to plan."

We left the building and started up the drive toward home, leaning on each other, Cisco trotting happily by our side. There was a touch of warmth in the air, the low-hanging sun signaling that winter had finally turned the corner and spring was just ahead.

It was about time.

A Note From The Author

This is the part where I thank everyone who crossed my path while I was writing this book, from the clerk at the grocery store to the Amazon delivery driver and, much like those tiresome Oscar speeches, these acknowledgement pages always go on much, much too long. I'm therefore going to keep it short and thank only the most important people: my readers.

I have said before that I will keep writing the Raine Stockton books as long as you keep buying them, and for sixteen books now you haven't let me down. You e-mail me, you post on social media, you write reviews, you send photos of your pups, and you never stop asking, "When is the next Raine and Cisco book coming out?" You are the reason—the only reason—that Raine and Cisco continue to live, play, love and search the mountains of North Carolina year after year... because you want them to.

So I thank you. Raine and Cisco thank you. Mischief, Magic, Pepper, Miles, Melanie, Casey, Aunt Mart, Uncle Roe and even Buck down in Mercy, Georgia, thank you for their chance to tell their stories. None of this would be possible without you.

Jagged Edges dealt with some serious issues that

were, at times, difficult to write about—particularly in a format such as this, which doesn't naturally lend itself to exploring dark subjects. But sometimes the most important stories are the most challenging to tell. According to federal tracking data from 2024, approximately 250,000 women and girls go missing in the United States every year. The Signal for Help described in this book is this:

Begin with the palm facing out
Fold the thumb across the palm
Close the fingers over the thumb, as though "trapping" the thumb.

The National Domestic Violence Hotline is
800-799-7233

They're here to help.

And for those of my favorite readers who keep asking, "When is the next Raine and Cisco book coming out?"—Good news! Look for *Bones from the Sky* within the year. Read on for an excerpt.

Excerpt

from
Bones From the Sky
Raine Stockton Dog Mystery #18

If dogs' prayers were answered,
bones would rain from the sky.
--Indian Proverb

After

In my dream, I am searching the debris field with Cisco. The smoke, mixed with the heavy mist of a mountain morning, smells like oil and burning plastic and other awful, unthinkable things. I use a flashlight to pick my way around broken branches, some of them still flaming, shattered glass, and half-buried shards of steel. Cisco is wearing his heat-proof booties, and bravely keeps his nose to the ground, desperately trying to pick up the scent of something, anything, that's still alive. Surely he knows, as I do, that nothing could have survived this. Nothing.

In the distance, muffled by the fog, I can hear the murmured voices of other rescue workers, the crackle of radios, the wail of sirens. A truck motor groans its way uphill, no doubt bringing supplies for what will be a long and arduous investigation. I'm not interested in any of this. I focus on the task at hand, on the placement of my footsteps, one after another, the sound of Cisco's breathing, the swish of his tail, the tug of the line in my hand. The beat of my heart, the knot in my stomach. The urgent, determined effort not to think, or feel or imagine. Just focus. Footfalls. Breathing.

There's something odd wedged in the fork of a tree just ahead. I shine my flashlight upward and as I get closer I can make it out. It's a passenger seat, upholstery unscathed, unmoored but otherwise intact. It survived; perhaps whoever was sitting in it did, too. I place a flag and move on.

A few yards later we come upon the remnants of a leather duffle bag, charred bits of clothing scattered about, a melted phone not far away. Our orders are not to touch or disturb anything, so I plant another flag for the investigators who will come after me, trying not to think about the person who had packed that bag so hopefully, never imagining that it would end up here, in a shredded and burned mess, in the middle of the Nantahala National Forest.

Suddenly Cisco barks and starts pawing the ground. I should know this is a dream because this is not something Cisco is trained to do, but nonetheless I rush forward and drop to my knees, pushing aside the soot and ashes and wet leaves to uncover the small circle of gleaming metal. It's a ring.

With shaking fingers, I pick it up. I wipe it off. I turn it over in my hand. I read the engraving inside. *To Raine, the forever girl.*

It's my wedding ring. The one Miles was supposed to place on my finger less than twenty-four hours ago. The one he'd been carrying in his pocket the last time I'd seen him. How could it be here, in this smoldering field of death and destruction, among the shattered remnants of an airplane that had exploded in the sky? How could it be? How could *he* be?

Not possible, I tell myself. Miles had not been on that plane. He couldn't have been. He mustn't have been. Not possible, not possible…

And just as my hysteria starts to spiral out of control and the trees above my head begin to spin, Cisco gives a sudden joyful bark and pulls the leash from my hand. I look around to see him running toward something, a shadowy figure that appears in the mist, moving slowly toward us.

"Miles!" I cry, leaping to my feet. He is alive, he is well, he is *here*. Of course he is. I'd known it all the time. Of *course* he is. I run toward him. "Miles!"

I fling myself toward him, but just as I reach out to embrace him, the figure dissolves into smoke. That's when I wake up.

And that's when I start to cry. Because it was just a dream. And that's not the way it happened at all.

Bones From the Sky

Raine Stockton Dog Mystery #18

Coming soon from Donna Ball

BOOKS BY THIS AUTHOR

The Raine Stockton Dog Mystery Series Books in Order

SMOKY MOUNTAIN TRACKS

A child has been kidnapped and abandoned in the mountain wilderness. Her only hope is Raine Stockton and her young, untried tracking dog Cisco...

RAPID FIRE

Raine and Cisco are brought in by the FBI to track a terrorist ...a terrorist who just happens to be Raine's old boyfriend.

GUN SHY

Raine rescues a traumatized service dog, and soon begins to suspect he is the only witness to a murder.

BONE YARD

Cisco digs up human remains in Raine's back yard, and mayhem ensues. Could this be evidence of a serial killer, a long-unsolved mass murder, or something even more sinister... and closer to home?

SILENT NIGHT

It's Christmastime in Hansonville, N.C., and Raine and Cisco are on the trail of a missing teenager. But when a newborn is abandoned in the manger of the town's living nativity and Raine walks in on what appears to be the scene of a murder, the holidays take a very dark turn for everyone concerned.

THE DEAD SEASON

Raine and Cisco take a job leading a wilderness hike for troubled teenagers, and soon find themselves trapped on a mountainside in a blizzard... with a killer.

ALL THAT GLITTERS: A Holiday Short Story e book

Raine looks back on how she and Cisco met and solved their first crime in this Christmas Cozy short story. Sold separately as an e-book or bundled with the print edition of HIGH IN TRIAL.

HIGH IN TRIAL

A carefree weekend turns deadly when Raine and Cisco travel to the South Carolina low country for an agility competition

DOUBLE DOG DARE

A luxury Caribbean vacation sounds like just the ticket for over-worked, over-stressed Raine Stockton and her happy go lucky canine companion Cisco. But even in paradise trouble finds them, and when someone she loves is threatened Raine must use every resource at her command to track down a killer before it's too late.

HOME OF THE BRAVE

There's a new dog in town, and Raine and Cisco find themselves unexpectedly upstaged by a flashy K-9 addition to the sheriff's department. But when things go terribly wrong at a mountain camp for kids and dogs over the Fourth of July weekend, Raine and Cisco need all the help they can get to save themselves, and those they love.

DOG DAYS

Raine takes in a lost English Cream Golden Retriever, and the search for her owner leads Raine and Cisco into the hands of a killer. Readers will enjoy a treasure hunt for the titles of all ten of the Raine Stockton Dog Mysteries hidden in this special tenth anniversary release!

LAND OF THE FREE

On a routine search and rescue mission Raine

Stockton and her golden retriever Cisco stumble onto something they were never meant to find, and are plunged into a nightmare of murder, corruption and intrigue as figures from her past re-emerge to threaten everything Raine holds dear.

DEADFALL

Hollywood comes to Hanover County, and Raine and Cisco get caught up in the drama when a series of mishaps on the set lead to murder.

THE DEVIL'S DEAL

Raine takes temporary custody of what may well be the most valuable dog in the world, but when lives are at stake she is forced to make an unthinkable choice.

MURDER CREEK

Raine and Cisco rescue a dog who is locked in a hot car in a remote Smoky Mountain park... and subsequently discover the owner of that car drowned in the creek only a few dozen yards away. Was it an accident, or was it murder?

ANGELS IN THE SNOW: A Raine Stockton Short Novella

While preparing for the annual Dog Daze Christmas party, Raine leaves on a secret Christmas errand and becomes trapped in a blizzard. Injured and alone, with a desperate criminal on the loose, a surprising canine hero comes to her rescue. But is it all a product of her imagination, or a genuine Christmas miracle?

Also available in in **DECK THE HALLS**: A HOLIDAY MYSTERY ANTHOLOGY

THE JUDGES DAUGHTER

In this pivotal fifteenth book in the ground-breaking Raine Stockton Dog Mystery Series, the death of an old friend leaves Raine Stockton with an unwanted inheritance, an old wound reopened, and the most challenging mystery of her life.

DEAD MAN'S TRAIL

Deep in the heart of the Smoky Mountains there a thousand things that will kill you... and one of them is human.

Raine and Cisco agree to help instruct a group of executives at a survival training camp. On a routine exercise, the group becomes stranded in the wilderness with an ice storm moving in. With all communications disabled, they are completely cut off from the modern world and being hunted by a man to whom killing is a way of life. As one by one their members are picked off, the survivors must rely on Raine and Cisco to lead them to safety. But as the killer draws ever closer, even Raine is no longer sure where safety lies.

Don't miss this thrilling first installment in The Hunter Saga, Raine and Cisco's most harrowing adventure yet!

~*~

The Blood River Mystery Series

UNFIXABLE: A Buck Lawson Mystery

Former sheriff Buck Lawson leaves the mountains of North Carolina to take a job as police chief of the small South Georgia town of Mercy, and soon finds himself in over his head. For one thing, his predecessor has been murdered…

WELCOME TO BETHLEHEM: A Buck Lawson Short Novella

Police chief Buck Lawson wants his first Christmas in his new hometown of Mercy, Georgia, to be a memorable one, both for his family and the police officers under his command. But while preparing to host the traditional police department Christmas party, Buck's home is burglarized by a Middle Eastern man who may be connected to far more violent crimes. As the investigation unfolds and unsettling connections to the past come to light, Buck fears this Christmas will be memorable for all the wrong reasons.

Also Available in the Holiday Anthology **DECK THE HALLS**

Unstoppable: A Buck Lawson Mystery

With the Fourth of July coming up and the Mercy police force already stretched to its limit, police chief Buck Lawson investigates a fraud complaint that leads him to a missing newborn and a terrified, runaway mother. At the same time, the skeletal remains of two young boys are discovered buried on the property of a prominent citizen. When a young woman is murdered, the web of secrecy protecting Mercy begins to unravel, revealing a network of illegal activity that has gone undeterred for decades.

UNDEFEATABLE: A Buck Lawson Mystery

The quiet little south Georgia town of Mercy is rocked by the brutal murder of one of its most unassuming citizens. Within hours of the discovery of the crime, the remains of another victim are found in the Blood River. And then another. Things like this simply don't happen in Mercy.

Until they do...

~*~

The Dogleg Island Mystery Series

FLASH

Dogleg Island Mystery #1

Almost two years ago the sleepy little community of Dogleg Island was the scene of one of the most brutal crimes in Florida history. The only eye witnesses were Flash, a border collie puppy, and a police officer. Now the trial of the century is about to begin. The defendant, accused of slaughtering his parents in their beach home, maintains his innocence. The top witnesses for the prosecution are convinced he is lying. But only Flash knows the truth. And with another murder to solve and a monster storm on the way, the truth may come to late... for all of them.

THE SOUND OF RUNNING HORSES

Dogleg Island Mystery #2

A family outing takes a dark turn when Flash, Aggie and Grady discover a body on deserted Wild Horse Island, and the evidence appears to point to someone they know—and trust.

FLASH OF BRILLIANCE

Dogleg Island Mystery #3

Aggie, Flash and Grady look forward to their first

Christmas as a family until a homicide hit-and-run exposes a crime syndicate, and dark shadows from the past return to haunt their future.

PIECES OF EIGHT

Dogleg Island Mystery #4

A deadly explosion at an archeological dig on Dogleg Island plunges police chief Aggie Malone and her canine partner Flash into a dark mystery from the past, while on the other side of the bridge, Deputy Sheriff Ryan Grady stumbles onto the site of a mass murder. As the investigation unfolds, Aggie and Grady see that the two cases are related, but only Flash knows how...and by whom.

FLASH IN THE DARK

Dogleg Island Mystery #5

Flash discovers an abandoned child on the beach, and the subsequent attempt to identify her leads to a secret organization with a plan for revenge that has been decades in the making. Unless Aggie, Grady and Flash can stop it they risk losing everything the love... even Dogleg Island itself.

FLASH OF FIRE

Dogleg Island Mystery #6

The beaches of Dogleg Island are targeted by a

group of environmental activists who insist upon exercising their right to peaceful protest in the most disruptive ways possible. When a series of apparently harmless break-ins result in the theft of explosives, Aggie begins to suspect the environmentalists are not as peaceful as they appear. And when a man is murdered, Aggie and Flash know that it's only a matter of time before the troubles on Dogleg escalate into a crisis.

THE GOOD SHEPHERD: A Dogleg Island Short Novella

A missing infant, a holiday pageant, and a priest determined to do the right thing no matter what the cost all come together to present Dogleg Island police chief Aggie Malone and her canine assistant Flash with one of their most unusual cases yet. When a routine call escalates into a kidnapping on the eve of the annual Dogleg Island Police Department holiday open house, Flash and Aggie are held hostage by a desperate man whose only chance for redemption may be the grace of the holiday season.

Also Available in **DECK THE HALLS**: A HOLIDAY MYSTERY ANTHOLOGY

FLASH OF FIRE:

Dogleg Island Mystery #6

Ecoterrorists threaten Dogleg Island, and the only person who can save the island from catastrophe may be more dangerous than the terrorists themselves.

A FLASH OF SHADOW

A notorious serial killer, come home to die. A young woman found hanging from a tree. A missing billionaire. In the quiet coastal community of Dogleg Island, nothing is as it should be. And for Police Chief Aggie Malone and her extraordinarily perceptive canine assistant Flash, time is running out.

~*~

Spine-chilling suspense by Donna Ball

SHATTERED

A missing child, a desperate call for help in the middle of the night... is this a cruel hoax, or the work of a maniacal serial killer who is poised to strike again?

NIGHT FLIGHT

She's an innocent woman who knows too much. Now she's fleeing through the night without a weapon and without a phone, and her only hope for survival is a cop who's willing to risk his badge—and his life—to save her.

SANCTUARY

They came to the peaceful, untouched mountain wilderness of Eastern Tennessee seeking an escape from the madness of modern life. But when they built their luxury homes in the heart of virgin forest they did not realize that something was there before them... something ancient and horrible; something that will make them believe that monsters are real.

EXPOSURE

Everyone has secrets, but when talk show host Jessamine Cray's stalker begins to use her past to terrorize her, no one is safe ... not her family, her friends, her coworkers, and especially not Jess herself.

RENEGADE by Donna Boyd

Enter a world of dark mystery and intense passion, where human destiny is controlled by a species of powerful, exotic creatures. Once they ruled the Tundra, now they rule Wall Street. Once they fought with teeth and claws, now they fight with wealth and power. And only one man can stop them... if he dares.

Also by Donna Ball

The Ladybug Farm series by Donna Ball

For every woman who ever had a dream… or a friend

A Year on Ladybug Farm

At Home on Ladybug Farm

Love Letters from Ladybug Farm

Christmas on Ladybug Farm

Recipes from Ladybug Farm

Vintage Ladybug Farm

A Wedding on Ladybug Farm

A Gift From Ladybug Farm

The Hummingbird House

Christmas at the Hummingbird House

The Hummingbird House Presents

ABOUT THE AUTHOR

Donna Ball

Donna Ball is the author of over 100 books under a variety of pseudonyms. Though she has been published in virtually every genre, she is best known for her work in women's fiction, mystery and suspense. Her novels have been translated into multiple languages and published around the world. Her most popular series are the award-winning Raine Stockton Dog Mystery series, the Dogleg Island Mystery series, The Blood River Mystery series, and the Ladybug Farm series. All are available now in paperback in bookstores everywhere, as audiobook downloads, and in digital format for your e-reader.

Donna lives in the heart of the Blue Ridge Divide in a restored Victorian barn which was the inspiration for the bestselling A YEAR ON LADYBUG FARM. She spends her spare time hiking, painting, and enjoying canine sports with her three dogs.

You can reach her at www.donnaball.net.

www.ingramcontent.com/pod-product-compliance
Lightning Source LLC
LaVergne TN
LVHW090553110826
845146LV00001B/111